W9-BKE-273

Whispers in the Wind

Books by Lauraine Snelling

*Golden Filly Collection One**
*Golden Filly Collection Two**
*High Hurdles Collection One**
*High Hurdles Collection Two**

SECRET REFUGE
Daughter of Twin Oaks
Sisters of the Confederacy • *The Long Way Home*

DAKOTAH TREASURES
Ruby • *Pearl*
Opal • *Amethyst*

DAUGHTERS OF BLESSING
A Promise for Ellie • *Sophie's Dilemma*
A Touch of Grace • *Rebecca's Reward*

HOME TO BLESSING
A Measure of Mercy • *No Distance Too Far*
A Heart for Home

RED RIVER OF THE NORTH
An Untamed Land • *A New Day Rising*
A Land to Call Home • *The Reapers' Song*
Tender Mercies • *Blessing in Disguise*

RETURN TO RED RIVER
A Dream to Follow • *Believing the Dream*
More Than a Dream

WILD WEST WIND
Valley of Dreams
Whispers in the Wind

*5 books in each volume

Wild West Wind • BOOK 2

Whispers in the Wind

LAURAINE SNELLING

BETHANY HOUSE PUBLISHERS
a division of Baker Publishing Group
Minneapolis, Minnesota

Published by Bethany House Publishers
11400 Hampshire Avenue South
Bloomington, Minnesota 55438
www.bethanyhouse.com

Bethany House Publishers is a division of
Baker Publishing Group, Grand Rapids, Michigan

Printed in the United States of America

Library of Congress Cataloging-in-Publication Data

Snelling, Lauraine.
Whispers in the wind / Lauraine Snelling.
p. cm. — (Wild west wind ; 2)
ISBN 978-0-7642-1006-8 (hardcover : alk. paper) — ISBN 978-0-7642-0416-6 (pbk.) — ISBN 978-0-7642-1007-5 (large-print pbk.)
1. Frontier and pioneer life—South Dakota—Fiction. I. Title.
PS3569.N39W47 2012
813'.54—dc23 2012006414

Scripture quotations are from the King James Version of the Bible

This is a work of fiction. Names, characters, incidents, and dialogues are products of the author's imagination and are not to be construed as real. Any resemblance to actual events or persons, living or dead, is entirely coincidental.

Cover design by John Hamilton Design

12 13 14 15 16 17 18 7 6 5 4 3 2 1

Whispers in the Wind is dedicated to:

Sandy Dengler, who, with her wild wit and wisdom, first introduced me to the intricacies of researching as a writer. I am beyond grateful that she has continued to make my life richer with her enduring friendship and assistance.

Colleen Reece, fiction teacher extraordinaire, who read my first horse book chapter, bled all over it, and then suggested where to send it and how. Colleen has remained a friend and advisor. All of us need cheerleaders like these two.

The many others who have left their marks on my life.
I am incredibly blessed.

Who am I? Daughter of the wind,
The wind that covers,
The wind that brings the mist.
I am she who breathes deep of that wind,
Hiding no longer,
Loves so that others
Yearn for the wind.

—Lauraine Snelling

1

Late October 1906
Bar E Ranch
Argus, South Dakota

"Are you telling me this ranch is not ours?"

Mavis Engstrom shook her head, wishing for a way to erase the anger she could read on her son's face. Ransom wore the ice blue eyes and steel jaw of his father when he was fighting for control. "No, that is not what I am saying. I said the ranch belongs to Cassie Lockwood too."

"How can this be? You've never mentioned it before." Ransom snapped off anything else he was going to say.

"No, I haven't, and that is my fault, but I couldn't see any sense in worrying about something that might never happen." Mavis scrubbed her sweaty hands down the sides of her full apron. "This is a long story, so I'll put supper on the table and then we can talk."

"This better be good," Ransom muttered as he grabbed the canvas wood carrier and stomped out to the front porch to bring in wood for the fireplace.

Mavis crossed to the front window, wishing she'd been able to convince Cassie to stay longer. Cassie Lockwood, the daughter of Adam Lockwood. What a wonderful surprise. At least in Mavis's mind. But Cassie and her guide, Chief, had elected to return to their camp closer to town. Amazing how she had recognized in the old Indian the young man who had guided her not-yet-husband, Ivar Engstrom, and his new partner, Adam Lockwood, in their search for both gold and land. What a long story she had to tell. Where to begin?

"Did they leave already?" Gretchen, Mavis's twelve-year-old daughter, asked. "I thought they would stay awhile. Did you see Cassie's horse? Mor, did you really know her pa?"

"Yes, I saw her horse. He truly is a beauty." Mavis paused, as if to say something else but then stopped. "Please set the table, Gretchen, and slice the bread. Oh, before you do that, will you go to the cellar and bring up a jar of string beans and one of applesauce?"

"We having pork chops?"

"Well, elk chops, and applesauce tastes good on them too."

"I thought the applesauce was for the gingerbread."

"Oh, that's right. It is." Mavis blinked as if coming awake. She shouldn't let the situation rattle her like this. But trying to explain the story from those many years ago to her two grown sons was not something she was looking forward to.

Gretchen came up the stairs from the cellar with two jars and a pint of jam. "I thought Juneberry jam would be good on that corn bread."

"Oh yes. The corn bread. We were going to have that."

"Mor, are you all right?" Gretchen set the jars down on the counter, keeping her gaze on her mother.

"I will be." Mavis forced herself to cross the kitchen and add wood to the firebox of her shiny black range with chrome trim. After rattling the grate to let the ash fall through to the box below, she opened the damper so the wood would catch more quickly. "Maybe a cup of coffee will help."

"Help what? Are you sick?"

"No, I am not sick. The arrival of Cassie and her guide was just a huge surprise." Shock might be a better term for the way she was feeling. Mavis tried to smile reassurance, but the look on her daughter's face told her she'd failed. "Besides, I need to get my thoughts together. This is dredging up a lot of memories, and I want to be sure I tell the story correctly." How much to put in and what needed to be left out. *Just be honest*, she reminded herself with the wisdom she had passed on to her children.

Gretchen went about setting the table before taking a loaf of bread from the bread box. "I thought we were going to have corn bread."

"We are. It is in the oven."

"Then why am I slicing bread?"

Mavis chuckled and shook her head. "You caught me." She could hear wood being stacked by the fireplace in the parlor. Not that it was really a parlor but instead the room where the family lived, other than the kitchen. With a huge stone fireplace on one wall, cottonwood frames with leather cushions for furniture, and a bear rug in the middle, the room invited everyone to come sit a spell. Right now Mavis would love to have done just that. A cup of coffee, a blazing fire, and time to ponder her situation.

Instead, she heard the men's boots on the back porch. After bringing in the wood, Ransom had milked the cow for the last time until she freshened while Lucas checked on the cattle. Ever since they'd had a fence cut in two places, they checked the herd morning and night to make sure all were accounted for. Cattle rustling was still considered a hanging crime unless, of course, one talked with Sheriff Edgar McDougal, a real by-the-law lawman.

Taking the pan of corn bread from the oven, she set it on the table on top of a pot holder and then brought the skillet of elk chops, along with the potatoes she'd baked. The gingerbread sat cooling on the counter, and Gretchen emptied the kettle of string beans into a bowl. The jar of Juneberry jam waited by the corn bread.

"Are we missing anything?" She turned to Gretchen. *Other than my mind, I think not.* She glanced up to see Ransom studying her.

"I strained the milk and set it in the tank. There wasn't even enough to fill a jug."

"I wonder if anyone else might have some milk for sale. It won't be long until Rosie comes in, so we can get along without if need be." As soon as they were all seated, she bowed her head. Tonight it was her turn to say grace, and she needed all the grace she could get. "Heavenly Father, thank you for this food and all the provisions you have given us. Thank you for this day, for my family, and please show us your leading in all matters. In Jesus' name we pray." They all joined in the amen.

Except for the occasional "please pass" and "thank you," an uncharacteristic silence settled over the table. The tension did a fine job of doing away with her appetite. *Lord, tell me what to say, where to start. Let these men of mine hear me out with ears of love. The furrows on their foreheads are deep.*

"Would you like dessert now or later?" she asked when the last plate was scraped clean.

"Both?" Lucas grinned at her, obviously trying to lighten the situation.

"Of course. There is plenty. I'll bring it into the other room."

They all picked up their plates and set them in the pan of soapy water staying hot on the reservoir. Gretchen set about putting the other things away, and Ransom retrieved small plates, cups, and saucers from the cupboard.

Mavis called, "Lucas, would you please cut the gingerbread and put applesauce on it? I need to get a few things." When he returned from the parlor, she ignored his questioning look and strode down the hall to her bedroom. The box she needed lay at the back of the shelf in her closet, resting there all these years. She debated just bringing the whole thing into the sitting room but hesitated, thinking through the treasures she had saved in this box. Mementos from the early years before she and Ivar were married, the contracts, later contracts, the journal Ivar kept in the early years before they turned to the leather- and cloth-bound ones they used now, a lock of hair from each of the boys when they'd had their first haircut, a baby rattle, a poem that Ivar wrote on the death of their son. She'd never known he could write poetry until then. Feelings he couldn't say, he put on paper.

Realizing that the others would be wondering what had happened to her, she took out the parchment packet that held the original ranch contracts between the Engstroms and the Lockwoods and, after setting the wooden box up on the shelf, returned to find that they'd served themselves and were waiting.

"I fixed yours too." Gretchen pointed to the table by the rocker Ivar had made for Mavis when she was expecting the first time. Why did everything remind her of Ivar? Perhaps the arrival of Cassie Lockwood had opened the floodgates of memory and she was swimming for all she was worth.

"Thank you." Mavis sat down and smiled into each of the three pairs of eyes watching her as if she might disappear at any moment. "I am going to start at the beginning. You all know that I was born in Minnesota and lived there until my father decided he'd rather live somewhere else and moved us to Rapid City, South Dakota. It felt like the end of the earth, but we settled in and I attended the local school along with my brothers and sisters. You've seen the place where we lived.

"But times were hard, and when I was in high school, my mother and father decided to return to Minnesota. I chose to stay here, as did your uncle Vernon. I went to work for the Graden family for my room and board so I could finish school here. Vernon went to work at the local lumberyard. We didn't see each other a lot but enjoyed the local dances in the fall and winter months. One night Vern brought a friend along, Ivar Engstrom. The next week, he brought a newcomer to town, Adam Lockwood. Vernon became fast friends with the two men, and they included me in many of their adventures. I think I was considered a bit wild by the proper ladies of the church, but we had marvelous times.

"Lockwood and Engstrom decided to try mining for gold, but Vern thought they were nuts and told them so, which caused some hard feelings. However, the two of them located a young man from the Rosebud Indian Reservation, who now goes by the name of Chief. He was quiet but an excellent guide."

And I was falling in love with Adam Lockwood. Mavis kept that bit to herself as she took a bite of gingerbread. She sipped her coffee and wrinkled her nose. Tepid coffee was not to be endured.

"I'll get the coffeepot," Gretchen offered before her mother had time to stand.

"Bring the gingerbread too," Lucas called after her.

"You come get that. My hands are full."

Mavis jumped up to go with her daughter. She cut another piece and made sure the applesauce came with it. Anything to keep from looking into Ransom's face. When they were all settled again, she held the steaming cup of coffee in front of her like a shield.

"So then what happened?" Ransom's voice rang insistent, icy hard.

"Well, they did find gold. Right here in this valley. They filed on the gold claim, and then Lockwood suggested they buy the valley for a ranch. That way, if the mine played out, they would turn to ranching, or if it did well, no one could move in on them. They built the cabin in time for winter and kept on tunneling, searching for the elusive gold." She paused and shook her head. "Gold fever is a terrible disease." *How do I tell them that I was becoming the bone of contention between the two friends? Or can I leave that out?*

"They pulled enough gold out of that hillside to pay for the four hundred acres of this land, and then the vein ran out. When they started tunneling again, the mine collapsed. It was thanks to their Indian friend, John Birdwing, now called Chief, that they were able to get out. They finally listened to the geologists and engineers and boarded up that tunnel. Since they owned the land jointly, they decided to go into the ranching business. But Lockwood got itchy feet."

She took a swallow of coffee. "One night at the saloon, they met a man who owned a Wild West show, quite an eccentric fellow. Lockwood won half title to the show at cards that night. He now owned half interest in a ranch with Ivar and half interest in a Wild West show with this Jason Talbot. Lockwood dreamed of developing a trick riding act and asked me if I would like to go along." She studied the dregs of her coffee cup. When had she drained that?

"I'll get it." Ransom stood, the set of his shoulders saying more than his mouth. "What happened then?" he asked as he refilled their coffee cups.

"Since I'd not had a home of my own since my folks left, I chose to stay here. Ivar asked me to marry him, and I did."

Did he ever know how much I loved Adam Lockwood? I traded love for security, and I'm still sure I made the right choice—most of the time.

"And Lockwood?"

"He promised to return some day. He left some money on the table to buy cattle and took off with Talbot. Your father and I lived in the cabin until we built this house—you know what a good carpenter your father was—and over the years we built up the ranch. We'd hear from Adam once in a while. Tales of his adventures made his letters a delight to receive. He married a Norwegian princess, or at least she was somehow related to the family of the king. Their Wild West Show traveled the world with Adam's and his wife's act the headliner. I heard they had a little girl who became part of the show, and then the letters stopped coming. I think I heard that his wife died; I'm not sure if it was in a letter or what. But I always figured he would come back when he got tired of the traveling life."

"And now his daughter showed up," Ransom said. "Or at least she says she's his daughter. Did she bring her copy of the deed?"

"She showed it to me, but she still has it. She is who she says she is."

"You don't know that!"

"Yes, Ransom, I do. Besides, I recognized the old Indian with her."

"May I see the deed?"

"Of course." She handed the packet to her eldest son. "It's all legal. They had an attorney draw it up. They both signed it. Your father took it to a judge one time when we'd not heard from Lockwood for a long while. The judge said it was absolutely binding and could be deeded by heirs, if someone ever showed up. If they didn't, well, the place was all ours. When your father died, the deed came to me, and when I die, it will be split between the three of you and Jesse. Our share, that is."

"But we are the ones who put all the work into this place. Doesn't that count for anything?" Lucas leaned forward, elbows resting on his knees. "Seems to me that all they have title to is the land—nothing else about the ranch."

"And the cattle purchased with the money he left."

"I suppose." The face Lucas made said he didn't really agree.

"If we had the money, we could buy her out."

Lucas turned to look at his brother. "Mighty big *if*. Might as well be worth millions." Shifting his attention back to his mother, he asked, "Any idea what the ranch is worth, Mor?"

"No, none. But I remember your father saying that something is only worth what someone else is willing to pay for it."

"What if she wants to buy us out?" Lucas raised his eyebrows.

"You just want to go homestead in Montana." Disgust riddled Ransom's tone.

Mavis shook her head. "I have no desire to start over on bare land in Montana or here or anywhere. I already did that once. If you want to go, you will go with my blessing, but I am staying here. This ranch is not for sale."

Even if we own only half of it.

2

CAMPSITE

"Well, what do you think?"

Chief shrugged.

Cassie Lockwood heaved a sigh. Her friend's lifelong scarcity of using a lot of words was hard to change, if not impossible. Especially since the aging Indian showed no desire to change. Had the meeting with the Engstroms gone well? She most certainly had been welcomed by Mrs. Engstrom. What an amazing woman to welcome them so warmly, as if she'd been expecting them. Cassie had a feeling the rest of the family would not be so forthcoming, although the daughter sure was likable.

After all, if she lived on that ranch and someone showed up out of the blue with another deed, how would she react? She leaned back in her saddle a bit and tipped her head back, staring up at the brilliant cobalt sky with nary a bit of white. A fall sky, Chief had called it. Although the sun was warm, there was surely a bite in the breeze.

She jerked her mind back to the situation at hand. She had a deed to half the ranch, signed by her father and Ivar Engstrom, father and husband of those on the ranch, who had conveniently died a number of years earlier. When her father last saw the ranch, what had it looked like? Wild and free, she suspected. So this family built the buildings, fenced it, and made untamed land into what looked to be a thriving ranch. She wished she were a mouse in a pocket back in that room, which like Mrs. Engstrom herself, invited them in to sit and be comfortable. Those two men riding up to the house were most likely part of the family.

No doubt now they were an angry part of the family.

Cassie's pinto, Wind Dancer, tossed his head, bringing her attention back to the matter at hand—riding back to camp.

So why had she not stayed when invited?

Because you were scared. That's why. Her internal voice showed no mercy. What was she to do next? Help make supper, finish cleaning the house-on-wheels wagon they all lived in and around, and go to bed.

"So what do we do next?" She raised her voice for Chief to hear her over the scuff of horses' hooves.

"We are nearly out of meat. Need to go hunting."

Cassie swallowed a sharp retort. Leave it to Chief; the old man was ever practical. "I meant regarding the ranch." *Now don't get snippy. You know he'll really get quiet then.* Counseling herself had become endemic through their weeks on the road, after they had left the failed Wild West Show and headed south to locate her father's valley of dreams—a place he'd always dreamed of returning to. His dream was to raise Appaloosa horses and beef cattle for the market. Both he and her mother had died before the dream could be realized. And then the Wild West Show was disbanded due to failing revenues. Poor management by her so-called uncle, Jason Talbot, is what she really figured, but it didn't matter now. The show was dead and left far behind.

She decided to try Chief again. "Regarding the ranch."

He glanced at her over his shoulder. "Go back. What else can you do?"

"I can go back to riding and shooting in Wild West shows."

But how could she leave her family? This family that was not related in any way, but a month of traveling together had given them a bond, a unity probably closer than most families knew. What if she left them? Chief could go back to his reservation. And Runs Like a Deer, the Indian woman they'd found with a broken leg on the way down? She could probably return to her reservation as well, but she didn't want to. And Micah, former animal handler for the show and always her friend and protector? What about him?

Cassie could sell the cattle and buffalo, but George, the bison bull she'd raised from a calf, was so old that someone would probably just shoot him. The others too would most likely be slaughtered. And Wind Dancer? She could always sell him, but how did one go about selling a piece of her heart? Unthinkable. Perhaps he could go with her. After all, she needed him in her act, the act she'd not practiced since they'd left the show. Instead of shooting clay pigeons and various targets, she'd learned how to shoot game birds from the trees and deer on the run.

They turned onto the trail that led to their camp, where

the others were waiting to learn what had happened. Her rangy dog, Othello, and Runs Like a Deer's dog both came bounding down the trail to greet them, yipping their delight at seeing her again. George, the buffalo, looked up from grazing and snorted his greeting before dropping that huge head and continuing to eat.

The fragrance of meat cooking over a campfire welcomed them in. Runs Like a Deer looked up from her task of sewing rabbit skins into mittens for winter and smiled. It was the first time Cassie had seen the woman really smile. What was Runs Like a Deer thinking about? Did she too yearn for a home, a safe haven, a place of peace? Like the ranch?

Micah looked up from checking the rabbit carcasses sizzling on sticks over a glowing fire. Even he smiled, if one could call a lightening of the eyes and a lifting of one side of his mouth a real smile. If Chief was miserly with his words, Micah was doubly stingy with his smiles.

These people were her family now, far more so than the Engstroms could ever be. She could not, she dared not, neglect their welfare when the hour of reckoning came. And that hour was not far off.

Cassie dismounted by the wagon, which had a charging buffalo painted on the sides with *Lockwood and Talbot Wild West Show* lettered in an arch over the picture. While the bright red and blue trim was starting to fade, the wagon was all that remained of the show she had called home. That and her skills as a sharpshooter and trick rider. She'd become a headliner of the show after her mother and father died and, like her father, had participated in shooting matches during the winter season when most of the shows disbanded until spring. This was the first year in her twenty years that she was fighting snow instead of enjoying warm sunshine and time to work on refining and adding to her act. But never had she had a real home, a roots-deep-in-the-ground, house-without-wheels, roaring-fireplace kind of home. Like the one she'd just left.

While her mind flirted with dreams, she pulled off her saddle and smiled when Micah exchanged a halter for the bridle and led Wind Dancer off to graze with the other animals. Othello shoved his nose under her hand, demanding his share of attention. She rubbed his ears without thinking, but when he whimpered, she bent over and stroked down his back, sending him into spasms of delight.

"I wish we all could be as delighted as you with so little." She straightened to see the other three pretending to go about their own chores and not pay attention to her. But she knew they were curious, their glances sliding away when she caught their gaze. Heaving a sigh, she motioned toward the chunks of wood that Micah had dragged in and sat on the one nearest her.

"That ranch is certainly the one my father's deed gives me part of. Mrs. Engstrom and her family own the rest of it. Mr. Engstrom was a good friend of my father's. She welcomed us with open arms and even recognized Chief as the young man who'd been a guide and friend to the two partners." She looked toward Chief. "He knows far more than he has ever let on. I do hope you will tell me more about those early days."

His shrug said he'd heard her but nothing more than that.

"Did she invite you to stay?" Micah asked.

"Yes." The memory of the woman saying *"Welcome home"* with such warmth shocked her anew. "But I have a feeling her two sons are not going to agree."

"So what will happen? What will you do?" Micah never raised his gaze from the wood he was carving, most likely into some other useful tool. Wooden spoons for cooking were his specialty, besides the crutch he'd fashioned for Runs Like a Deer.

"What will *we* do?" she responded. "I don't know. I guess it depends on how they all act. Maybe we can build a cabin somewhere on the ranch."

"There was a cabin up in the woods by the mine," Chief said, finally taking part in the conversation.

"Indians are not welcome around here," Runs Like a Deer said as she smoothed the rabbit-skin mitten she had just completed.

"Mrs. Engstrom didn't seem to have any bad feelings about Indians. She was happy to see Chief."

"But what about those in town?"

While the pastor had welcomed them to Argus, a couple of loudmouths had made their dislike clear. So they had left town immediately and found this place to camp on their way to the ranch.

Runs Like a Deer lifted the lid on the simmering kettle and stirred the contents with a long-handled spoon, one carved by Micah. "Supper's ready."

She dished up the stew as everyone held out their plates, and Micah broke pieces off the crispy rabbit for each of them.

Cassie cut up a chunk of potato that the Brandenburgs had given them right out of their garden. She closed her eyes, the better to savor the flavor. "Do you think we'll be able to plant a garden here? If we get to stay, that is."

"There were lots of gardens in Argus." Micah licked the meat juice from his fingers.

Cassie looked from Runs Like a Deer to Micah. "Either of you ever made a garden?" When they both nodded, Cassie forked a piece of carrot, from the same garden as the potatoes.

"So you would know how?"

More nods.

Mrs. Brandenburg had said she would teach her to cook, so perhaps she could teach her to garden too. At least she knew how to sew, but not with skins and hides. Her mother had insisted her daughter learn to repair her own costumes. Not that there would be much call for fancy clothes out here. And if she needed clothes, she had plenty in the trunk. Wrapped up in her own thoughts, Cassie finally realized someone had called her name. She looked up, a rabbit bone in her hand. "What?"

"When are you going back?"

"I don't know. What do you think?"

"Winter coming soon."

They'd already waited out one storm not long after leaving Dickinson, where the show disbanded. The wind and cold had been like nothing she'd ever experienced. How would the four of them live in this tiny wagon for months at a time?

Cassie sopped up the gravy with the bit of biscuit she had left. How were they going to survive on the little money they had left, plus feed the animals?

The load she'd managed to shed since arriving in Argus climbed back onto her shoulders like a monkey she'd seen in one of the newfangled circuses, an entertainment that seemed to be surpassing or even destroying Wild West shows. Monkeys were popular exhibits in zoos too, and she'd seen some big ones, especially in Europe. Only the monkey on her back was bigger than she was.

Her last thought before diving into the well of sleep was to take the deed with her and go back out to the ranch in the morning.

Digging into the trunk as soon as she was dressed and her hair was in its usual braid, Cassie retrieved the packet of papers she'd found in the wagon cubbyholes on the trip south. Just when she heard the jingle and snort of an approaching horse and rider, the two dogs started announcing that company was arriving and one of the horses joined in. Cassie tucked the papers back in and shut the trunk before stepping out the door.

The sight of two riders made her pause until she recognized the young girl with the wheat-colored braids, Gretchen Engstrom.

"Hi, Miss Lockwood. I'm here on an errand for my mother. She said to tell you she hopes you will come back to the ranch this morning and to please bring . . ." The girl paused, and the man riding beside her finished for her.

"The deed to the ranch, if you have one, and any other things your father may have kept."

"This is my oldest brother, Ransom." She frowned at him, his cold tone being obvious to her too. "I have to go on to school, but he'll take your answer home to Mor. I do hope you are still there when I get home."

"That is, if you have—"

"Ransom Engstrom, that is rude." She glared at her brother and turned back to Cassie. "He isn't always like this. Sorry."

"You better get a move on, or you'll be late."

"I know. Bye." She waved and reined her horse around to lope back out on the trail.

He barely touched the brim of his hat. "And your message for my mother?"

"I'll be there soon." *Of all the nerve.* On one hand she could understand his obvious resentment, but manners were manners. It was a shame he didn't live up to his rugged good looks. As she watched him turn and leave without even a polite good-bye, she clenched her teeth. This sure didn't look good for them having an amicable meeting.

3

Bar E Ranch

Ransom hated making mistakes, even more than most people did.

His horse turned into the ranch lane without being guided, which was a good thing, since Ransom's thoughts were everywhere but on his riding. His mother would have been truly disappointed in the sarcastic way he'd spoken to Miss Lockwood. One never treated guests with anything but graciousness; that was a cardinal rule of her training of both daughter and sons. No matter how one felt, being polite was not negotiable. And Gretchen was just like their mother. Now she was disappointed in him too. What a great way to ruin a perfectly fine fall day. He had planned to spend the day stripping branches off the downed pine trees to get them ready to run through the saw and make posts for shoring up the cave-in that had happened so many years ago at the mine.

After nearly losing his life in the cave-in, his father, Ivar, had boarded up the mine and ordered everyone to stay out of it, saying there was no more gold and the mine shafts were unstable. But Ransom kept on believing that in spite of the opinions they'd received from mining experts, there was still gold in that mine. The first step was to clear the debris of the cave-in and fit the tunnels with new supports to prevent a reoccurrence. They had borrowed a steam-run sawmill from a neighbor, and as soon as there was time, the two brothers would saw the downed pine trees into six-by-sixes.

His mind still on the mine, Ransom unsaddled his horse at the barn and let him loose in the small pasture. The fragrance of baking cinnamon rolls met him on the back porch, where he pulled his boots off at the jack. His mother was indeed rolling out the red carpet for this probable land thief.

He thought back to the amazing story his mother had told her children the night before. The more he thought about it, although she'd never said so, he wondered if his mother had been in love with Lockwood. The wistfulness in her eyes as she told her story suggested that. Had their father started his heavy drinking when he realized his wife loved another man? That would make many a man start to tip the bottle. He entered the kitchen.

"So what did she say?" Mavis looked up from rolling pie dough.

"She said she'd be here soon," he said, adjusting the thong that held his hair back.

"Why didn't you wait for her?"

"I thought you'd want to know she was coming. Where's Lucas?"

"Checking the herd and the fences. Said he'd watch for company. Remember the other night when he returned from town and said he'd seen the woman of his dreams?"

"Ja, a bit of superlatives from our ladies' man. I think we've heard that before."

"I believe the woman he was swooning over was Cassie Lockwood."

"Figures. He always goes for the new skirt in town."

Mavis looked up from her pie dough. "What burr got under your saddle?"

"Do you actually believe her story?"

"I do. No one could make all that up. I've seen her copy of the deed. And when she shows you that deed and how it matches the one I have, you will have to believe too. It's not like she can take the ranch away from us, son. We own half the land and all the improvements. If we need to divide the land, we will still have a fine ranch."

"Two hundred acres is not enough to run the number of cattle we have now, let alone allow us to increase the herd." He poured himself a cup of coffee and propped his haunches against the counter. "I might as well tell you before Gretchen comes home all indignant. I was rude to Miss Lockwood. Gretchen called me on it." Sipping from his cup, he tried to ignore his mother's raised eyebrows as she laid the just-rolled top crust over the apple filling in the second pie. "Do you think she'll stay long?"

"I hope so. They need to move their wagon closer to here. I thought by the barn for now. They can run their stock in the small pasture until we all decide what to do."

"So you are planning on their moving here, no matter how Lucas and I feel?"

Mavis sighed and slid the two pies into the oven. She shut the heavy oven door with a thud before turning to her son. "Think this through, Ransom. She has a legal deed to this place. Because of that, she can live here if she wants to. She could probably go to the law and have the sheriff serve us a warrant or whatever the legal process is. Do you honestly want that to happen?" She crossed her arms and leaned against the counter, matching her son. "Besides all that, her father was your father's very good friend, and mine as well. Do you expect me to turn his daughter away from our home?"

Put like that, Ransom knew there was no need for further argument. "No, she would be welcome here." But inside he wondered, if he had shown up at the Wild West Show, would Mr. Lockwood welcome him with such open hands? All on the basis of a very long-ago friendship?

"Thank you. Now you might want to fill your brother in on our conversation before he comes storming in here."

"And asks her to marry him?"

Mavis grinned and then chuckled. "Ransom Engstrom, you never cease to amaze me."

Ransom went out the back door, hoofing it to the barn, where Lucas was unsaddling his horse. "Mor wants me to make sure you understand that we are to welcome Miss Lockwood as a long-lost relative or friend."

"Whyever wouldn't I?" He arched an eyebrow. "I take it something happened already today that I am not aware of?"

"Don't ask. There goes the warning bark. I'll bring her horse down here and put him in the small pasture with ours."

"I could do that," Lucas offered.

"But I've already met her. You haven't. Mor has cinnamon rolls waiting."

"Honored guest?" The two men headed back up to the house, Ransom splitting off to go to the front door.

"Good morning again, Miss Lockwood. I'll take your horse to the barn and let him out in the pasture, if you like."

The look she gave Ransom might have made him smile were he in a more hospitable mood.

"Thank you." She dismounted and dug a packet of papers from her saddlebag.

"Go right on in. Mor knows you are here."

"Your dog announced it to the entire country."

"He's good at that." Ransom stroked her horse's nose and led the pinto away.

Cassie stood alone, her dreams and her father's, her whole future wadded up and tucked under her arm. Now what? Other than the cold chill vibrating her breastbone?

In spite of the young man's instructions, Cassie raised her hand to the knocker, but the door opened before she could rap the metal E brand against the iron plate.

"Come in, Cassie." Mavis Engstrom held the door open wide, matching her smile.

The chill abated, just a bit. "Thank you." She stepped through the doorway, inhaling the fragrance that inundated her. "What smells so good?"

"I baked cinnamon rolls this morning. Thought you might like a taste of home."

"The cook at the show baked cinnamon rolls sometimes, but they sure didn't smell like yours." She held her packet close to her side and looked around the room, delighting again in the welcome of it.

"Did you bring the others?" the tall woman asked.

"N-no. I thought perhaps we should talk about some things first."

"Well, you have a seat, and I'll—" She turned to see Lucas come through the door carrying a tray with the food things.

He smiled at Cassie and set the tray on the low table made of the same wood as the furniture. "Hello. I'm Lucas."

"Miss Lockwood, Mr. Engstrom," Mavis said, putting the emphasis on manners.

Cassie smiled and nodded. While the older brother seemed stern, the younger, with his short hair curling around his ears, had his mother's engaging smile and easy way. "Pleased to meet all of you."

"My sister is in love with your horse."

Just then Ransom came from the kitchen. "Your horse handles easily."

"Wind Dancer is used to other people taking care of him. He and I grew up together—at least that's what my father used to say. That's probably why we can read each other's minds."

"Please, sit down, all of us. Do you take cream and or sugar with your coffee?"

"No. Black will be fine." The fragrance of the rolls was making her mouth water. Would that she could learn to bake like that someday. Not just bake but cook in general. She sank down into the leather chair, not allowing herself to relax against the back. After all, she was really there on business and things could go all wrong in an instant.

Mavis passed the plate of rolls, and Cassie took the one on

top. Manners said one should never eat until all were served, but when Lucas took the first bite of his, she followed suit.

"My mother makes the best rolls and apple pie anywhere."

"Lucas, whatever happened to not talking with your mouth full?" Ransom glared at his brother.

Cassie took a small bite, to make the treat last longer. So there was more than a bit of hard feelings between the two brothers. The thought that her presence might be causing the rift made her want to leave without showing them the deed. She set her roll down and picked up the cup, something to hide behind. When she glanced at Mrs. Engstrom, the gentle and welcoming look nearly undid her. How could she be so gracious when she knew the reason Cassie was there?

"Go ahead and enjoy your roll," she said with a smile. "Sometimes ignoring a conversation is easier than answering."

"Maybe we'd better get the hard talking over with right away."

"Are you in a hurry?"

"N-no, but . . ." The coffee now tasted bitter, something like the fear in her heart. Obviously Ransom did not want her there at all. Lucas was charming, but this was still his ranch, and Mrs. Engstrom made her want to be part of this family, even more so than wanting to live on the ranch. A home. All she wanted was a home. She'd not thought about having a family, other than her three traveling companions, with that home.

"I have the deed and all the papers of my father's that I could locate." She laid the packet on the table. "I mean, to prove who I really am."

Ransom looked like someone had carved his face in stone. Lucas leaned forward, but the smile had disappeared.

Cassie slid the deed from the papers and laid it on the little table before Mrs. Engstrom. "As far as I know, this is legal. I do know that is my father's signature."

Mavis laid a matching paper beside it. The other deed. "And I know that both those signatures are the real thing. According to the deed, you own half of this ranch. There is no mention of including all the improvements we have made through the years. When Adam and Ivar bought this land, the first thing they built was the log cabin up by the mine. They both lived there while they were digging for gold. They used the gold to pay for the land, with plans to build two houses. When Lockwood left with the Wild West Show, he said he would return one day."

"But he died before he could realize that dream. I always thought the valley was just a dream, one that I wanted to find. But only when I discovered the deed in the show wagon did I know he already owned a part of the land. I do not want to take what you have created. I only want a place to live and some pasture for the animals I have. My father dreamed of raising Appaloosa horses and herds of cattle. I don't know anything about breeding horses and raising cattle. I am willing to learn if someone wants to teach me, but the only world I know is the show world that I came from."

"What will you live on?" Ransom's eyes never softened. "Feeding cattle, the few you have, takes pasture and hay and some grain, especially for the horses."

"I know. I've thought of that. I am sure that once I inform show people of where I am and that I would be interested in participating in shooting matches, I can perhaps earn enough to support us." She met his eyes, stare for stare.

He turned those granite eyes away from her. "No need to

go getting all stiff and upset. But building a house takes time, and winter is nearly here."

"They will live in the cabin," Mavis said with finality. "Perhaps the two women could sleep in the cabin and the men in the show wagon. We have plenty of pasture and hay put up for the winter. You can run your animals in with ours. Are they all branded?"

"Yes, with the L and T of Lockwood and Talbot." Cassie paused, smiling at the thought. "Chief said he was always in charge of the branding when new stock entered the show and when the babies were born in the spring." And now Cassie could hardly talk. All she wanted to do was run over and throw her arms around this woman who was offering her more cinnamon rolls—and a life.

But would her sons go along with her? Or did they really have a say?

"How long will it take for you to bring your wagon and the cattle out here?"

"I thought . . . I mean, are you sure?"

"Of course we are. I was hoping you would all be here for dinner, but supper will be fine. You can park the wagon by the barn for now."

"But, Mor, that cabin needs work to be fit for people to live in it." Lucas looked from Cassie to his mother.

"I know. I was just up there recently, remember? With all of us working, we should have it cleaned and repaired in a couple of days, and then we can move their wagon up there." She paused for a moment. "Actually, you could share a room here in the house with Gretchen, if you would like. I know she'd be thrilled."

Cassie shook her head. "No, no I can't do that. The cabin

will be wonderful." She kept from looking at Ransom, sure that the granite had not begun to crumble. But then again, all she knew about granite was that it was extremely hard, so she was not surprised. So far it seemed that all the giving was on their side and all the taking on hers. She had to earn enough money to pay her own way—hers and her "family's." Surely there would be some names of people in the show world in those papers she'd saved in the wagon. If only she had paid more attention, but Jason Talbot had always promised her he'd take care of her.

Well, he'd done that for sure. Only a canyon ran between his idea of caring for her and hers. And she was sure Talbot's shortcomings would have distressed her father too. If only he were there to celebrate with her. *"Welcome home,"* Mrs. Engstrom had said. Could this indeed become the home she'd always dreamed of? And even more so, the home her father had dreamed of?

4

Cassie leaned forward and patted Wind Dancer's shoulder. "I still can't believe we will have a place for the winter. Nothing like we were used to, but no matter—it'll be better than the wagon. At least it seems that way for right now. I sure wonder what the whole story is about those early years." Wind Dancer's ears flicked forward and back as he listened to her voice. "I guess talking with you isn't a whole lot different than talking to Chief or Micah. No one answers much."

The horse snorted, making her smile. "I apologize. Of course you listen and answer. But I have to warn you, there will be no warm stall for you this winter, and we are going to find out what winters in South Dakota are really like. Chief says they can be brutal. I wish I knew what he meant by that. I guess we will learn."

On the other side of the road from the entrance to the Bar E Ranch, another road ran off to a different ranch. This one didn't have the attractive pole with the ranch name carved into it. She wondered who lived there. Would the other ranchers in the area accept them like the Engstroms had? *If* they had.

Mavis. Lucas. Ransom. Each so different and yet obviously so close. A family. Ransom's anger burned into her, so unbending, defying her to quench it. Mavis was the leader, the matriarch, so surely he trusted his mother's . . . trust! That was it. Ransom did not trust her, did not fully believe her. There was no reason he should, she realized, but neither was there any reason he shouldn't. There'd been many times when others had been angry with her for some reason. The moment had always passed. But never had she been deemed untrustworthy. If distrust formed at least part of his attitude, his refusal to trust her ate at her worse than his anger ever could. But was she right about that?

Since she had no answers, she switched her thinking to the money situation. What would it take to set up some shooting matches? How did one go about getting invited to participate? Tonight she would go through those papers and learn whatever she could, no matter how long it took. She turned into the narrow road that led to the camp. At least tonight she wouldn't have to worry about those ruffians from Argus finding them and causing more problems. She didn't allow herself to imagine what those problems might have been.

Othello did his dance of greeting, and Chief and Runs Like a Deer looked up from working on the deer hide they had been curing. Runs Like a Deer had said that she wanted to finish the job, whatever that took, so she could make something from it. They watched and waited for Cassie to dismount and tie her horse to a wagon wheel.

"They want us to come today. They've invited us for supper.

There is a log cabin by the mine that will be ours for the winter."

Chief nodded. "I remember that cabin. We all worked to build it."

Cassie stared at him. What other information was he not sharing about those early years? Most likely everything that had happened. If only she could get him talking about those times.

"How big is it?"

"Bigger than the wagon for sure."

"The older brother, Ransom, wants to clear out the mine where it collapsed and search for gold again."

"The vein quit."

"I have no idea about that. Anyway, Mrs. Engstrom said that they would all help us get the cabin ready for winter."

"Good." Chief looked around. "You ready the wagon. I will bring in the team. Micah will round up the cattle and buffalo."

"Should I use the water from the barrel to kill the fire?"

"Yes. We can refill it there." Within an hour they were ready to leave the campsite. Cassie, on her horse, stayed behind to make sure they had everything and then followed Micah and the animals down the road. Chief was driving the wagon, with Runs Like a Deer sitting beside him.

By the time they drove into the ranch, Cassie's butterflies had returned to have a party in her middle. Was she doing the right thing? Were there any other things she could do? Should do? Why was it that taking from these strangers who really didn't feel like strangers did not sit well with her at all?

You are living your father's dream, she told herself. *Living here is where you need to be, on the land he owned with these people. You are now a half owner of this ranch.* She repeated that to herself. *I own half this land, this ranch.* She had never owned anything in her life but her clothes, her guns, and her horse, but now she owned half a ranch in South Dakota. A place to live. A safe place for her and her friends.

Following the instructions Ransom gave him, Chief halted the wagon on the west side of the barn. Ransom opened the gate to a fenced-in pasture, and they drove the three buffalo and the cattle through. When she and Micah had dismounted, she introduced them to Ransom.

"So you really knew my father?" he asked, shaking Chief's hand.

"I did. A good man."

"Were you here when the mine collapsed?"

"Yes."

"I wish you would tell us about that some time."

Chief only shrugged.

Cassie watched the exchange, wondering, as she was sure Ransom was wondering, why Chief didn't volunteer more information. But then, she knew Chief, and he never volunteered anything. While Micah unhitched the team, she unsaddled her horse and they let all the horses loose in the pasture where the other animals were already grazing. They had stopped by the water tank and filled up the water barrel at the pump. Setting up camp was easy, for they had brought their dry wood along with them to start a fire.

"Mor is planning on all of you coming for supper. We'll eat at about five."

"Thank you. This is Runs Like a Deer, and Micah is our animal handler."

"We call men who take care of cattle 'wranglers.'"

"Oh. Then Micah is our wrangler. Micah, meet Mr. Ransom Engstrom."

Both Micah and Runs Like a Deer nodded but with no hint of a smile showing. *He must think we are an unfriendly group,* Cassie thought. *Unfriendly and come to take part of his land. Possibly untrustworthy. We haven't made much of a good impression, I'm afraid.* But she kept her thoughts to herself, making sure she was wearing her company face. Not the performing smile but a public one. It wasn't hard to understand why he seemed less gracious than his mother, who had recognized the deed immediately, since she had one to match it. She had an idea that this whole land ownership thing was as new to the brothers as it was to her. She wasn't sure what made her think that, but there it was.

"Can I get you anything else?" Forced politeness again. It was a shame his younger brother wasn't out here instead.

"No, thank you." Polite for polite.

"Then I'll get on with my chores. If you need more firewood, the back porch has shorter wood cut for the stove, and the front porch has longer for the fireplace. Help yourselves."

"Thank you." Cassie watched him walk off and then turned to Runs Like a Deer. "I'm going to sort through some more of those papers." What she really wanted to do was go spend the afternoon with Mrs. Engstrom.

"I will finish up the deer hide. Chief said to go hunting in the morning."

Cassie heaved a sigh. "All right." Going hunting never rated high on her list of pleasurable things to do. But they did need to eat, and more and more she was seeing the value of the hides. She'd worn the mittens that Runs Like a Deer made for her and knew that when winter hit, she'd be even more thankful. There were now enough rabbit skins to make her a vest, she'd been told. She climbed into the wagon, pulled out a drawer, and started digging.

As she sorted through the letters again, she watched for anything to do with acts in shows, but mostly, she wanted contacts for shooting matches. Nothing. Where had she put them? She pulled out another of the built-in drawers along the long wall and, sitting back down at the table where she had the kerosene lamp set up, attacked another stack. It was a shame she had not separated them all out the last time. When she finally located the correct stack, all the addresses were for cities on the East Coast or in the South. What could she do to get to them? She had no money, no contacts, and no experience in this organizing part. In the past, she'd had Jason Talbot to do this and her father before that. Whom could she ask for advice? Alone and lost hardly began to describe her feelings.

If only she had copies of the letters Talbot had sent out. Did he never keep track of anything? Anger at him and his poor business practices sputtered and revived in her middle. No wonder he'd gone bankrupt. But what did he do with the money the show brought in? He'd paid the payroll, usually on time, he'd fed them all and provided housing and must have paid other expenses until he declared them bankrupt. But how much money had he taken with him? She'd never know, so she smashed the thought before it could continue to eat at her. She didn't really want to see him again anyway.

One night earlier she'd read through one of the account books her father had kept. The show had been healthy then, with a solid worldwide reputation, only to be disbanded in Dickinson, the most westerly point of their circuit. Her mind wandered back to the glory days, as she was beginning to think of them. For several years after her father died, the show had done well. In the winter months she had participated in rehearsals for new acts and in exhibitions that Talbot had set up. Had organizers invited them to take part or had Jason set them up? The latter seemed less probable now, as she realized his lack of ambition, or was it his lack of ability? She'd never get answers to her questions now, and she'd been too trusting before. It was a shame it had taken such a major shock to wake her up.

Cassie glanced up to see that the daylight coming in the window of the door had started to dim while she was sorting. Mr. Engstrom had said supper at five. Was it nearing that? She eyed the stacks and drawers left to search through. *Please, Lord, let there be something in all this to help us. Someone. You know we need money to get through the winter. Not just the winter. How do I make sure we have enough to take care of us and the animals?* The weight of responsibility hung on her like the chains that had locked down the wagon on the train cars when they traveled between shows.

She looked up at a knock at the door. None of them knocked, so it must be one of the Engstroms. "Come in."

Gretchen stuck her head around the door. "Mor sent me to remind you that supper is nearly ready, if you'd like to come up to the house."

"Thank you. Let me put things away here, and we'll be right there. Are the others nearby?"

"Around the fire." She hesitated.

"Would you like to come in?"

"Mor said I shouldn't bother you if you were busy."

"I just ceased being busy. You are welcome to look around. The wagon is an interesting home."

Gretchen stepped in and shut the door behind her before staring around. "I've never seen so many drawers and doors. It's like a playhouse."

"That it is." Leaving her guest to continue her inspection, Cassie gathered up the stacks she had sorted through and put them back into separate drawers and cubbyholes. No sense mixing things up again. The stack of helpful papers was mighty short. Surely there had to be contact people somewhere out there.

Reverend Brandenburg from Argus. He must know a lot of people in the local area. She'd ask him when she went to town the next time. Maybe she would need to make a special trip. Closing the last door, she smiled at her guest. "Okay, I'm ready. How was school today?"

"Good. Two boys got in trouble for not having their homework done."

After they stepped outside, Cassie nodded to the others. "You ready?"

"We could stay here," Micah offered.

Gretchen's face fell. "Please don't. My mother likes to have company, and we're all excited to get to know you."

Cassie kept from rolling her eyes. If she knew anything about people, the two Engstrom brothers were not excited. Resentful was more likely. Purely angry obviously fit the older son, and resentment and anger were not excitement. She didn't blame them; at least she tried not to. She tried to pay attention to what Gretchen was saying, but the closer they came to the front steps, the more she wanted to hang back. She glanced over her shoulder, feeling like she was leading the parade and the others would rather not be in it. She didn't blame them either.

"I hope you'll tell us all about your life in the Wild West Show," Gretchen said as she opened the door and stepped aside for them to enter.

"Welcome back," Mrs. Engstrom said as she dried her hands on her apron. She reached out to take Cassie's before turning to the others.

"Mrs. Engstrom, I'd like you to meet Runs Like a Deer and Micah, who is our wrangler." There, at least she'd used the right word. They both nodded, but their smiles remained hidden.

"I'm glad to meet all of you. Welcome to the Bar E. If you'll make yourself at home, supper will be ready in a minute or two." She gestured toward the leather sofa and the chairs. "My sons will be here in just a couple of minutes."

"May I help you?" Cassie had no idea what she could do, but it seemed proper to offer.

"No, thank you. Gretchen and I have everything under control."

Cassie took one of the chairs so that the others would do the same. Besides, she liked just looking around the room. Three racks of antlers hung from the rock face above the mantel. She wasn't sure what they came from, other than a deer, and the two really long horns she knew came from cattle, longhorns like those they had from the show. For some reason, people back east really liked longhorns.

The rocking chair by the fire made her think of pictures she'd seen in magazines—pictures of homes with parlors or a chair by a stove. Sometimes waiting beside the chair was a small table with a lamp on it and perhaps a Bible, and often there was a braided rug in front, although this bearskin rug served just as well. Always with a feeling of love and comfort, parts she thought of as a home. She'd never realized how badly she'd wanted a home until she met Reverend Obediah Hornsmith and his wife in Belle Fourche, their first real stop on their way south. Their house was like this room with good smells coming from the kitchen and a fire dancing in the fireplace. Homes should be like this.

She glanced over to see Micah and Runs Like a Deer sitting on the edge of the sofa as if afraid to lean back. Chief was standing by the fire, his deeply lined face without expression. But when Cassie caught his eye, he raised one eyebrow and his mouth twitched. Was that almost a smile? He glanced over his shoulder, up the wall.

"What is the largest set from?" she asked.

"Bull elk. Bigger than a deer. Much bigger."

"You've hunted them before?"

A nod. He must have used up his allotted supply of words. The thought made her smile. Ah, if only he would tell her more of what he knew about her father, and now the Engstroms too. How could she get that to happen?

Mavis came to the kitchen door. "Please, come and eat."

Cassie stood and glanced at Runs Like a Deer, who looked like that is exactly what she wanted to do—run away. Micah met her gaze and shrugged the slightest bit. Again, she led the way. Sometimes she allowed herself one little bit of wishing that someone else would step forward and lead for a time. Maybe once they were moved into the cabin, things would be different. The thought of the cabin nearly made her smile.

Until she walked into the kitchen and met the stare of the older son. Ransom was not prepared to give an inch, she realized. *"Don't expect anything and you won't be disappointed."* One of Jason Talbot's pet phrases came back to her. Far better to remember her mother's words. *"Give thanks to the Lord in all things."*

They sat down in the places indicated. Mrs. Engstrom at one end and Ransom at the other, her three companions on one side of the oval table, while she sat at Mavis's right, with Gretchen next to her and Lucas next to his brother.

"Ransom, if you will say grace, please."

"Thank you, Lord, for this food and this day. Amen."

Short and sweet. Another man of few words. All of a sudden, Cassie missed the lively discussions around the supper tables of the show cast. Rehashing the day, swapping tales of days gone by, general teasing of folks who knew each other well. She clenched her teeth against the lump in her throat. What brought that on? Was there any chance that they could become friends, this family and hers, or would there always be the tension she felt around this table?

5

I think yesterday went very well, getting to know them." Ransom's mother hustled about in the kitchen, and she was smiling. "Now tonight's supper will be less tense, I'm sure."

Ransom was not smiling. "You accept her without any more questions than that?" Ransom thought about those two deeds. He had studied them carefully and critically, hoping that he would see something wrong, anything wrong. They had obviously been signed at the same time, since all the signatures matched; in fact, the two were virtually identical.

"What is there to question?"

"I don't know, but shouldn't there be a trial time? Something that says if this doesn't work out, we can have her removed or she would just leave?" Ransom paced the length of the room and back. "I can't believe we are locked into this—this agreement, for want of a better word—without talking with someone else."

"Like whom would we talk to? The man who drew these up is long gone, like your father. The law will abide by the printed deeds unless something shows up that negates the deeds. Short of offering her half of the land, I think in the long run, this is what's best for all of us."

Lucas came back in the house, whistling a tune.

"You certainly sound happy." Ransom did not feel happy, so how could Lucas?

"Why shouldn't I be? Now that I have met her, I am even more convinced that she is indeed the woman I have always dreamed of."

Ransom snorted. "What about Betsy? You've been walking Betsy home for a year or so now. I bet she thinks that any day you will propose, and she will gladly become Mrs. Lucas Engstrom."

Lucas winced. "I guess I better talk with her, huh?"

"Lucas, you don't even know Cassie. How can you say you are in love with her?" Mavis shot her younger son a questioning look.

"I didn't say I'm in love with her. I said I want to marry her. I know I'll fall in love. I can feel it coming."

"Oh—" Ransom cut off the rest of his sentence. Arguing with Lucas would do no good. Better that they put their heads together to figure a way out of this. "Maybe she would like to go homestead in Montana."

"Would you buy her out?" Mavis dropped her comment into the discussion.

"With what?" Ransom stomped over to stand in front of the stove. "It's getting colder out." He stared at his mother. "You did say all of us should work on the cabin, right?"

"I did."

"What about all the other chores we have to do around here to get ready for winter?"

"I—" Mavis sucked in a deep breath. "We can't let them freeze to death in that cabin the way it is."

"Let them fix it up. They're the ones going to live there. Besides, when we were up there, I figured it was pretty much weatherproof. I was planning on staying up there while I worked on the mine."

"You are going to go ahead with that, then?"

"I thought that during the winter the snow and cold don't really get deep into the ground. With Lucas helping, we should be able to get the mine repaired before spring." Why did he keep trying to convince her? Changing his mother's mind when it was made up was as impossible as stopping a snowstorm.

"You don't know how much there is to do there."

"Probably, but we have the pine trees cut, so we are nearly ready to run them through the saw."

"Perhaps Chief and Micah would be willing to help around here."

"We can't afford to pay them."

"True, but if you asked, they might like something to do. Once that cabin is fixed up and they have wood for the winter, what will they have to do? Other than hunt."

"Since they're running their livestock with ours, they can help feed them and maintain fences." Lucas poured himself a cup of coffee. "And like you said, they could help in the mine. Personally, I'd like to see how well Miss Lockwood can shoot. If she starred in a Wild West show, she must be pretty good at what she does. You've got to admit, that is one flashy horse she rides."

"Maybe if you ask her nice, she'll give a demonstration. I know Gretchen would be absolutely delighted."

"Speaking of Gretchen and making nice"—Ransom decided he might as well get this over with—"sooner or later she is going to tell you that I was less than polite when we went down to the barn to talk with them earlier. Talking with some young woman who is going to waltz in here and take half our ranch is . . . was . . ." He glared at his grinning brother. "I find it very difficult to be polite at all times."

"How bad was it?" Lucas raised his eyebrows, losing a halfhearted fight with the grin that Ransom seriously considered wiping off his face.

"Just accept that I told you, and now I am going out to split more wood."

"That riled, eh?"

"You can come do the same. Let's see who gets the largest pile before chores time."

"You're on!"

Mavis watched them go. This way they'd at least work off some of their animosity, and today's meals would be far more pleasant. She hummed along with the rhythm of dueling axes, looking forward to getting to know her soon-to-be neighbors better. What furniture and supplies could go up to the cabin to help make it more comfortable? Maybe she should first ask them what they had. But if the wagon was like she suspected and Gretchen had confirmed, with tables, chairs, and beds all built in, they most likely had nothing.

There was the rocker she kept in her bedroom, which could go. And the old table out on the back porch. It was pretty weathered and scarred but serviceable. But what for chairs? While there was a built-in bed at the cabin, the remainder of her furnishings had been made for this house, used here as the family grew. If Ivar were here, he would build chairs with ease. Strange what brought about thoughts of him again. Even after all these years, some days she just wanted to sit down and let him tell her what he dreamed about doing on the ranch next. He'd always had big dreams. And he had looked forward to the day when his sons would be old enough to take an active part in the ranch.

Well, Ivar, here they are, and good, strapping boys you would be proud to claim. She would make an apple spice cake next.

You could have offered Cassie and her friends the bunkhouse. The thought stopped her in midmotion. Of course she could have, so why didn't she? Pondering that question, she covered the remains from breakfast with a dish towel and got out the ingredients to make the cake. By the time she had refilled the stove and slipped the cake with sliced apples on top into the oven, the thunk of alternating axes was slowing. She looked out the kitchen window to see both of her sons shedding their vests. The determination etched into their faces said that their shirts would be next to go.

All they needed was for them to catch the grippe out there, but she didn't try to stop them. They'd be much more amenable around the dinner table if they were exhausted. She also refused to let her mind worry over dividing the land. She knew that Ivar and Adam had planned on ranching this land together, not dividing it. *Dear Lord, let that happen. Let this be a good addition to our ranch, not an insurmountable problem.* Washing the cooking things in the sink always brought her time with her Lord. If someone asked her what her favorite praying place was, she'd have to say the kitchen sink.

Father, I keep seeing that young face and thinking she could have been my daughter, had I gone with Adam. Never in all these years had she allowed her thoughts to take such a turn. She'd made her choice and had lived up to that faithfully, never looking back. Well, if she were going to be totally honest, not that she knew how to be anything but, once or twice when Ivar was passed out drunk, she had felt sorry for herself and let what-ifs play in her mind for a bit. But every time, God saw her through.

And now they are both gone. His wife is gone too, and I am left with our children. Lord God, give me all the wisdom I need here. I know you will, and I thank you for that.

Lucas had shucked his shirt. Good thing he was in the sunshine. The pile of split wood had doubled. She should go out there and stack for a while, but instead she went into the other room to build up the fire in the fireplace. After poking the coals back to life, she added wood and it caught immediately. She sat down in the rocker and picked up her Bible. Setting the rocker in motion always calmed her. Ivar had finished the chair in plenty of time to welcome their firstborn, Ransom. Ivar believed every mother needed a rocking chair for nursing babies. The creaking song of it spread peace throughout the room and into her heart. As she flipped through the New Testament, her gaze lighted on Jesus' words *And lo, I am with you always.*

She repeated the verse aloud. *Father, I thank you for the reminder. What a promise.* She read several other passages, finishing with the love chapter in Corinthians. *Charity suffereth long, and is kind . . . beareth all things, believeth all things, hopeth all things. . . . but the greatest of these is charity.*

No more thudding. She rose and returned to the kitchen to

check on her cake. She stuck a broom straw in the cake and it came out clean, signaling that it was done. She drew the cake from the oven to set on a rack on the counter. Glancing at the clock, she figured Cassie and her entourage would be up from the barn any time now. Both men were buttoning up their shirts and then shaking hands.

Truce called. For two men who were so different, usually they got along remarkably well. The woodboxes always benefited when they chose to solve their differences with the axes. One time the fence on the south edge of the south pasture came to life rather quickly for the same reason.

Sometime later she heard the dog bark. Company coming. They were here, although she could not think of them as company. They were so much more than that. She kept herself from running to the front porch and waving them in. Let the boys take care of this part. While she wanted to fetch Cassie and spend the rest of the afternoon visiting with her, she decided to take it easy. Gretchen had mentioned that several of them had gone up to the cabin to reconnoiter and decide what would be needed.

She took out the big crockery bowl she used for mixing most anything and measured in the ingredients for chocolate cookies. For some reason that sounded especially appealing. Gretchen loved them.

"Mor, they are back." Gretchen burst through the door after school when Mavis was removing the last pan from the oven. "Oh my. What smells so good?" Picking up a still-hot one, she tossed it from hand to hand to cool before taking a bite. "I thought maybe Cassie would be in here."

"I'm sure they have a lot to do at the wagon too. Put the cooled ones in the square cookie tin."

"Okay, but I was hoping to go see her horse, and her, of course. Are those people with her really real Indians? I mean, Indian Indians. They really are, aren't they?"

"They are."

"Will she tell us about it? I want to hear all about it."

"We shall see. Go ahead and set the table now too. The roast is in; we'll add the vegetables later. Help me think of things we could send up to the cabin for them."

"A cat to kill the mice."

"That's a good idea. One or two of those half-grown cats from the barn would be the thing."

"Two. One cat and it will come right back here. Or some traps."

"Or both."

"I wish she would stay here. My bedroom is big enough."

"Thank you. I wish so too, but hopefully we'll have her here a lot." *Adam Lockwood's daughter.*

They gathered up a featherbed and some quilts, along with the table and rocking chair, added the vegetables to the roast, and set the table. It was all that could be done as dusk began to settle more tightly over the valley, a slight fog rising with the cooling of the coming night.

"You go remind them that supper is about ready, all right?" Mavis smiled as Gretchen flew out the door and down the slight slope from house to barn. The boys had reservations, but Gretchen was obviously enamored with Adam's daughter.

Adam Lockwood's daughter, his only child.

Mavis had finished cleaning up the kitchen by the time she heard voices out front. She laid a hand on her middle to calm the flutters of anticipation and went to meet them at the door.

6

Mavis, Gretchen, and Cassie kept the conversation going at the supper table. Cassie could see Micah was beginning to relax, as he had second helpings at Mavis's request, but he, Chief, and Runs Like a Deer were their normal taciturn selves. The sons were very quiet. Were they always like this at the table, or had Cassie's appearance changed things that much?

"Thank you, ma'am. This is delicious." Micah caught Cassie's glance, and one corner of his mouth twitched.

Chief only answered with a nod or shake of his head when spoken to directly, as in "Would you like more gravy?" Finally he raised his hand, palm out, and said, "No more, thank you." Runs Like a Deer just shook her head.

Lucas seemed about ready to laugh, and Ransom passed things without a word, but at least he didn't seem quite as dark and forbidding as before.

"So how old were you when your father gave you Wind Dancer?" Gretchen was full of questions.

"About twelve, maybe eleven. No wait, Dancer is ten, so I guess I was a couple years younger than you are." Cassie smiled at the eager girl. "He was newly weaned and not happy to be taken from his mother. I thought he was the prettiest thing I had ever seen. He fit right in with George and me. The two of them would follow me around the corral. I was about your size, and strangers would be horrified to see that big bull buffalo taking carrots or hay from my hand. He has a place right above his eyes that he loves to have scratched. He does not like to get a bath. Wind Dancer does, though, unless the water is too cold."

"I had a pony for a while, but he got old and the wolves got him one winter." Gretchen spoke matter-of-factly, as if everyone lost a friend like that.

Mavis turned to Chief. "I have a question for you. Do you want me to call you Chief or John Birdwing?"

Cassie stared from her to her friend. "She called you that the first time we met. John Birdwing really is your name?"

He nodded. "Most everyone knows me as Chief."

"John Birdwing. That is a great name. Would those on the reservation remember you by that name?"

He nodded again.

Then this is your new life. Take whatever name you want. We can adjust. But Cassie kept her thought to herself to bring up to him when they were alone sometime.

"Mr. Chief?" Gretchen asked.

"Just Chief."

"But . . ." She glanced at her mother, who nodded.

With a shrug she continued. "You were friends with my father. Right?"

He nodded again.

"How did you meet him?"

"I heard that he and his friend were looking for a guide into the Black Hills, so I went to talk to them."

Cassie smiled at Gretchen and nodded to encourage her. Maybe he'd continue answering her instead of only grunting or ignoring the question.

"They were looking for our ranch?"

"No, they were looking for gold."

"And you helped them find it?"

"Yes."

"How did you know where to look?"

"I had found some shiny stones in a creek, and I took them there."

"I thought the Indians were trying to keep the prospectors out," Ransom said, finally joining the conversation.

"Most were and so was the army, but my family was starving."

"Oh." Cassie caught herself from saying more.

Gretchen ignored the look her mother gave her and asked what Cassie wanted to know. "What happened to your family?"

"Died. Sickness one winter. I stayed with Lockwood when he joined with Talbot."

"The Wild West Show."

"But you were there when the mine caved in?"

He simply nodded.

"Yes." Mavis added to the story. "John Birdwing nearly gave his life to save those two crazy white men who had insisted on digging deeper when the vein they found quit on them and they should have stopped. It took that to convince your father to close the mine."

Gretchen used the ensuing silence to change the subject. "The Wild West Show. Are all of you from the Wild West Show? I mean, the cattle and buffalo and . . ." She hesitated. "The Indians and all?"

Cassie laughed. "Even the dog. You see, people back east just love western things, and most of them have never seen a buffalo or an Indian. They would ooh and aah over George. If we wanted to really impress some important person, we'd let him feed George a carrot."

"So all he had to do was stand there?" Gretchen flushed slightly and looked from face to face across the table. "What did the Indians do?"

Chief shrugged. "Put on some costumes and gallop around the arena."

Cassie added, "And Chief was quick to explain to me that they were costumes, not real regalia. The costumes they wore usually weren't even from their own tribe."

Cassie realized she'd better change the subject. "Mrs. Engstrom—Mavis—this is delicious, and I am so grateful to be here. I've never been on a ranch before."

Lucas gave her a surprised look. "I thought you were from out west."

She smiled. "Wild West shows don't play well out west. We traveled around the East. I lived in the wagon and on the trains with the show all my life. I've never lived in a house before."

Even Ransom looked surprised, a nice change from that scowl.

She explained. "Usually right after the shows at Dickinson, we would travel south for the winter season, getting ahead of the winter storms. We'd be invited out to visit a farm sometimes, or a shooting match would be held on some big spread, but then we'd return to the wagons right away. We never stayed where the matches were held."

Lucas looked fascinated. "You really took part in shooting matches?"

"My father used to be a big name in the matches, and he took me along too. People were always amazed at how well I shot. You'd think that after Annie Oakley became so famous, and other female shooters too, that I'd be taken for granted, but I started out in my younger years, and that's what surprised people, I guess. Men don't like to be outshot by a fifteen-year-old girl."

"You won?"

"Not always, but usually, and I improved through the years. You don't know of any such events going on out here in the West, do you?" There, she'd asked one of the questions she really wanted, no, needed, an answer to.

"No, but I could look into it. Not to be nosy, but how do you get paid for performing?" Leaning forward, Lucas looked a lot more interested in the change of topic.

"The organizers or sponsors offer a pot to be given to the winner. Sometimes there is money for second place or even third too, if there are a lot of shooters. But if there are only two, then the winner takes it all."

Mavis rose. "Let's move into the other room. Gretchen, help me clear the table please. We'll bring dessert in there."

Cassie stood too. "I would like to help."

Mavis waved toward the door. "You just go sit. We have it taken care of."

Cassie glanced at Chief, and he motioned slightly toward the back door. She ignored him and led the way into the other room. She was afraid the other three would head back to the wagon, and it was time they learned to be part of the rest of the world—all of them, including her.

That night Cassie tossed and turned in her hammock in the wagon. Finally she threw back the covers and, wrapping in her coat, added more wood to the embers that had not had time yet to burn away.

"You all right?" Runs Like a Deer asked from the bunk bed.

"Just can't sleep. Do you mind if I go back to searching through the paper work? I need to locate people I can contact about shooting matches. Will it keep you awake?"

Runs Like a Deer gave a gentle snort. "No, don't worry. Now that I know you are all right, I'll go back to sleep."

"Thank you."

Within moments the woman's breathing signified she had done just as she said. After lighting the lamp, Cassie pulled more stacks of paper from the remaining drawers and cubbyholes with doors.

The pile was dwindling, with only a few sheets added to the pile of letters with contacts. She gave a deep sigh and rose to add more wood to the fire. Her eyes had begun to feel the gritty sand of sleep, but she returned to the sorting. There wasn't that much left to go.

How would she ever let enough people know where she was so that she could get invited to shooting matches? Why hadn't Jason Talbot kept better records, or at least kept her father's correspondence? Could there be anywhere else he might have put it all? She had washed out all the storage places. Or had she? She studied the wall behind her, but nothing snagged her attention. Had she pulled all the drawers out? As far as she could tell, she had.

She looked up, studying the ceiling, praying for some kind of wisdom. She could hear Mavis's voice. *"God always hears our prayers, and He always answers. Just sometimes we don't like His answers." So very true,* Cassie thought. *I prayed my mother and then my father wouldn't die, but here I am. Maybe I just didn't pray hard enough.*

In the circle of light reflected on the ceiling from the lamp, she saw a board that looked like it had warped. Great. Now the roof would probably start leaking. She pulled out the chair and climbed up on it to see if she could push the board back in place. Poor old wagon. No one had really taken care of it since her mother died. She pushed on the board, and instead of tightening, it loosened, hanging down even further.

Something glinted in the light. So she dug in with her fingertips, trying not to dislodge the entire board. The chair wiggled, and she jerked. Now she could see a piece of chain. She tugged on the chain, and a locket—her mother's gold locket that she always wore—dangled from the chain clamped in her fingers.

Her breath stopped. Her mother's locket! Why was it stuffed in the ceiling? She'd not seen it since her mother wore it last. At least she didn't remember seeing it. Who hid it in the ceiling? Why? She sank down on the chair, memories flooding like a rain-swollen river. Tears burned and then trickled down her face. Her mother's locket. She started to put it on but realized one part of the clasp was missing. Instead she wiped her face and began putting the papers all back, placing the locket in the front of the drawer with the small stack of papers she would study soon. Her mother's locket. Who would she find that could mend the chain?

When she climbed back in her hammock, she lay for a few moments, thanking God for this treasure. Part of her mother. Could this be classified as a miracle? She hugged the secret to herself, deciding not to show it to anyone until she could get it fixed. And then she would wear it proudly.

7

"That went better than I thought it would." Lucas leaned against the counter, arms crossed over his chest. "They sure seemed anxious to leave, though."

"I'm glad you think so." Ransom dumped another load of wood into the box.

Mavis wiped the table clean, not that it wasn't clean already. "So you'll both go up to the cabin with me in the morning?"

Ransom glanced at his mother after putting the canvas wood-hauling bag on the hook behind the woodbox. "Do you leave us any choice?"

"No. I could be a big help too, you know." Gretchen hung up her dish towel.

"You will be. Going to school is your job, and you will do it well."

"You know what I mean." Her eyebrows came together in the frown that she'd inherited from their father.

Ransom tweaked her single braid as she walked past him. "You know that you can't get out of school unless you're deathly sick."

Gretchen rolled her eyes. "I miss out on all the fun."

"You think it will be fun working on the cabin? Why don't we wait until Saturday, and you can take my place." Lucas grinned at her. "Mor has never let her children skip school for any reason. Ransom and I can attest to that."

Gretchen glared at him through narrowed eyes. "Did you ever skip?"

"How could I with my big brother always around?"

"You didn't answer my question." Her chin squared. "You did, didn't you!" She paused, counting briefly on her fingers. "It had to be after Ransom graduated. You were still in school after that."

"All right, so Hudson and I went fishing one time." He made a disgusted noise. "And we didn't even catch anything."

Mavis studied her younger son. "And that was the only time?"

"Yes. We knew if we got caught, there would be fireworks for sure, so we thought about it sometimes but never did it again."

"What did you use for an excuse the next day?"

"Mor, that was a long time ago." When she persisted in staring at him, he shrugged and shook his head. "I wrote one for him, and he wrote mine for me."

"And you signed my name?" Now Mavis crossed her arms and glared steely eyed at her younger son.

"Well, no, not exactly. I scribbled his mother's name, and Hudson scribbled yours. But the teacher didn't ask for our notes, so we threw them away. What is this? The inquisition?

It was a long time ago. I was just a kid, and I learned my lesson." He glared at Gretchen. "See what you started?"

She shrugged. "It's not my fault. I didn't skip."

"Well, I'm glad to hear it was a one-time thing. So what time will you be ready in the morning?"

"As if we have a choice."

"Right after breakfast, then. We'll load the cleaning supplies into the wagon—oh, and bring some firewood so we can heat water. Ransom, you'll see to all the tools?"

He nodded.

"Good, then. If anyone wants coffee, I'll bring it into the other room." Mavis raised a finger. "Oh, and we'll take food along for dinner too."

"'Night, everybody." Gretchen hugged her mother and headed down the hallway to her room. "At least I don't have to milk a cow in the morning."

Ransom muttered, "It don't take long to milk out a quart or less." But no one was listening.

A minute later Gretchen returned, a letter in her hand. "Sorry, Mor, I was so excited I forgot to give this to you. From Jesse."

"Oh, well. Glad to have it now." She smiled at her daughter, pulled out the paper, and read aloud.

"Dear Mor and all,

I am sorry that I do not write more often, but all of you are always with me in my mind. Thank you for writing even when I don't.

School is going well. I am grateful for all that I learned before coming here. Ranch living is a far better training ground for life than living in the cities, or at least it seems that way to me. I was so hoping to come home during the summer for a few days, but my job made that impossible. Jobs aren't real plentiful for part time, so I knew better than to even ask.

I know the matter of the mine is causing difficulties, like you said, but I think I agree with Ransom. Something about that hole in the ground intrigues me also. I have no idea why, but I am glad to hear Ransom is hanging on to that idea. Perhaps it is not gold to be found, but maybe something else. Times are changing and new minerals are being discovered and found uses for. Wouldn't it be a cosmic joke if that were the case, and Pa was sitting on another kind of gold mine?

I better get back to my studies. I am hoping to graduate in May, so have already been investigating medical schools. My professors assure me that since I am in the top three of my class—we keep taking turns as to who is first—I will have my choice of where to go from here. May graduation depends on several things, so I will let you know when I know for sure.

My love to you all, and thank you for the money. Every little bit helps.

Your son,
Jesse"

Mavis sighed. "What a perfect ending to a rather exciting day."

"Wait till Jesse hears about all this," Ransom muttered, his hand sweeping to encompass the wagon too.

Cassie hardly slept, she was so excited. Any dread she had felt about approaching the Engstroms with her deed had disappeared. This place was hers, and she was becoming part of it. An actual home. The next morning she was up early. Breakfast completed, she and her traveling companions sat around the fire drinking coffee and watching embers dance. Waiting. She'd often waited, but this time was different.

Lucas and Mrs. Engstrom walked up to the four. "You about ready?" Lucas asked.

Cassie leaped to her feet. "We are. Can Runs Like a Deer ride in the wagon?" She pulled on her gloves.

"Of course," Lucas said. "I take it the rest of you are riding?"

"Unless you want Chief to drive the wagon."

"He can do that. We've got the bed pretty full of supplies. Mor found some furniture that she thought you might be able to use."

Perhaps Chief was as eager as she, for he was already on his feet and smothering the fire.

In a few minutes, with all the people loaded or mounted, they headed out across the pasture toward the hills lining the west side of the valley. Micah rode on one side of Cassie, and Lucas reined in next to her.

"I thought I could point out the landmarks as we go. I'll give you a bit more information about the ranch."

"Thank you. I'd appreciate that."

"Have you really always lived in that wagon?"

She nodded. "Except for on the trains when we hauled our show to a town far away."

While she answered his questions, she kept looking ahead at the trees with silver bark that wore gold and brass leaves, only a few on the branches and the rest painting the ground in drifts of color.

"What kind of trees are those ahead?"

"Those losing their leaves are aspen. The tall evergreens behind them are pine trees. You can see the cabin partway up the hill now."

Cassie looked to where Lucas was pointing. The cabin seemed to blend right in with the land, as if it had grown up there. Come to think of it, it had. She twisted to look back the way they had come. The barn and ranch house gave her that same feeling from a distance, a oneness with the land. It all fit together: the fences, the buildings, the cattle in some of the pastures. She could see George and their other animals in another enclosure, all grazing peacefully, as if they knew they had come home.

At the southern end of the valley, the three monolithic rocks that looked like fingers pointing to heaven kept guard. No wonder her father had fallen in love with this valley. How could he bear to leave it? But she remembered his love of adventure. The romantic, larger-than-life Wild West Show had surely appealed to that love. And if he'd not done that, he'd not have met her mother, and she would not be here. She wished he were the one showing off the land to her now, returning triumphantly to live out his dreams of flashy horses and grazing cattle.

She saw Ransom in the distance cantering his horse away from them. "Where is your brother going?"

"Over to check real quick on the pine trees we felled to make into support posts for the mine. He has the harebrained idea that there is still gold in there."

"And that machinery?"

"The sawmill we borrowed to cut the logs into the right sizes."

"Oh." So much to learn.

"You and I need to talk more about the shooting matches. I have an idea."

She could feel her eyebrows rise. "You do?"

"I'm going to talk to a man I know in Hill City. He likes sponsoring events."

"That would be interesting."

As they rode farther up the hill, she studied the cabin. Made of logs, it had a door and a window facing down the hill. A chimney that reminded her of the fireplace wall in the ranch house rose along the left wall. They would probably park the wagon along the right wall. Chief had been correct. It was a lot bigger than the wagon. A huge oak tree behind it seemed to shelter the back of the cabin. There were other trees farther up the hill that were neither pine nor aspen. She wanted to know about them all.

There were no fences up here, no corrals or paddocks. Where would they keep their riding horses? Wind Dancer would come when she whistled for him, but the other horses were not so well trained. She saw no shelter for them either.

She asked, "What do your animals do in the winter?"

"None of them live in the barn, if that is what you are asking. We take hay to them out in the pastures. Load it in a wagon and then pitch it off. You'll see us doing that every day. We keep the herd in one of the closer pastures."

"But . . ." What should she ask, or rather, how should she ask it?

"They grow thick, heavy winter coats. Once it snaps cold and stays cold, they do fine."

They were entering the yard in front of the cabin now. She stopped Wind Dancer and waited for the wagon to join them. Up close, she saw how tightly the logs fit together. Some of the shingles on the roof, or shakes—whatever roof pieces were called—had broken away, exposing the underlying boards. No doubt that would have to be fixed. Tree leaves and broken branches had fallen on the roof, and others lay around the area.

The window was dark; the place looked abandoned. She chided herself. Of course it was abandoned. Everyone on this ranch lived in a warm, inviting house now, a real home. This cabin was leftover from the past, and now it was Cassie's immediate future. And to think her father helped build this, had actually lived in it.

She had so much to figure out and so much to learn. And everything she did that was new, everywhere she went, more questions were generated, lots of questions and few answers. Almost too many questions, it felt like.

One of the biggest: When would her new home here really come to feel like home?

That night after the house quieted down, Mavis sat down at the kitchen table in the pool of lamplight, but before applying pen to paper she stopped and prayed for wisdom. Tonight she surely needed it. If only she could explain things in a way that Jesse would not join with the anger of his brothers.

Dear Jesse,

So good to hear from you. Since the letter I sent you was in September, I have some astonishing news for you.

And something to confess. Back in the early days here on the ranch, your father was engaged in a partnership for the ranch. He and a close friend, Adam Lockwood, discovered the gold, thanks to their Indian guide, John Birdwing, and bought the four hundred acres of ranchland. Adam won half interest in a Wild West show and left here, promising to return one day. After a time we no longer heard from him, so your pa and I decided not to bother mentioning the agreement.

Mavis studied the letter. What a shame that Jesse must learn of this secret through the mail. But she was not making that mistake again. No more secrets. While she was sure her boys would forgive her eventually, not telling them years earlier was certainly an unwise course of action. But it had seemed right at the time.

Recently a young woman, Cassie Lockwood, showed up at our house with the other copy of the deed, matching the one I have always kept in a box on my shelf. Ransom and Lucas were incensed but are growing in acceptance. There are no alternatives, since she cannot buy us out, and we cannot buy her out. She and her companions are living up in the cabin, and all is working well, as only events orchestrated by our God can do. Lucas decided before even meeting her that she was the woman of his dreams and said he was going to marry her.

Other than that, all is well. The men have sawed braces for the mine and plan to work up there this winter. Gretchen is doing well in school and idolizes Cassie as the big sister she never had.

We send you all our love, and if Cassie can find a shooting match—I did not mention that she was a star trick rider and shooter in the Wild West Show, taking after her mother and father—in Denver, we will be able to come visit you. Wouldn't that be marvelous?

Your Mor

Laying down the pen, Mavis reread the letter, shook her head, and folded it to put in the envelope. Why was it that she missed Jesse more when she received a letter from him than at any other time? But then, she had always known he would not stay on the ranch like the rest of them.

8

So here she sat on her horse in the yard of her first real home. What a strange turn of events. Two months ago she could not have imagined any of this, and today she was gazing on a cabin her father had built and lived in, the place where now she would live.

Lucas was studying her. "Not much of a home, I'm afraid."

Cassie smiled. "It's beautiful. It doesn't have wheels."

He laughed out loud, the first good belly laugh she had ever heard from any of the Engstroms.

"Where did they get the wood to build this?"

"They took out the trees right here, and trimmed and sawed them to length. They split cedar for the shakes on the roof and used rock from higher up the hill for the fireplace. There's a cast-iron stove in there now—it's easier to cook on. Ransom remembered the shakes, so we'll patch the roof. But just about everything you see here is the way it was a generation ago." He swung off his horse and dropped the reins.

"What do I tie my horse to?"

"The wagon wheels will be fine, but I brought along hobbles so they can graze. They'll clean up the long grass around the house." He added as if he'd just thought of it, "Most horses around here ground tie. That means you drop the reins and they stay put. But we can build you a hitching rail to use until you get them trained."

"I have good memories of living here," Mrs. Engstrom said, joining them beside the wagon wheel.

Cassie swung down. "You lived here too?"

"Oh yes. Ivar and I lived here the first two years we were married, while we were building the house. We moved into the ranch house almost before it was done, because by then we had Ransom. The next year Ivar and some of the neighbors built the barn." She pulled a bucket out of the wagon, along with a broom and mop, and headed for the door. "We would get water from a pipe that came down from the stream that used to run from up the hill, but that dried up after we had moved to the big house. I'm afraid you're going to have to haul water in barrels for a while."

She set her bucket down to open the door. When it stuck, she turned and slammed her shoulder against the wood. With a squeal, it opened slowly, in jerks. "We'll need to work on the door too, I guess. Come on. Let's get at it."

Micah tied his horse to the other wheel and followed the instructions to take things out of the wagon bed and haul them inside. Runs Like a Deer did the same while Chief unhitched the team and hobbled them. After unsaddling the other horses, including Wind Dancer, he hobbled them to let them graze.

Carrying a wooden crate from the wagon bed, Cassie followed the others into the dimness of the cabin. She set her load down and took time to look around. A single big room with a bed built into one corner, a window on the wall opposite from the fireplace, cupboards and shelves on the other side of the fireplace, along with a black iron stove larger than the one in the wagon but not by a whole lot. There was an odd dry smell to the place—not exactly musty but softly whispering of age and neglect. So this was to be her first home that did not move.

"I know it looks pretty primitive, but you will be warm and dry. We brought a table along and a rocking chair, one of two that Ivar built for me. The ropes on that bed are going to have to be restrung, but you'll find it comfortable. I have some extra quilts and a feather bed we can put on it. You do have cooking things and so on in the wagon, right?"

"We have all we'll need, I'm sure. I . . . I mean, this looks huge after living in the wagon."

"Well, good to know the place will be loved again. Ransom, why don't you and Lucas go up on the roof and take care of those missing shakes. Chief, if you and Micah want to see about the wood supply, I think there are some fallen trees a little way up the hill. You could drag them down here. There used to be a bucksaw stand hanging on the wall behind the cabin. We women will clean the inside. Let's get a fire going to heat the water that's in the barrel."

She opened the lids on the iron stove. "A bit rusty, but steel wool will take care of that. Cassie, please bring in that wood we brought. I put kindling in the wagon too." She grabbed the wire handle on a black pot from one of the boxes and handed that to Runs Like a Deer. "We'll use this to carry and heat the water."

With the fire going and the water heating on the stove, Mavis handed Cassie the broom. "You need to sweep the ceiling first and then the walls. We'll start on the cupboards and shelves. We've had mice in here. No doubt we still do. We can catch one of the cats down at the barn, or maybe two so they'll stay together, to live here and get rid of the mice for you."

Cassie took the broom and started sweeping the ceiling. "Why is there a ladder on the wall?"

"Oh, we used to use the upstairs for storage. It's not really high enough to stand in except in the middle, but Ivar laid boards over the rafters so we could store supplies up there. He used to go out trapping some in winter, and once the skins were dry, he'd keep them up there until he had enough to sell."

Dust and cobwebs ran before Cassie's attacking broom. She sneezed at the dust but kept on. This was actually not work at all; it was too much fun. She finished the ceiling and started on the walls. By the time she'd completed her task, the two other women had swept and washed down the cupboards and counter, the smell of lye soap permeating the air.

Cassie listened for a moment to the men up on the roof, boots rattling the shakes, the hammers ringing loud every once in a while. She heard an ax thunking too, so Chief must have returned with the dry wood.

When Mavis called a halt for dinner, they took their sandwiches outside to enjoy the sunshine.

"You can see forever from here," Cassie said, sitting on the wagon tailgate, her feet swinging as she chewed. Before her, nearly the whole valley spread out in graceful curving lines stitched with trees. Browns and yellows and greens and the clear blue of a cloudless sky. How lush it all was, with even the brown patches a rich, vibrant brown. The country might be dying of autumn, but it was still full of life.

Mavis nodded. "I know. That was one of the things I really missed when we moved down into the big house. I had a bench by the wall, right over there, and I'd bring my coffee cup out here to watch the men fencing down below or the cattle grazing. We didn't have many then. Deer used to browse in the field over there. Those trees have taken over much of what used to be my garden plot. But we can rip them out."

"You had a garden up here?"

"Of course I did. So should you, come spring. Plowing up my garden space was one of the first things Ivar did that first spring. He'd plowed it once in the fall to break up the sod. We didn't put any fields into grain then, just pastured it all and raised hay. I remember the haystacks. He built fences around the stacks and let the cattle go through one stack at a time so they didn't waste any. He was a really good rancher."

"That was all after my father left?"

"Yes. As you know, we weren't married yet when the two of them built this cabin to live in as they worked the mine. They bought and paid for the land with the gold they found and were digging deeper, because they figured the vein hadn't actually quit, it had just shifted or something. That's when the mine collapsed. It is thanks to John Birdwing—your Chief—that both of them made it out."

"Were they injured?"

"Not much. Cuts and bruises. But had John not been there to dig them out, no one would have ever known what happened to them."

Cassie looked over at Chief, who was sitting cross-legged

on the ground, along with Micah and the two young men. Why would he never tell any of the stories of their early days?

"John, do you remember the bear that kept visiting the cabin?"

Chief nodded. "Nailed his hide to the back wall."

"The bear kept showing up, and one time when they all came home, the bear had broken into the cabin and raided their food supplies. I guess they went after the bear and shot him, and we used that hide on the floor as a rug until a few years ago, when it was looking pretty ratty. I still have it up in the attic at the house. That is, unless the mice have gotten into it."

Chief pulled a thong from under his shirt and held it out. There were three long claws on the thong. "From that bear. Sold the rest."

Mavis turned to Cassie. "Would you like that bear rug to lay in front of the fireplace here again?"

She nodded, a smile spreading wide. "I would. What do you think, Runs Like a Deer?"

Nodding, the woman drank her coffee and tossed the dregs off to the side. They all rose and stretched.

"Back to it." Mavis turned to look at the cabin. "Ransom, I've been thinking."

Cassie hid a grin at his groan.

"You know the slab wood you'll have from the pine trees—what if we built a shelter for the wagon right beside the cabin there and made it big enough for a couple of horses. That way they could keep at least two up here to use to catch the others."

"If we ever get to use that sawmill."

Micah looked to Ransom. "I will help you, if you want. Chief too."

Ransom stopped in midstride. "We can use all the help we can get. Thank you." He paused. "Can't pay you, though."

Micah stared at him. "You already have."

Chief waved up the hill. "Can we hunt up there?"

"Of course. We have deer and elk, lots of rabbits and squirrels, wolves, coyote. I'm sure you'll hear grouse and plenty of other critters. You're right on the edge of the wild country up here."

"Good."

Lucas punched his brother on the shoulder. "We'll get your posts sawed yet. Even if I still think you are crazy to want to go work in that hole."

Cassie caught the look that Ransom sent his brother. Was this the source of their antipathy? Or did they disagree about more than that?

9

Keeping a somewhat friendly look on his face was getting more difficult by the day, or the hour. All Ransom could think was that his days of fair weather were streaming past and he was locked into helping people he did not want to help, especially since Cassie Lockwood had him in a tight squeeze. He realized this deed of ownership was not her fault, but had she never found the deed, they would not be in this situation.

And his mother, keeping this destructive secret all these years. Why had she never told them about it? She said it was because she did not want to worry them in case it never happened. Well, now it had happened, and they were stuck with giving half their ranch to this kid who knew as much about ranching as he did about wearing a top hat and attending the opera. One of these days he and Mor would have to have another discussion, just to clear the air.

So they had all worked together to repair and clean the

cabin. They'd driven that circus wagon up there the next day. But now his mother wanted him and Lucas to build a corral at the cabin. And when the slab wood was cut off the logs, she expected them to build a lean-to to house that gaudy, useless wagon that the group was living in. Or rather, the women were. The men had been sleeping on the ground, but here at the ranch they had moved into the barn. Now they had the cabin to sleep in. Frankly, Ransom would have preferred the barn.

Come to think of it, did all these things need doing right now, or was Mor just making up work projects to keep him from working on his gold mine? She just might do that.

And where had Lucas gone?

Where is your Christian spirit, Ransom Engstrom? If only there were a way to throttle the insistent little voice that nagged at him constantly. *Love thy neighbor.* Yeah, right. He'd let Lucas do the loving part. Besotted was the only possible word to describe his younger brother. All over Miss Cassie Lockwood.

The bane of his existence.

He heaved the last of the cut poles into the wagon bed. That was another thing they were going to have to do, should do, this fall. Go up into the woods and look for straight, slender poles for the stack they kept constantly available in case a pole-and-post corral had to be repaired or a new one was needed. His father always got all that advance work done in a timely way. Why could Ransom not keep up?

Tomorrow was Sunday, so at least he would have that day off. Lucas was planning to go hunting this evening with Miss Lockwood and Chief. He didn't know why; they had not seen the elk herd recently. He climbed up into the wagon seat and hupped the team forward. When he arrived at the cabin, Micah and Chief were still digging holes for the posts. Even Ransom couldn't fault the two men, the way they took his instructions and went to work. The old man sure put a lie to the old adage that all Indians were lazy. Of course Ransom knew that from experience already, but still the thought ripped through his mind.

They unloaded the poles and stacked them in the middle of the circle. He'd brought up the six-foot posts earlier. This wouldn't be a high corral like down at the barn, but a three-rail fence, enough to keep unambitious horses in. "Micah, why don't you keep digging and Chief can help me set these."

Micah wiped the sweat off his forehead with his arm, his shirt sleeves rolled up. While it was a brisk fall day, it had frozen hard the night before, and digging postholes raised a sweat. He nodded and stepped off the next ten-foot section, eyeing the other holes to keep the circle true.

"I can help," Cassie said as she joined them.

Ransom started to turn down her offer but instead slammed a post into the hole. "Hold this straight up while we put the dirt back."

She nodded and did as he showed her. All without talking, which surprised him even further.

If Lucas knew she was out here working with them, he'd have been right here. *Where is he?*

He drove the heavy steel rod down to pack the soil tight around the post. "You'll have to hold it straight and steady while we tamp it down." When she didn't answer, he gave the post a bit of a push to straighten it. "Like that."

"Sorry."

He eyed the post when they were done. Straight. On to the

next. Straight. On to the third. He shook his head. "You can't let it lean like that. If it turns out not straight, we'll have to dig it out and tamp it down again."

Othello rose and came to stop at her knee. He looked up at her as if asking if she was all right. Then he stared at Ransom.

As if she needed a bodyguard. The next time he started to say something, he would have sworn the dog understood every word. The dog's eyes lowered, and he took one step forward.

"It's all right, Othello. Sit."

The dog sat, but he never stopped watching Ransom.

The next time, Ransom moved the post himself, said nothing, looked at her through slightly narrowed eyes.

She smiled wanly. "Guess I need lessons in straight up."

"I guess so." He kept his voice very gentle. The dog actually smiled. Ransom stared at Cassie, who stared right back, but she had rolled her lips together.

"Is he always this protective?"

"Yes."

They stepped back to see how all the posts looked. Ransom clamped his teeth together. Three more to go. "I do hope you can keep these straight." While his tone was absolutely polite, he wanted to say plenty. But he didn't. The three posts ended up straight. Guess she finally got the hang of it.

With the three of them working and him and Chief alternately shoveling the dirt back into the holes and tamping it solid with the rod, they caught up with Micah by the last hole. Once all the posts were set, again they stepped back. Well done—at least adequately done.

"Start the rails?" Chief asked.

"We should let those set for a few days, but we're under the gun here. I was hoping to start the sawmill on Monday."

Already he'd been out at the pine trees before daylight, ready to continue lobbing the branches off as soon as it was light enough to see. Daylight was needed to limb logs, or one was liable to lose a couple of toes.

He'd been out to the mine today too. He practically had it memorized, but still he wanted to look at it, to assay the first steps he must take. Once upon a time the path between the cabin and the mine had been beaten bare by many wheels and many hooves and feet—his father's feet and sometimes even his mother's in their youth. Now the trace was barely discernible in the brown grass. Ransom's feet had followed that path.

"Will you need us at the sawmill?" Micah's question brought him back to the moment. "If not, we can nail the rails up."

Ransom thought a moment and glanced up to see where the sun was. "We could go down to the trees and get a lot of the limbs off before dark. Let's let the poles settle until Monday."

"What about tomorrow?"

"Tomorrow is church. We honor the Lord's Day here." Sometimes only because Mor was adamant . . . but he didn't bother telling them his secret feelings. Yes, he wanted to do as the Word said, but surely God understood when there were things that had to be done before the snow flew.

"You have more axes?"

"There are two down there. You have one?"

"Needs sharpening."

"Two can chop and one can pile the branches out of the way."

"I can haul branches." There stood Cassie at his side.

Ransom stared at her. She'd been working right beside

them without slowing down, but . . . He shook his head. "Mor would have my hide if I let you do that."

"Let me?" Her eyebrows raised and she straightened. Othello, who'd been supervising their efforts, returned to stand by her side, keeping Ransom in his sights.

Ransom stared from Cassie to her dog and then to Chief, who might almost be laughing if Ransom was reading him right. Micah coughed into his sleeve to cover the snort that escaped. Obviously, she was going to be coming along with them.

"Bring the wagon, please." He and the two men started down the hill. He could feel her glare but ignored it. He should have offered to harness the team.

"I'll be there in a few minutes." Micah turned and headed back. Ransom glanced over his shoulder to see him and Cassie sliding the horses' bits into their mouths. What was there about her that made him act like he'd never learned any manners? If Mor caught wind of this . . .

He looked back again. Micah was riding with Cassie on the wagon, and when she stopped the team beyond the felled trees, he unbridled them so they could graze. Animal handler, huh? These people sure weren't ranchers. They didn't even speak the right kind of English.

Chief and Ransom set to splitting the branches off the downed trees, tossing the limbs aside as they worked.

"Where do you want the branches piled?" Cassie asked.

"Out of the way. We'll drag the logs down to the sawmill, so off to the sides would be better."

"One pile, or does it matter?"

He shrugged. "We'll probably burn them after they dry some, so a couple of piles."

"Some look good for firewood. Can we cut and use them?"

"If you want. But you should know that oak and maple burn longer and don't soot the chimney up like pine does. Alder's good too. Hardwood. Not pine."

"I see. But why waste this?"

Now she sounded like Mor.

"Do what you want."

"How about I chop for a while," Micah said to Chief, and the old Indian handed him the ax.

As the dark encroached, Ransom decided they'd better quit before someone got hurt. He set the tools in the bed of the wagon. "I'll sharpen those axes before we go at it again. Chief, you want me to sharpen yours too?"

"I'll sharpen it with a file," Micah said. "We need it to cut firewood."

"I'll bring up the crosscut saw when I come. I'm sure Mor is expecting you for dinner tomorrow. Will you be attending church with us?"

Cassie thought for a moment. "We'll see. What time do you leave?"

"Gotta leave here by nine to get there in time. I know the Brandenburgs will be delighted to see you there. Come down to the house. There will be room in the wagon." He stepped up into the wagon seat. "Thanks for your help."

"Thanks for yours too." Cassie started to walk up the hill, dog at her side, the two men flanking her. She turned to look at him and raised her voice. "Will we be hunting in the morning, since we won't be going tonight?"

"No, sorry. We don't hunt on Sundays either. Lucas must have forgotten what day it was."

"Okay, but hunting is all right up behind the cabin?"

"Yes. The elk and deer frequently come down into the pastures too. Probably not tonight, since we've been working up here. Makes 'em skittish."

She raised her hand in acknowledgment and kept on walking.

Ransom started down the hill and then turned to watch them. *I should have said just her and Micah for church, but I couldn't do that. Sure do hope she figures it out.* The realization that the three were all slogging along as if they were exceedingly weary made him realize he was tired too. Having another pair of hands would have lightened the load. Leave it to Lucas to be gone.

Lucas was sitting at the kitchen table when Ransom walked in.

"I thought you were going to help us today." Ransom knew a belligerent tone would not sit well, but his brother's not showing up didn't sit well with him either. He stopped at the sink to wash his hands.

"Sorry, but I got involved in town."

"Sure."

"I kept a plate hot for you," Mavis said, probably before another argument could heat up. "Lucas, I need some more wood in both woodboxes."

Ransom saw the look she gave her younger son. She meant business.

"I didn't realize he wasn't up there until he came in all excited about a shooting match in Hill City, or a possible one."

"So that's where he went." Ransom dug into his meal. The lunch she had sent with the work party had ended a long time ago.

She frowned. "You didn't know about it either?"

"Nope." The sound of wood being dumped into the box came from the other room. "Where's Gretchen?"

"Spending the night with Jenna."

"I'm surprised she didn't come up."

"Said she'd pass on the fencing."

"I invited them to church in the morning." He forked another potato into his mouth.

"Good. Do you think they'll come?"

"Some folks wouldn't be too welcoming to Chief and Runs Like a Deer, you know."

"Land sakes, how could I not think of that?" She sat down at the table, a cup of coffee between her cupped hands, and stared into the dark liquid. "I want them to be happy here."

And I want them to be on their way, without claiming half of my—our—land. But he figured that wasn't about to happen.

Lucas dumped a load into the kitchen woodbox and dusted off his hands. He poured himself a cup of coffee, raised the pot to ask Ransom, and set it back down at his brother's no. Sitting down at the other end of the table, he laid his arms out on the table and leaned forward. "I talked to Mr. Porter at the Hill City Hotel about sponsoring a shooting match, and he got real excited, especially when I told him Cassie Lockwood is living right here."

"He knew of her?"

"He knew of that Wild West Show and her father. He remembered seeing a performance up in Dickinson a few years ago, so the name Lockwood rang a bell."

"Thought you were going to help us up at the cabin."

"Well, I was, but then I got to thinking that Miss Lockwood

is worried about having money to get through the winter, so I headed for Hill City instead."

Mavis frowned. "Why is she so concerned about money? We have plenty of everything here, and they are welcome to whatever they need."

"I think she has a hard time asking for what she sees as favors." Lucas sipped his coffee. "She's mighty independent."

Except when it comes to taking our land. Ransom tried to ignore the voice again. At least when he was limbing pine logs, he didn't have to listen to it. Calling himself a sorehead did nothing to help that.

"Did you tell Miss Lockwood that you were going to do that?"

"I told her I had an idea for a shoot in our area, and she seemed amenable."

"Always running ahead," Ransom said. "What if she doesn't want to do that? Now you've put her into a difficult situation."

"Well, at least I'm doing something, not just grousing about her taking half our land."

"Just another of your harebrained schemes."

"Me? There's nothing like a fool looking for gold when the vein quit years ago." Lucas half stood and leaned forward. Ransom half rose too.

"All right, you two. That's enough! I'm getting real tired of hearing arguments like this. The contract is a done deal, so let's hear no more about it."

The two glared at each other but subsided into their chairs. The crackling of the fire was the only sound for a bit, if one ignored the gnashing of teeth.

Ransom shook his head and pushed his empty plate away,

deciding to try another tack. He looked at his mother. "I still have a hard time understanding why you never told us any of this slice of family history." He thought for a second. "And Pa didn't either. Never made a reference to a partnership, not that I can remember."

"We agreed not to discuss it, at least until you boys were old enough to understand."

"Well, I'm old enough, and I'm having trouble understanding all the secrecy. Feel like I've been lied to all these years when speaking of *our* ranch. The Bar E, the Engstrom spread." He knew his voice was getting louder and pretty intense, but he didn't try to stop the torrent.

"Ransom, I—"

"I've given this ranch everything I've got to give, and now I have to pretend to be pleased when this long-lost person shows up with deed in hand?"

"No one is asking you to pretend. I'm asking you to just accept the reality. And we'll go on from here."

He slammed the flat of his palm on the table. "What would Pa say?"

"What could he say? He signed the deed too."

"Oh, I imagine he could say a lot," Lucas said with a half shrug. "Pa was never one not to say his mind."

"I never lied to you, Ransom."

Let it go. He ignored the voice. "You didn't tell the whole truth, though. You always said that was the same as lying."

"I apologize for making such a horrendous error. I . . . I . . . Looking back, I can see that."

Ransom tipped his head back. This was getting them nowhere. *Maybe if I find some gold in that mine, we can buy her out and the ranch will be all ours again.* He reached out and laid his hand over his mother's. "I'm sorry, Mor. Something good will happen. You always say that. We just have to stick together." Guilt stabbed him at the sorrow in his mother's eyes.

Please, God, let it be so. Maybe after church tomorrow, he could catch the town lawyer, Daniel Westbrook, and ask him a question or two. Like his pa used to say, *"Never leave a stone unturned."* But it looked like they were fast running out of stones.

10

Cassie lay in the bed she now shared with Runs Like a Deer, who was snoring softly. How she loved watching the dancing flames from the fireplace reflected on the ceiling. While she had been out working with the men, Runs Like a Deer had been stitching rabbit skins into a vest for her. And cooking supper. Cornmeal biscuits had made the simmering pot of beans and dried venison taste even better. While they were tired of beans, she'd not complained, nor had the men.

The chair from the wagon sat pulled up to the weathered old table that Mrs. Engstrom had brought them. Micah said that when the weather closed in, he'd make three more, but for now, he dragged in the same chunks of wood they'd used on the trail. Her trunk sat at the foot of the bed, and the chifforobe that had ridden all the way on top of the wagon finally had a place of its own against what she now knew to be the south wall. The front door faced east, looking across the valley. The bear rug might be missing some hair in a few places, but it was back in front of the fireplace where it used to lie, according to Mrs. Engstrom.

Did she want to go to church in the morning? That was the question keeping her from much-needed sleep. She wanted to, but what about the others? Chief had made it clear that he and Runs Like a Deer would not be welcome there. That shouldn't be the case, but "should" and "is" were two different things. And remembering their hasty flight from town, she figured he was probably right. But if this was to be her home, she needed, wanted, to get to know the people. The Brandenburgs had been so kind and generous to them. What would it be like to be a member of the church? Of this church? What did they do besides having services on Sunday mornings?

She moved her head from side to side. By the time they had quit hauling branches, the aches of different work had started attacking her back and arms. On Chief's recommendation, she'd used kerosene to remove the pitch from her hands, and now her hands stank of kerosene, in spite of the lye soap she'd used to get the kerosene off.

Back to the original question. Should she get dressed in the morning and drive the wagon down to the ranch house and go with the Engstroms to church? She'd been to church a few times in her life, usually during the winter months when the show remained in one place. After her mother died, her father lost interest in church, and they didn't go again.

She should have taken a dress out of the chifforobe and hung it to let the wrinkles fall out. There wasn't a sadiron in any of her things. She should probably purchase one, particularly if she was going to attend church regularly. She kept hearing Mrs. Brandenburg promise that if they stayed in this area, she would love to teach Cassie how to cook. Mrs.

Engstrom would most likely offer too, if asked. Maybe, just maybe, she could turn this cabin into a real home.

If she could find a way to earn money to feed them and the livestock . . .

Since she couldn't seem to get to sleep, she could have been sorting those papers again, but they were all out in the wagon, and she wasn't going to go get them now. *So go to sleep.*

Rolling over carefully so she wouldn't disturb Runs Like a Deer, she stared at the dying fire.

Someone was rattling around. She opened her eyes to see Chief starting the fire in the stove and Runs Like a Deer braiding her hair by the again-crackling fireplace. How had he or they done all that and she had slept right through it?

"I'm thinking of going to church with the Engstroms."

"We'll be cutting wood."

"We need a saw. That's for sure."

"Ransom said he had one we could use. I'll ride down with you and bring it back."

"Will you all come for dinner after church?"

He shrugged. Runs Like a Deer copied him.

"I'm sure Mrs. Engstrom will have a good meal."

"Hard to get wood in when going there."

"True." Cassie reached back and released the curtain they had hung around the bed to create a separate room. Sleeping in nightclothes again had made her feel she was no longer a traveler. She belted her wrapper and padded to the chiffo-robe to choose clothes to wear. How she would love to have a bath, to wash her hair, and then wash the clothes she'd been wearing day after day. Choosing a dark serge skirt and a cream-colored waist, she dressed and sat down to lace up her dress boots. Brushing the snarls out of her hair took a bit of doing, but she managed and then used some of the heating water to wash her face.

Micah came in, along with Othello, and gave her an appreciative grin. "You look nice."

"Why, thank you. I'd almost forgotten how to dress." She smoothed the front of the skirt. The waistband was plenty loose. She'd never been the slightest bit heavy, but she'd lost weight during their long trek south. Micah didn't have any extra fat on him either.

Chief rattled the lids on the stove back in place after feeding the fire. He set the frying pan on to heat. Runs Like a Deer cut up some of the leftover rabbit and dropped it into the pan. When it sizzled, she added eggs and stirred.

"Eggs. I can't believe we have eggs again."

"Thanks to Mrs. Engstrom. In the baskets of food she brought." Runs Like a Deer glanced over her shoulder.

Cassie nodded. Good things were happening. The other woman was talking more and going ahead and cooking or sewing or tanning leather, the jobs she set for herself. While Runs Like a Deer still limped at times, her broken leg had healed straight, thanks to the weeks she'd spent with her leg strapped to a board.

"Food is ready." Runs Like a Deer took the tin plates off the shelf and dished up their meal. Cassie sat in the chair, for they had all insisted she take the one chair, and they sat on the blocks of wood. When the meal was finished, they put their plates and utensils in the pan of soapy water on the stove.

"We'll put the barrel in the wagon, and I will fill that too." Chief glanced at the others. "We will go down for dinner."

It was a statement, not a question. Albeit reluctantly, Micah and Runs Like a Deer nodded. They knew a mandate when they heard it.

"Good." Another thing conquered. She knew they'd rather not. But that would be rude. After all the Engstroms had done to help them, rude was not an option. Cassie dug through her trunk for the reticule she remembered storing there, but when she failed to find it right away, she abandoned her search. Grabbing her coat off a peg on the wall by the door, she headed outside, then returned for her hat. A wide-brimmed felt that had already seen plenty of duty was not fashionable, but that was the only hat she had. While she had brought dresses and her show outfits, she'd not thought to stuff in a hat.

Chief was already sitting up in the wagon box and waiting. She must have wasted too much time looking for her reticule, for he and Micah had already harnessed and hitched the team, and the two men had loaded the empty barrel into the wagon bed.

Like so many other things, the Engstroms were also to be thanked for the loan of this wagon. It was more a buckboard than a wagon, with dry wood and rusting springs. They said it was an old one they could spare, but to Cassie it was a blessing, for their only wheeled transportation was the show wagon they had been living in.

Micah helped her up into the wagon box and smiled her on her way. Were they treating her differently because she was dressed up? That was something to think about. But getting in the wagon had been far easier in men's britches. Well, her britches. They'd never belonged to a man; she just bought a small size. The first time she'd donned britches, her father had raised his eyebrows, but he never said anything. Daily on the show lot, and now with all their traveling, life was far easier—and more modest too—in trousers.

"You stay here," she told Othello when he started to follow them. She looked back to see him flop down next to Dog and stare after her. He could do sad better than many people. All they needed was for him to decide he didn't like the Engstrom dog. They did not need a dog fight.

She gazed out across the valley as they followed the track back down the hill. When they approached the ranch house, George raised his heavy head and looked at her, then went back to grazing, the other buffalo near him. Wind Dancer nickered and trotted up to the fence. He stamped a front foot and tossed his head, obviously wishing for a run, or at least some attention.

"Tonight," she promised him and then turned when Chief snorted. Cassie ignored him. She needed to give Wind Dancer a good brushing and get the tangles out of his mane and tail. Would she be able to use him in an exhibition type of act? They could do their routine without music or the extra props. Maybe now that they were getting settled she could take time to practice again, both the riding and the shooting.

Riding was no problem, but shooting took a lot of shells, something of which she was running short. What she had left, she needed to use for hunting. Everything always came back to the money issue. She'd never had to even think about it, and now it rode in the back of her mind like a specter waiting to pounce.

The Engstrom wagon was hitched up and waiting at the front gate. Chief stopped the wagon, and she climbed over the edge to use the wheel to step down. "Thanks." She smiled up at him. "See you this afternoon?"

"We'll come when we see the wagon return." Chief started to loop the lines around the whipstock, but when Ransom stepped out on the porch, he stopped. "Can we use the saw? Need to fill the water barrel too."

"Go on over to the pump, and I'll bring the saw. You need anything else?"

Chief shook his head and flipped the lines to the team, turning them to head over to the windmill that ran the pump that kept the stock tank full in a corral near the barn.

Cassie looked toward the house just as Lucas and his mother came out the door.

"Good morning, Miss Lockwood," Lucas called. "I'll be right there to assist you."

Mavis's cheerful greeting made Cassie feel welcome all over again.

"I am so glad you decided to come. The others will be joining us for dinner, won't they?"

"Chief told me they'd come down when they see the wagon returning home."

"Good, good." Mavis firmed her foot on a little iron step bolted into the front wagon panel, took a deep breath, and launched herself up and in. She more or less arranged herself into a space as narrow as possible, and Cassie climbed up beside her. That little iron step was sure nice.

Lucas brought his horse up. "I could drive if you'd like, Mor."

"That's all right. Ransom will do just fine. Three of us can fit on this seat."

"I can sit in the back."

"No, we'll let Gretchen sit in the back on the way home." While they waited for Ransom, Mavis patted Cassie's arm.

"I am truly glad that you are going to become part of our congregation. You met the Brandenburgs, right?"

"Reverend Brandenburg let us set up camp by the church, and then they invited us all for supper. We put the animals in their corrals with water, and he even pitched in hay. He was so nice. Then they sent us home with eggs and potatoes from their garden, and the next morning he brought us a loaf of fresh bread."

"Why did you not stay there longer?"

"A crowd gathered, and a couple of men from the back of the group started in about not wanting Indians in Argus. So we thought to stave off any problems, we'd better leave town. I was afraid they might follow us, but they didn't."

Mavis fell silent, suddenly grim.

Had Cassie said something wrong? The only way to know was to ask, so it wouldn't happen again. "What did I say?"

"Nothing, dear. Nothing. It's not you. I'm pretty sure I know who that man was. He is a constant troublemaker, a worthless man who leads his cronies into trouble with him. I know I shouldn't say that, but if there are problems of any kind, there is where it starts." She smiled. "I'm sure that is really not the feeling of the rest of the town."

Cassie smiled. "The rest of the town probably thinks we are Gypsies. I put Wind Dancer through a couple of his flashier tricks, and that made the children happy. But then some woman muttered something about Gypsies and hustled her children away. There was a little girl there who had a lisp. She was so sweet."

"Yes, she is. Her family goes to our church. I'm sure you'll meet them today."

"Sorry I'm late." With no further comment, Ransom hauled himself up into the seat and picked up the lines.

Mavis gathered her bag in close on her lap in anticipation of the wagon lurching forward.

Away they went, these others who knew everybody, not just in the church but the whole town, and Cassie, who knew nobody. It reminded her again of how much she must learn, how many people she must meet, how hard she must work to make her new house a real home.

And it would all be worth it. Wouldn't it?

11

What amazing country. Cassie fell in love with the valleys, the ridges, every time she gazed on them. Golden aspens, deep green pines, meadows that could not decide whether to be lush tan or quiet green. And she owned some of this! Her head was fairly comfortable with that fact now, but her heart still had trouble grasping it.

As they rattled along toward town, Mavis pointed out the other ranches and told her a bit about the families. Cassie showed them the track that led to the place where they had camped. Lucas told a story about one of the families, which made her laugh. What a pleasant time.

Lucas rode along beside, just off the right wheel. "So how do you like the cabin?"

"I love it. Thanks to all your help, it already feels like a home. Not that I have a lot of experience in homes, but we are comfortable." *And safe from the weather, and safe from more traveling.* She thought a moment. "What is it like to live in one place all your life?"

He frowned and then shrugged. "I have nothing to compare it to, so in my mind this is the way life should be. What was it like for you?"

"Yours seems so much more simple and peaceful. But then, one gets used to all the hubbub of taking everything down, traveling, and setting up again, with people around all the time, constantly moving from place to place. That is the life I grew up with. We all ate in the kitchen tent, so we saw the same people all the time, like a great big family. Getting ready for a show was always a tense time, but once those gates opened and the parade began, everyone did their job and we entertained the guests. We gave them a good show and taught them something about the West and life in the West at the same time."

"And you had a trick-riding act as well as a sharpshooting act?" Mavis was asking more than stating.

"I did. My father trained Wind Dancer and me together. I started with a pony when I was six and became part of the act when I turned seven. Both my mother and my father were the act for years. When Mother died, it was just my father and me. He loved shooting and taught me. Together we got up a good act. After he died, I was the headliner."

"Why did you leave the show?"

"We didn't. The show left us. The owner, Jason Talbot, announced at the end of the Dickinson run that the show was bankrupt and everyone would need to find other jobs. Just like that. Boom. Done." Cassie did not look at either Lucas or Mavis but kept her gaze focused on the beginnings of the town. When they had left town that other day, she'd not paid a lot of attention to its outskirts, just concentrated on getting out of there without trouble. Now she could look around.

"Oh, how awful." Mavis patted her arm. "See, that's our church just ahead and to the right. You can see the steeple. I'm sure you already know that's the general store. Yonder is the doctor's office and other businesses. Of course you can't miss the grain elevators by the tracks, and the cattle yards are there."

Cassie nodded. "That's where we kept the horses and cattle that night."

Ransom turned the team into the field where they had camped and drew the horses up to a halt beside another wagon and team. Lucas swung off and gallantly assisted both Cassie and his mother to the ground. He obviously enjoyed being the ladies' escort.

"Thank you," Cassie said with a smile, ignoring the butterflies cavorting in her middle. She could still hear that man hollering at them. What if he was in church today? She'd ignore him, if possible. But from what someone else said, he was most likely sleeping off his night at the tavern.

Lucas offered one arm to his mother and the other to Cassie. Hesitantly she slid her hand through the crook in his arm. Ransom followed behind.

Gretchen met them at the base of the steps. "Oh, Miss Lockwood, I'm so glad to see you here."

"Thank you. I'm glad to be here." *Or I will be when I get in there and all sat down.* She felt as though all the eyes in the building were staring at her while she followed Mrs. Engstrom down the center aisle to an empty pew. Mrs. Engstrom went in first, and then Gretchen. Cassie followed the girl, and then she realized that Lucas was right behind her. She wanted to find out where Ransom was, why she had no idea, but when they all sat down, Lucas's shoulder was right up next to hers. He pulled the hymnal out of the pew rack, looked up at a list of numbers on a rack on the wall, and then turned to the first one.

Could eyes be drilling into her back? It surely felt like it.

Gretchen leaned closer. "Just follow me and I'll show you what we do."

Cassie nodded. What she wanted to do was exit fast and return to the safety of the cabin. When a man took his place at the organ in the front to the side and music poured forth, she sat enthralled. Rich and powerful, the music picked her up and soared with her right up and out of the peaked rafters high overhead. When he began another song, everyone stood and Lucas held the hymnal for them. Gretchen shared one with her mother. At some point Ransom had sat down on the other side of Mrs. Engstrom.

"Hymn number 376," Reverend Brandenburg announced from the chair behind the pulpit. The organ played, the people joined in the singing, and Lucas pointed to where the song began. Cassie followed the words, never having learned to read music. They stood, they sat, they prayed, they sang. The pastor read from the big leather-bound Bible, then preached a sermon, prayed, they sang, and finally they stood as Reverend Brandenburg raised his hands to bless them.

"'The Lord bless thee, and keep thee: the Lord make his face shine upon thee, and be gracious unto thee: the Lord lift up his countenance upon thee, and give thee peace.' Amen."

Cassie felt he was talking right to her. Bless her and keep her. Surely God's face was shining on her to bring her here, to the ranch where her father had dreamed of living.

Lucas closed the hymnal and slid it back into the rack.

When the organ played again, they all began talking to those around them.

Mrs. Brandenburg had been sitting right in front of them. She turned and, with a wide smile, held out her hands. "Why, Cassie Longwood! No, it's Lockwood, isn't it. You didn't leave the area. And you met the Engstroms. How wonderful." She paused and stared from Mrs. Engstrom to Cassie. "Did the Bar E turn out to be the place you were looking for?"

Cassie took the hands offered. What could she say? "Yes. And the Engstroms have been most gracious to us."

"Well, of course. Mavis couldn't be anything but gracious. I'm sure there's a real story here, but right now I want you to know how happy I am to see you again."

"Thank you." Cassie looked at Gretchen, who motioned her to return to the middle aisle. Lucas had not left her side. Once they were out of the pew and heading toward the door, the Engstroms introduced her to those around. Cassie immediately forgot the names, but most of the people smiled and welcomed her. All except for a young woman who was glaring at her. At least it seemed that way, but Cassie couldn't figure any reason for that, so surely she was mistaken.

When they made it to the door, Pastor Brandenburg shook her hand, covering her hand with his other.

"Well, Miss Lockwood, what a delightful surprise to see you in church with us this morning. I rode out to the place where I figured you had camped, but your wagon was gone. I was so disappointed. But here you are and with some of my favorite people." He turned. "Thank you, Mrs. Engstrom, for bringing her back to us here in town."

"Thank you. This was a lovely service." Cassie wasn't about to tell him how uncomfortable she had been because she'd not been to church in she didn't remember how many years. But maybe next time, she'd be a little more comfortable.

Smiling brightly, Lucas immediately stepped up beside her and extended his arm, elbow cocked. She smiled in return and accepted his escort, his mother on the other side. They strolled down the street toward their wagon, basking in the friendliness of the people and the music that made her feel like she was flying. She was sure she had not a care in the world.

"Where's Ransom?" Mavis asked her son.

"I think I saw him talking with Daniel Westbrook."

"Oh, really?"

Was that a note of concern Cassie heard in her voice? Whoever this Daniel Westbrook was, she'd not met him. The name didn't even sound familiar. She glanced at a house across the street and sucked in her breath.

There he was! That fellow who didn't want Indians in Argus! He was walking this way on the other side of the street with two companions, heading straight toward her. There was not a shadow of a doubt that he would recognize her the moment he saw her.

She snatched her hat off her head. Her hat would be even more recognizable than she, and she would be the only woman in the world to be wearing a hat like that. She turned her face away from the street, which put her in the awkward position of being escorted by a man she was carefully looking away from. The fellow had never seen her in skirts—that would work in her favor. Maybe.

Lucas lowered his voice. "What in the world are you doing?"

"The big burly man across the street, in the brown shirt. He's the Indian hater."

Mavis clucked. "Yes, I thought that's who you were talking about."

"Want us to go over there and explain a few things to him?" Lucas asked. "I'd be glad to."

"And I'd be happy to join you," Ransom said from behind them.

"No!" Cassie tried to muffle it, but it burst out much too loud. "No, please don't. That won't help anything."

"She has an excellent point." Mavis continued toward the wagons, her voice taking on its no-nonsense, don't-even-think-of-disobeying tone. "We will go home."

Acting rather pouty and disappointed, Lucas assisted both his mother and Cassie back up into the wagon. Gretchen climbed into the back and sat down on a bench they had there, her back resting against the inside of the wagon box. Ransom backed the team. They waved good-bye to those waving and headed out of town, with Cassie carefully keeping her head tucked down.

After a couple of blocks, Cassie let out a breath and felt herself relax. He'd not seen her. "Thank you for bringing me with you. People seemed really nice. With that exception, of course. The music was so beautiful."

"Yes, for a church our size we have a good organ and a man who loves to play it. He gives music lessons too. If we weren't so far out of town, I'd love to have Gretchen take lessons."

"But Gretchen doesn't really want to take lessons, so it's all right" came from the girl on the bench who twisted around on her knees and locked her elbows up over the back of the seat. "Mor, did you notice Betsy's sister? She sure looked mad. I thought she was going to stab Lucas with something. But I didn't see Betsy."

"She was there earlier. She must have had to leave early or something."

"She was probably upset that Lucas was sitting next to Miss Lockwood." Ransom flicked the lines and the horses picked up a trot.

"Surely not," Mavis answered. "At least, I hope not."

Cassie had no idea what they were talking about, but she listened politely and watched the houses go by, and then they were back out in ranching country. She'd not seen the little girl with the lisp at the service. But then the man with the big mouth hadn't been there either. Seeing him out on the street was frightening enough. There sure was a story to tell about her and the Engstroms, but she was not going to be the one telling it. That would be up to Mrs. Engstrom. Cassie just wanted to have a home, and the cabin with her adopted family was it.

Lucas rode beside the wagon, and when they arrived at the ranch house, he helped Cassie and his mother down before riding his horse down to the barn. Ransom drove the wagon on down too.

"They'll unhitch and dawdle long enough for us to get the table set." Gretchen walked with Cassie, following Mavis into the house. "Let me take your coat and hat, and I'll hang them on the tree by the door."

Cassie did as asked and, when she turned, let her gaze wander the room again. Such a welcoming and comfortable place.

"You can sit in here if you'd like," Mrs. Engstrom told Cassie, "while we get dinner on the table."

"Isn't there something I can do to help?"

"It's about ready. I have the meat and vegetables in the oven, and they should be about done by now. We're having baked Hubbard squash. I had to take an ax to that big squash to cut it into small enough pieces. I'll send some home with you so it doesn't go to waste. Nothing tastes better than Hubbard squash with butter and brown sugar cooked into it. And it goes equally well in stew or soup."

Cassie just nodded. She'd learn all this about food and cooking if it killed her. Should she just ask questions, or try to pretend she already knew something about it? Anything about it? What was so ordinary and humdrum to these people was completely alien to her.

"Do you want to help me set the table while Mor makes the gravy? We'll need to slice the bread too and put out the pickles and the pickled beets."

"All right." *At least I can set a table, can't I? I mean, how difficult is that?*

Gretchen waved an arm about. "There's four of us and four of you. The plates are in that cupboard and the silver in that drawer. I'll get the napkins."

Cassie did as Gretchen showed her, managing to slice the dill pickles into a dish and fork the beet pickles into another. The fragrances that came from the oven, and then the stove, made her mouth water.

"Ransom, will you carve the meat, please?" Mrs. Engstrom asked when the two men came into the kitchen. "Lucas, do we have any cider left out in the springhouse?"

"We do, but it's probably pretty hard by now."

What could he mean that the cider was hard? Another one of those things that confused her.

"That's a shame."

"No it's not. Now is when it's the best."

"I should have canned that leftover, so it wouldn't turn." She handed Lucas a bowl of potatoes and another of carrots, onions, and turnips. The squash took up a platter of its own. When all the food was set on the table, the dog's barking announced that Cassie's people had arrived.

"You want to go meet them?" Mavis asked, smiling at Cassie.

"Of course." Cassie went to open the front door and welcome the others into the house. "You're just in time. Everything is on the table."

Runs Like a Deer nodded and followed Cassie to the kitchen, where they took the chairs assigned to them.

"We're glad to have you here," Mavis said with a warm smile. "We should always have company around the table for Sunday dinner." When they were settled, she bowed her head. "Gretchen, it is your turn to say grace."

After grace was said and the serving dishes were all passed, Cassie looked at her plate. She'd not had such a variety of food on her plate for a long time, if ever. And never food that had been grown right there on the land they called home.

"This is elk meat," Gretchen informed her. "Lucas shot it right out in our pasture."

"Have you had elk before?" Mavis asked.

"I . . . I don't know. We shot a deer on our way down here but not elk." She cut a piece of the meat and put it in her mouth. The rich flavor of meat and gravy sank into her tongue and made her smile. "This is delicious."

"Good. Maybe we'll get another one tonight." Lucas smiled at her.

"I thought hunting wasn't allowed on Sundays."

"Sunday morning is for church, and then dinner and chores, and then we can go hunting if we want."

"I see." But she didn't really and looked to Mavis for confirmation.

"If you've shot a deer . . ." Lucas was looking at her.

"That was hard. He was so beautiful, with huge warm eyes, but we were getting hungry and tired of beans all the time. Chief kept us in rabbits too, with his snares, so we had enough to eat. He and Runs Like a Deer smoked a lot of the deer."

"We call deer meat *venison*," Gretchen told her.

"Why?"

"I don't know, but that's the way it is."

"Just like pig meat is called pork." Lucas grinned at her from across the table.

Cassie just nodded. There was so much to learn. She glanced at Ransom, who kept on eating as if no one were talking. Did he dislike her and her friends so terribly much that he couldn't even be polite? Was there anything she could do, other than leave the ranch behind forever, that might help this situation?

Probably not, and that saddened her. The last thing she wanted was to cause a rift in this family.

12

Mavis stood up with her empty plate in hand. "We'll have dessert in the other room."

While the men rose and followed Ransom out, the women began clearing the table. Runs Like a Deer scraped plates and stacked them while the others put the food away and Cassie set out the plates on the counter for the apple pie.

The plump brown pies smelled wonderful. "When did you have time to bake apple pies?"

"Oh, yesterday, when you were all working at the cabin. This is Lucas's favorite dessert; the apples came from the trees up by the cabin. In fact, we planted the apple trees before they finished the cabin. Ivar built a high fence around them at first to keep the deer and elk out. Had to do the same with the garden."

"Will I be able to have a garden next spring?"

"I don't know why not. It would be good if we could get it plowed before winter, so the snow and frost can help break down the sod. You'll have to take those young trees out. Digging out the roots is hard, so the easiest way to is just to pull them out with the team. It doesn't take the forest long to take over a field again. Some of them will make good corral poles, the straight ones."

Cassie listened carefully. "You hitch the team to a tree?"

"Yes, with chains. You can use the chains off the barn wall."

Oh, how I hope Micah or Chief knows what she is talking about.

Mavis smiled at her. "Don't worry. Lucas or Ransom will show the others how, if need be."

I hate feeling so stupid. "Thank you. How will I ever repay you for all your kindness?"

Mavis paused, then came over to stand right in front of Cassie. She clasped Cassie's upper arms. "There is no payback here. You are your father's daughter, and in my book that makes you family. Your father, Ivar, and I were the best of friends and then partners. God put us all together for a reason, many reasons in fact, and now we are privileged to be able to continue."

"But your son . . ."

"I must confess that Ivar and I made a terrible mistake in not telling our family about the partnership. And now we are paying the price for that. Ransom will come around. He's a fine man and honorable. We just need to be patient with him."

We. What a fine word. Cassie couldn't speak, so she nodded.

"Good. Now let's get that pie in there. I know Lucas is dying to talk to you about his new idea."

"I will finish the dishes," Runs Like a Deer said as she set another plate in the rinse water.

Mavis snorted. "On second thought, the men can wait a few minutes."

Gretchen picked up a towel and a stack of four plates. Four at once? She dried the top and bottom of the stack with a few practiced swipes. Then she slipped the top plate to the bottom and dried top and bottom again. Again. Again. The stack was done.

Cassie realized she was staring. Not only did she have so much to learn, she was going to have to learn all the little tricks like this that made long chores much simpler. She picked up the last two plates and dried them as Gretchen had, an experiment. It worked.

"Will you show us some of your trick riding?" Gretchen asked, putting away the dishes that Cassie had dried.

"Of course. I need some practice. We could use the big corral."

"Oh good. When?"

"Is tomorrow soon enough?"

"Right after school?"

"Wind Dancer will be real happy. Othello too."

"Is he part of your act?"

Cassie nodded. "Both in the trick riding and the shooting."

Gretchen turned to her mother, who was dishing up the pie. "Can Jenna come too?"

"If her mother says so."

Gretchen asked, "Are you really going hunting tonight?"

"I believe so. I'll need to go change clothes first. How far do we have to go? Or is the morning better?"

"Lucas hunts the most here. He shot the last ones right on the edge of the pasture."

Mavis tidied up the last of the counter. Her kitchen, as

always, was now spotless, another thing Cassie would have to learn.

"He got our last deer up the hill and over the ridge from the cabin. The deer bed down in the thickets up there. I'm surprised you've not seen any around the cabin yet."

"Othello was barking during the night. Maybe he chased them away."

Mavis ordered, "You carry the coffeepot, and Gretchen, you get the tray with cups. Runs Like a Deer and I will bring the pie." Like a parade, the four of them filed into the other room. The men looked up from the antler buttons Lucas was showing them. When everyone was served, Cassie took her first bite of the pie. If anything could be better than cinnamon rolls, this was it. "Can I learn to make pies like this?"

"Mor makes the best apple pie of anyone, anywhere." Lucas raised his plate in salute.

"It's all in the crust. There's more if anyone wants another piece."

"Who all is going hunting?" Lucas asked, scraping the last of the pie juice from his plate.

"Chief and I. Micah, are you going?"

He shook his head. "I need to learn to shoot first."

Lucas waved his fork at him. "Good point. We can set up targets out behind the house. I put one on the barn wall one time, and my pa about took my hide off. Put holes in the wood so rot could start. Not a wise move."

"I'd like to go."

Wide-eyed, the two Engstrom men stared at their mother.

Mavis looked from man to man. "Is that a problem?"

"Not at all. We'll shoot 'em, and the others can do the dressing."

Cocky was a good word for him. Were the elk so plentiful they'd get more than one if they got any? Cassie cleaned up the last of her pie. No wonder this was Lucas's favorite dessert.

"Need to fire up the smoker. We can do a half in there, if need be." Lucas again.

Mavis turned to Cassie. "I salt some down, but I have canned the meat too, when we got a warm spell. Smoking is our favorite way of preserving meat."

"In strips like Chief smoked the venison?"

"Oh no. We cut some pieces, grind some, and smoke the rest in big chunks, like the shoulder, the loins, and the hindquarters. If it turns cold enough soon enough, we can freeze a lot of it."

Cassie thought of the cold they'd experienced in the snowstorm that stopped them for a couple of days south of Dickinson. Anything left outside would have frozen, all right. She'd been afraid they would freeze inside the wagon. She glanced at Chief, who nodded.

"May we have the hides?" Runs Like a Deer asked.

"Of course. We have plenty. What did you do with the last one, Lucas?"

"It's down in the barn, curing."

"Oh. No, then we don't want that one." Runs Like a Deer shook her head. "Not when you are intending to use it."

Lucas shook his head too. "We don't have any plans for it. It's just that we were raised to never throw away anything useful. You can always find a use for hides."

"More coffee anyone?" Cassie raised the pot.

When they shook their heads no, Runs Like a Deer gathered up the plates and took them to the kitchen.

Mavis started to object, exchanged a look with the Indian woman, and acquiesced. "Thank you. When do you want to leave?"

Lucas shrugged. "Let's wait until a little later in the afternoon. Say four o'clock? We'll be riding."

Her Sunday clothes tucked away in the chifforobe and her legs back in her familiar trousers, Cassie rode down into the Engstroms' yard as the others were saddling their horses. Wind Dancer jigged in place and tossed his head, ready for a real ride. Cassie patted his shoulder and smiled down at Gretchen. "If you want to ride him sometime . . ."

"Oh, really?" Gretchen stood in front of the horse and held out a carrot chunk on the palm of her hand. Wind Dancer crunched it and nosed for another.

"You have made a friend for life. He bribes so pitifully easy. You know who else loves carrots?" When Gretchen shook her head, Cassie continued. "George. He grew up loving carrots. Not your normal buffalo feed, but no one told him he was a buffalo for a long time. He thought he was a horse. He and Wind Dancer were buddies."

Mavis laughed and patted her mount's shoulder. "Ah, this feels good. I need to ride more often."

"Do you want me to fix something for supper?" Gretchen asked.

"I thought we'd have leftovers from dinner. We'll heat them when we get back."

"We could have fried liver," Lucas suggested as he joined them.

"You are just too smug." Gretchen shook her head at her brother. "Serves you right if you miss."

Ransom nodded and tugged at her braid. "You tell him."

"You'll see. Let's go." Lucas and Chief urged their horses forward and led the group out past the corrals.

Cassie and Mavis rode side by side, something else new for Cassie. It had been so many years since she'd ridden with another woman. Not since her mother died. Her best friends on the show cast and crew had not been the other key performers but rather people who were pressed into service for the crowd scenes. None of them seemed to care to ride for pleasure. Everyone had multiple jobs to keep the show going.

"This is so beautiful," she said, looking up toward the western hills. The sun was already starting to coast lower and paint the scene silver with just a touch of mist. Soon, Cassie knew, that silver would turn to gold.

Mavis sounded wistful. "I know, and I ask God to keep reminding me so that I never take this for granted. One of my favorite verses is, 'I will lift up mine eyes unto the hills.' I see God in the beauty all around us."

"That's something my mother would have said. She talked about the mountains of Norway the same way. There are no mountains like these back east. She would have loved it here."

"I know your father did."

Cassie had been thinking about all she had to learn about ranching. She didn't even know many important things about her own father and his life before the show. In some ways this warm and welcoming lady knew more about her own background than she did.

13

Does Wind Dancer miss his old life with the show? Cassie would have to guess yes. The pinto loved performing, and he was probably forgetting some of his tricks, it had been so long. He loved getting out too, and with all this hustling to prepare for winter, Cassie had been neglecting him of late.

Lucas dismounted and opened a gate for them to leave the fields and head up into the hills. When he'd closed it again and remounted, he pointed to a faintly visible track going up the hill. "Game trail. Elk and deer often use it coming down into the valley. But if the entire elk herd comes down, they don't bother with the trails."

He fell in beside Cassie. "One time we found them bedded down up the side of a hill, and we didn't even see them because they had disappeared so well into the vegetation. A sound spooked them, and all of a sudden the hillside erupted and the whole herd charged up the hill. You could see all the light rumps moving up in the dimness of the trees. Pretty awesome sight."

"What might have spooked them?"

"Oh, a horse snorting or a tumbling rock. They always have one animal on guard to signal the warning. Herd animals are wise that way."

Cassie turned to Chief. "Did you ever shoot an elk?"

"Many of them. An elk can feed a lot of people."

Lucas said, "We only shoot the young bulls. They will have much smaller horns. Like deer, the number of prongs on the horn tell the animal's age. The fewer the prongs, the more tender the meat. Those big bull elk with the massive racks may be exciting to see, but they're sure tough to chew."

As they entered the wooded area, Lucas called a halt. "Mor, why don't you and Miss Lockwood settle in by one of these trees on the edge of this meadow and keep an eye out. This is the area where they'll come down if they're coming tonight. Chief and I will go see if we can locate the herd."

"All right. Two horses make a lot less noise than four." Mavis looked about. "Where should we leave the horses so they don't get shot?"

Lucas snorted but let the dig pass. "Tie them over that way or hobble them. If they're grazing, they won't bother the elk any. Elk are used to horses out grazing."

Cassie and Mavis did as he said, taking their rifles and ammunition with them. They made their way back and found a place on the downside of a huge evergreen tree. Cassie had not liked shooting the deer, and she wasn't looking forward to this either. But they had to eat, and another hide would help keep them warm when it turned really cold.

"Have you ever shot an elk?" she asked Mavis when they were settled.

"Years ago. I used to be a pretty good shot, but I haven't done much shooting these last years since the boys became men. Lucas loves hunting, and Ransom doesn't mind butchering them out. We hang them in the barn, and now that it is colder, the meat will be able to hang longer. Hanging it a while brings out the flavor."

Cassie settled herself comfortably and the women ceased making any noise. They sat listening carefully. Above and behind them the forest scowled, brooding. Before them a sloping glade opened up downhill, ever expanding until it reached the open valley floor. Cassie loved the colors, the meadow adorned with pale grass and vivid bushes, all in the hues painted by autumn. Here and there, baby trees in dark green poked their heads above the grass.

Forest noises one usually didn't even hear became audible, more noticeable—something skittering through the dried leaves, a bat that hadn't yet gone into hibernation diving, flitting, and cleaning the air of bugs. They heard a dog barking far away. Not Othello. This wooded hillside seemed somehow to smell moist, even dank, although it was dry. Perhaps it was the layer of duff they had disturbed. She could smell the pines too, faintly, a gentle aroma that soothed the soul. The shadows were long across the valley; a slight mist rose from the ground. The grazing horses seemed to float on a silver whisper.

Cassie rested her rifle across her raised knees, her eyes scanning the valley, watching for any unusual motion. Where were Chief and Lucas? She was surprised they had not returned.

She felt a tap on her arm and turned to see Mrs. Engstrom

gesturing subtly to her left. A shuffle of leaves, a snapping branch. Elk were moving down the hill right in front of them. Cassie saw nothing; then she could make out a brown form inside the brown forest edge, and another and another. The parade passed before their eyes while they froze, immobile. Cassie quit counting at ten. As they reached the meadow, the elk spread out. Magnificent animals. One with a huge rack of antlers that was odd. Remembering the elk rack over the Engstroms' fireplace, Cassie would have expected the branches of these to be more slender, pointier. Instead, they were thick and soft looking, with blunted tines. The big bull stood at the side and watched all about while the others lowered their heads to graze.

Mavis motioned to a male that was straight down from Cassie with antlers but only one tine and mouthed *You*. She pointed to another one and tapped her chest. Cassie nodded. Together they silently shifted positions, raised their rifles, sighted.

Cassie's target, the elk with one prong on his blunt little antlers, raised his head and then dropped it again. He took a few steps downhill, nibbling here, nibbling there. He turned, still browsing, turned some more, and now he stood broadside of her. Perfect. She took careful aim at the spot behind his front leg and raised her rifle muzzle just a hair to compensate for the distance.

Their guns fired at nearly the same moment. Cassie's young bull reared up and leaped forward, and for one brief moment she was sure she had missed. Then he dropped heavily onto his side in the dying grass. Mavis's bull had fallen motionless as well. The rest of the herd, heads high and noses thrust out, charged off up the hill, bounding, crashing, fanning out, disappearing into the trees. Farther up the hill, a rifle fired twice in quick succession.

The two women grinned at each other, shook hands, and made their way down the hill to their fallen elk.

Mavis warned, "Be careful at this point in case one is not quite dead. Those horns might be small and in velvet yet, but they can be deadly. Come up on it from behind, like this." She nudged the hindquarters of the one she'd shot and, when it didn't move, stepped in behind its shoulders and grasped an antler. She took out her hunting knife and slit the animal's throat to bleed it out and then handed the knife to Cassie.

Cassie walked on down the slope to hers. She shoved a foot against the elk's hindquarters. Then for long moments she simply stood and stared down at the beautiful creature that had been so wild and free, so alive just minutes before. "I'm sorry, but we need what you can give us." She leaned over and gripped an antler. It was furry, not nearly as soft as it looked, a hard core, but furry. She stabbed the point of her knife into the warm neck, slicing like Chief had shown her so that the animal bled freely.

Mavis raised her gun in the air and fired two rounds in quick succession. "That's to tell Ransom to bring the wagon. We made a kill."

"Someone shot above us too."

"If they also got one, we'll have to rig new tackle. We can manage two at a time in the barn all right, but not three." She smiled at Cassie. "That was mighty fine shooting."

"You too. I almost feel guilty. They made it so easy." She sniffed and blinked away a couple of residual tears. "Sorry. I hate doing this. I love shooting, but the killing is hard to get used to."

"I remember when I shot my first deer. I felt terrible. I knew we needed the meat, and we don't waste anything, but they are so beautiful, so graceful, walking, running. They seem to float. I had to laugh one time when I saw two of them, standing on their rear legs, eating apples off my trees. Ivar said I should scare them away, but they were so perfect. I used to sit and watch the fawns play when the does brought them out. That was when we still lived up here on the hill, in the cabin. They don't come around the ranch house down there."

A horse whinnied from up the hill, and one of theirs answered.

"Here they come." Cassie tried to spot Lucas and Chief but could see nothing.

Mavis waved an arm toward where the sloping meadow descended onto the valley floor to become open pasture. A light bobbed way down there in the gathering darkness. "Ransom is coming with the wagon."

Chief and Lucas emerged from the trees. Lucas cackled. "Well, will you look at that." He grinned at his mother. "You each got one, eh?"

"We heard you shoot."

"And missed. They came up that hill like a pack of wolves was behind them."

Cassie smiled at Chief. "You taught me well."

He nodded, and she detected the slight smirk that suggested a smile without actually delivering one.

Lucas dismounted and stopped at the elk his mother had shot. "Three-year-old. He's nice sized. Did you have a hard time seeing the horns, close to dark as it is?"

Mavis cradled her rifle in the crook of her arm. "These two stayed on the uphill side of the herd, out in the open.

Easy targets. I notice several cows had calves with them. The herd looks to be in real good shape."

"Should be. There was plenty of rain for forage this summer." He grabbed Cassie's elk by the antlers. "Two-year-old. Did you see that big bull?"

She nodded. "He was magnificent."

"He has a nice harem. We've watched him for the last several years. In the fall the bulls try to take cows away from other bulls. When you hear an elk bugle, the hair stands up on the back of your neck. I think of it and can hear them so plain, as if they were right here. I'm surprised he let these young bucks remain with his herd."

"They're probably not old enough to challenge him yet." Mavis turned to Cassie. "One of the things I love about living on the ranch is learning about all the wildlife around us." She motioned to Chief. "He trained Adam and Ivar in the way of the woods. They were willing to work hard. Your father sure did love guns and shooting them. I wasn't a bit surprised when we heard he had a shooting act."

Here came Ransom, and his team was acting nervous. The blood, Cassie realized. They smelled the blood.

Lucas laid a hand on the near horse's bridle as Ransom climbed down out of the wagon box. "Would you believe the women each got one and we got skunked?"

"Gretchen will never let you live that down." He walked over to the larger one and gave it a shove with one foot. "Mor, you got this one?"

"I did. Haven't lost my touch."

"So you missed your shots, huh?" Ransom grunted as the three of them heaved the heavy carcass up to the wagon bed and slid it in.

"Yep. Got two off, in fact, but the bull got away. Doesn't happen often."

"And Mor and Miss Lockwood both got theirs."

"Rub it in, why don't you?"

"Just thought it's worth mentioning."

So Lucas had fired both shots. Now Cassie knew that Chief had not pulled his trigger. When he'd been so insistent that she learn to hunt a few weeks ago, she'd realized that his eyesight was dimming and he couldn't see well enough to make a clean shot any longer. But today it was obvious to her that he still relished the chase as much as ever. He walked down to help load the second elk.

Mavis climbed up into the box and drove the wagon down to Cassie's elk. The three men had a little easier time loading hers, since it wasn't quite as huge.

"So you decided not to gut them out here," Mavis said as she stepped down from the wagon.

Chief brought the other two horses in. At the smell of blood, Wind Dancer tried backing away but Cassie laid firm hands on his head and talked to him, calming him down.

"Easier at the barn with decent light." Ransom climbed into the wagon and clucked the team off down the hill, headed for the barn.

As she mounted, Cassie asked no one in particular, "How heavy are they?"

Mavis replied, "At least five hundred pounds. Of course, if you gut them in the field, it's quite a bit less weight to have to throw around."

Considering that this might be called an evening of death, Cassie still felt elated, and the elation surprised her. She was providing food for them all, and that was no small accomplishment. Only one shot too. The darkness had brought with it enough cold to call this day *winter*, though of course it was not. And it was going to get much colder, she knew, when the real winter arrived. She could see a certain wisdom in taking the show south during the winter, to places where snow rarely fell.

Lucas swung the gate closed behind them, and they were back in civilization, the wagon rattling along a well-worn track. "I have a great idea. How about having a shooting contest right here at the ranch?" Lucas asked when he pulled up to ride beside her again.

Cassie wanted to turn it down, since she was low on shells, but realized that might not be a good idea, especially if he was interested in finding someone to sponsor a match. "All right. We can do targets, or clay pigeons, or toss something in the air. Whatever." She turned to Mavis riding on the other side. "Do you buy ready-loaded shells or load your own?"

"We do both," Lucas said. "How many guns do you have?"

"Six. Rifles, shotguns, and pistols. Some of them were my father's." Wind Dancer had apparently decided the smell of blood was tolerable, since he'd settled down again.

Ransom said, "Micah went up to get Runs Like a Deer when we heard the rifle shots. We can hang both at the same time. Gretchen can start the supper warming, but it'll be awhile before we get there for that."

"It's a good thing we weren't depending on Lucas to bring home the liver." Mavis turned to tease her son.

"Mor, even I miss sometimes."

"Obviously."

When she heard Chief audibly chuckle, Cassie almost fell off her horse.

Back at the barn, Micah and Runs Like a Deer were waiting. Ransom drove the wagon right in through the big doors.

Runs Like a Deer looked in the wagon as it passed and nodded. "Good."

When Mavis explained that she and Cassie shot the two elk, Runs Like a Deer glanced at Lucas and raised an eyebrow. "Very good." Her face betrayed a tiny twitch of a smile.

"Do you need us to help?" Mavis asked.

"Nope. There are plenty of hands here to do the job. But I sure am getting hungry." Lucas dismounted and started pulling the saddle down off his mother's horse. "I'll take the horses back out to the pasture. You want to take Wind Dancer up to the cabin?"

"No. He can go back to the field. Thanks." Cassie dismounted and walked into the barn to see Ransom and Chief already slitting the skin on the elks' back legs and pushing a bar through, between bone and sinew. They attached the tackle that hung by pulleys from the rafters and, with Ransom pulling on the rope, raised the smaller elk right up off the wagon bed, letting it hang free. Runs Like a Deer lighted a lantern, giving Cassie's elk a ghostly hue as it swayed slowly back and forth.

Mavis motioned. "Come on, Cassie. Let's go help Gretchen get supper on the table. Half an hour?"

Lucas nodded. "About that. You want the intestines?"

"Yes. I'll clean them tomorrow."

The two walked up the rise to the ranch house. "That was some hunting trip," Mavis commented. "I'm sure glad I went along."

"Me too."

"It might be a long time before we let Lucas off the hook. This might take his cockiness down a peg or two."

He was entertaining. That was for sure. At least they weren't going to go hungry and didn't have to accept everything from the Engstroms. Cassie had to find a way to make enough money, to buy ammunition at least. Five dollars was all she had left, not taking into account the gold piece she had found during that first pawing search through the drawers. That was her absolutely-only-in-an-emergency backup.

Hopefully they wouldn't have to use it.

14

Now if only the sawmill will start right up.

Once they'd finished breakfast, Ransom made sure all the tools they would need were in the wagon, and he headed to the sawmill set in the pine trees. Finally they would be able to get the sawmill going and begin cutting the timbers for the mine. He was driving the team up there, and Lucas was supposed to ride his horse in case they needed him to go back down for anything else.

Micah and Chief would be helping too. They could finish cutting off the branches while he and Lucas set up the mill. He should have asked Dan Arnett, the owner of the portable sawmill, to come over to supervise. The thought had come to him more than once, but he hadn't gotten around to doing it. Like so many things in his life.

He could go over there now, but that would take a lot more time. The old man was quite a talker and age had slowed him down a lot. On the other hand, he probably would have loved a home-cooked meal. The thoughts went back and forth. He looked ahead to see Micah and Chief coming down the hill. Looking back, no Lucas was in sight. Probably finishing his last cup of coffee. When it had to do with something Ransom wanted him to do, he could always be late, sometimes Ransom referred to as *Lucas time*.

And Lucas was the one most familiar with the instructions on how to set up the mill. Ransom jogged the horses up to where the mill waited. He remembered helping his father when he cut the logs to build the smokehouse. Old Mr. Arnett wasn't so old then; it was maybe ten years ago. They ripped a couple of pines into one-inch slabs, the width of the boards being whatever the width of the log might be. In fact, they still had a few pieces of that siding on a rack up in the barn. Well-seasoned by now. Sometimes he wished they had bought the sawmill when Arnett first had it for sale. If they had any money now, it could stay right where it was and they could log off some of the upper timber too. Maybe some oak. Sell it. His dreams nearly took off with him. They needed to do something to bring in more money. Maybe the sawmill was it.

"Morning." He greeted the two men, who started taking tools out of the wagon.

"You want me to hobble the horses?" Micah asked.

Ever the animal handler, that fellow. "No thanks. We'll be using them soon. You know anything about steam engines?"

"A little. You build the fire under the boiler and get up the steam that will do the work—turn the belts to run the sawmill, in this case."

"You ever worked on one?"

"Just to fill the water tank and keep the fire burning. The show had a steam calliope for a while when I first started working for them, but I was new there and wasn't supposed to mess with it. We could use the cut branches as part of the firewood."

"I brought up some dry firewood. Easier to start. We'll stack it near the boiler. Chief, you ever worked with a steam engine?"

"No. I took care of horses and wagons."

"I thought Micah here was the animal handler."

"Show that size took two people to keep up with all the stuff that broke. Lucas coming?"

"Said he was." He never should have gone off and left him behind. Should know better by now. Castigating himself was easy. Leave it to Lucas to slow down the action. He paused, frowning. "So what happened to the calliope? Didn't blow up, did it?"

"Owner lost it in a poker game. Drew a queen, shoulda been a king."

"Mm." Back to business. Ransom lifted a set of chains out of the wagon. "We'll drag the trimmed trees down by wrapping these chains around them. Same way you'll be pulling those trees out of the garden area by the cabin. Mor said Miss Lockwood is asking about a garden place for next spring."

Since it didn't look like Lucas would be coming anytime soon, Ransom looped the chains around the whippletree and let the horses drag them up to the trees.

"You wrap the choke chain around the tree and the other end around the whippletree. The team will drag it down. We'll set up skids to get the logs up onto the saw bed. Roll the log up."

"Sounds simple enough." Micah unwrapped one of the chains and took it over to the end of the nearest log. He studied the log and the chain, nodded, and turned to Ransom. "That rod we used for packing the dirt around the posts?"

"In the wagon."

"We can roll the log with that, I think."

Ransom nodded. "Good idea, since we don't have a peavey. Let's do it." Ransom retrieved the bar. Chief took the end of the chain with the hook, and together they got the chain around the log with Ransom planting the weighted steel rod and leveraging the log to get room to hook the chain solidly.

"Check it again. Nothing more dangerous than a broken chain."

They looped the other end around the whippletree, and Ransom gathered up the lines. "Stand way back out of the way." When the other two were well clear, he clucked the horses, and they leaned into their collars. The chain tightened, choking down on the log. Ransom flipped the lines and the horses dug in. The tree slid forward and they dragged it down a slight grade to the flat area parallel with the sawmill.

Ransom backed the horses a step to release the tension, and they removed the chain from the log. Breathing a sigh of relief, Ransom started the horses back up for a second log. They had skidded three logs down to lie side by side when Ransom saw two men riding across the pasture. *Well, look who's coming*, he muttered to himself. *But who is with him?*

"Sorry I'm late," Lucas said, dismounting. "But I knew I didn't know enough about that sawmill, so I went and got Arnett."

"Good to see you," Ransom said with a smile. Leave it to his brother to do something so perfect without telling anyone, and here he was ready to lay him out. "Thanks for coming. I figured I could handle moving the logs."

The old man, with a twinkle in his eye, nodded. "You did a fine job, for a youngster. I see you had helpers."

"Yes. Chief, Micah, meet one of our neighbors, Dan Arnett. He owns this sawmill and is going to tell us what to do."

"Good to meet you." Arnett nodded then turned to the machinery.

Half an hour later they had the boiler heating, the belts checked, oil in the right places, and knowledge of how the machine would work. With Arnett giving instructions, they finished setting up the rest of the gear, and by the time the sun stood straight overhead, the first log was heading into the spinning blade. With a mournful, drawn-out scream, the first side of slab wood fell off, and the milling had begun.

They stopped long enough to eat the meal Mavis brought to them, and then continued, log after log. The stack of six-by-sixes grew. The pile of slab wood grew, the pile of sawdust grew, and the number of trees on the ground diminished, as one by one they were skidded down to the mill, rolled up onto the platform, and turned into usable timbers.

They burned the dry wood that Ransom had brought up and many of the branches from the piles. Chief kept the fire stoked, while the others fed the whining blade. At the end of the day and the last log run through, they shut the mill down. The silence made Ransom blink.

"Mor will have supper ready. Let's go eat." Lucas and Arnett rode ahead. Ransom loaded the tools back into the wagon bed, and with Chief and Micah in the wagon too, he drove back to the ranch house.

When they'd washed and sat down at the table, with the women serving, Ransom gave the blessing, and they dug into the meal.

He glanced over. The old man was carefully, thoughtfully, working each bite around in his mouth, like a cow works its cud only much more thoroughly. A faint smile graced that grizzled old face, and it was obvious Dan Arnett needed to be with other people more often.

Ransom broke the silence. "Getting that done sure makes me wish we could cut some of those big trees above the cabin. Think what we could do with seasoned oak or maple. Pa made great furniture. I'd like to try my hand at that this winter."

Mavis frowned, a questioning look. "Dan, how long does it take green wood to season down to furniture wood?"

"Depends." He swallowed. "Two or three years should do it. In warm weather they cure faster than in cold weather, but on the other hand, felling trees this time of year takes a year off the drying, 'cause the sap's all run down out of the trunk for the winter. Takes a lot longer for a log cut in spring when it's fresh and sappy. Then your close-grain hardwoods will take longer'n softwoods, and oak and maple take longer'n alder or cottonwood. And you'll want to rip the logs into planks less'n two inches thick. Then it'll dry faster."

"Besides," Lucas added, "how can you work in the mine and make furniture too?"

"Don't know, but it bears thinking about. Two or three years? You sure?"

"Long as you keep it under cover. Say, why can't you just keep the sawmill awhile?" Arnett asked around a mouthful of potatoes and gravy. "I haven't had a meal like this since the last time I was here. My own cookin' ain't too appetizing."

"I'm sorry, Dan. You need to come here more often. Do you want to stay in the bunkhouse tonight, not ride home in the dark?" Mavis passed the serving platter of meat around again.

"That would be right fine, if'n it ain't too much trouble. Workin' with all these men for a change—that was some good time." He speared himself a chunk with stuffing.

"Gretchen, I'm sorry we didn't get to show you Wind Dancer's tricks today," Cassie said as she passed the platter. "Maybe we can do that tomorrow." She and Runs Like a Deer had been helping with pickling the tongues and cleaning out the intestines of the elk to use as sausage casings, so the elk were probably pretty well processed. Mavis had stuffed and baked the hearts for supper.

"That's okay. Maybe right after school tomorrow?"

Cassie nodded her assent.

Ransom glanced around the table. Everyone had been working together well, and look what all they had accomplished. He took another piece of the corn bread from the passing plate. "So you don't mind if we keep the sawmill awhile longer?"

"Not a'tall. I'm getting too old to use it. Need to sell it, but there ain't no one who wants it. You can use it, you keep it here. Maybe I could help you again, like today."

"You want to go up and look at those other trees tomorrow?"

"Can't hurt none."

"Do you have any chores that need doing at home?" Lucas asked.

"Yeah. I'll need to feed the chickens, make sure they got water, pick the eggs. Don't have so many anymore. The chickens was Mabel's doing. When they all die off, I won't have chickens no more. And the dog needs to be fed. He usually gets table scraps, but this here meal, this here's for old Arnett, not no dog."

Lucas chuckled. "Tell you what. I'll go by and take care of that for you tomorrow, and you and Ransom go up and look at the trees. I need to go into Hill City again anyway."

Ransom looked from his mother to his brother. Was Lucas pursuing the shooting match idea? He'd not talked it over with Miss Lockwood yet. What if that wasn't what she wanted to do? He thought about it only a moment. That was Lucas's problem, not his.

"I was hoping we could get those trees pulled out of the garden spot up there tomorrow," Mavis said with a smile at Cassie. "Since the team won't be needed for the sawmill, maybe we can do that?"

Ransom shrugged. "We can get it started on our way up to the higher timber. Micah, you and Chief got anything planned?"

"To pull trees out, I guess," Micah said. "And put those rails up on the posts. They should be set by now. Probably ought to wire them as well as nail them, in case one of the horses gets all excited."

Ransom nodded. "That sawdust could be spread over the garden plot. It will help kill off the sod for the spring plow. When we clean out the chicken house, we can bring a load up to the garden. Also that old manure pile by the barn. Mor usually scatters that on our garden too."

"And leaves from under some of those trees around you. We get all that dug in, and you'll have a good start." Mavis smiled at Cassie. "I have plenty of seeds saved. I left some carrots in the garden last year, and they went to seed, so I even have carrot seeds. As we eat the squash and pumpkins, I save the seeds from those too. And the last of the potatoes get cut up for planting as soon as the ground thaws."

Ransom caught himself from adding anything else. What was going on here? He didn't want Miss Lockwood to stay at all, yet here they were all talking like any family about things that needed doing for next spring. There was plenty of work in the garden down here. Why did they need to start another one?

"Thanks for all your help today," he said to Chief and Micah when they were ready to take their wagon up to the cabin. "The extra hands made the milling go so much faster. You want to ride up to see the other trees, I'd be glad to show you another part of the ranch."

Chief gave a nod. "Tomorrow."

"Thank you for all the lessons today," Cassie said to Mavis. "I learned so much . . . and want to learn more."

When the others had left, Ransom turned to the old man. "Come on, I'll show you where things are in the bunkhouse. We'll get a fire going in there, and you should be comfortable. Your horse will be fine with the rest of ours."

"Thank you, son. This has been a real good day. And, Lucas, I thank you for coming for me. I wouldn'ta missed this for anything."

Mavis stopped them. "Just a minute. I'm not sure if there are enough blankets on that bunk. I'll get another." She loaded a couple of blankets and a pillow on Ransom's arms. "We should have gone and cleaned that place before we put company out there."

"Don't you worry none. I'll see you in the mornin'."

They walked the distance to the bunkhouse, and Ransom opened the door.

"I'll get a fire going in the stove. You just make yourself at home. Shame you didn't bring your dog with you."

"He'll be right lonesome. He's good company, ya know."

Ransom dug the tinder out of the box kept for that purpose, rattled the grate on the stove that hadn't been used since he couldn't remember when, and after laying in the tinder, added some small kindling and lit the match. With the flames curling around the bits of wood, he added more kindling, then a couple of small sticks from the woodbox, and put the lids back in place. Opening the damper wide, he turned to see the old man spreading another blanket on the bunk and putting the pillow in place. What would it be like to live alone like he did?

Ransom could hear the fire starting to crackle and opened the front lid to add some larger sticks. "You want to add some more here in a few minutes? I'll leave the lantern on the table. So when you are ready you can turn it out. Do you need anything else?"

The old man sighed. "Not a thing. 'Night."

Ransom looked upward as he strolled back to the house. It would freeze again tonight, and tomorrow they'd go look at that timber. What he'd thought to take three or four days was done in one. The stars stood clear and bright in the cold air. He sucked in a deep breath and let it out. Now he'd better have a talk with Lucas. Looked like he would be putting the cart before the horse, and they might all be sorry for that.

15

Guts. Yards and yards of flat, slimy white guts.

Cassie jerked awake, feeling in desperate need of washing her hands—repeatedly. The smell when cleaning the intestines, even though they'd done it outside, was beyond belief. They'd cleaned out the elk intestines to be used for sausage casings. She understood the necessity, but the process made her want to run screaming back to a Wild West show—any Wild West show.

She had asked to learn how to do all those homemaking things that Mrs. Engstrom did so effortlessly. She was eager to learn, was all excited. Whatever had possessed her? This bad dream that had so violently awakened her was so real she sniffed her hands.

The coals of the fire barely winked, so the room was already beyond chilly. Somehow this winter, they would have to wake up once or twice during the night—maybe even more often—to stoke the fires. But it wasn't winter yet, and she didn't want to leave the warmth of her cocoon of covers. Runs Like a Deer lay perfectly still. Had she awakened her with her jerk, or had she dreamed that too? When the hanging elk meat had aged enough, they would be grinding and seasoning the ground meat and running it through a cast-iron machine called a sausage stuffer. Mrs. Engstrom had demonstrated; turning the crank handle is what pushed the meat through.

That part was intriguing. Mrs. Engstrom had said they would hang the ropes of sausage in the smokehouse with the other cuts of elk. She threw out words like *brining* and *packing in crocks* that had no meaning whatsoever to Cassie. She also didn't understand what Mrs. Engstrom had meant when she said the carcasses hanging in the barn were aging so the meat was more tender.

And today they were to pull trees out of the proposed garden area. Was that like pulling weeds? Weeds that were nearly twenty feet tall? Well, maybe not quite that big but taller than she was, taller even than the roof of the cabin. And spindly. Most were scraggly, with limbs far apart. Others formed a perfect cone of dark green needles. She swallowed a sigh and closed her eyes again. *Think sleep.* She must have returned to slumberland until she felt Runs Like a Deer trying to leave the bed without waking her.

"I'm awake," she admitted.

"I'll start the fires."

Cassie waited only a few minutes before leaving the bed to pull the curtains and get dressed. Today she would ask Mrs. Engstrom if they had a bathtub. Soaking in a bathtub would be the height of luxury. That had been one of her mother's demands, that a high-backed copper bathtub accompany the show. She had refused to succumb to the barbarian practice, her words, of washing and rinsing standing in a low basin and using as little water as possible. She'd said that washing in the rain was far preferable, but a bathtub would go with her or she wouldn't go.

But then her mother had always believed that getting all heated up and perspiring and then rolling in a snowbank was a healthful, perfectly splendid idea. Her father never had agreed to that one.

The bathtub had disappeared when her mother died. But then, who would ever imagine, Cassie especially, that one day she would own land and be settling down?

Perhaps she could wash their clothes down at the ranch house too, so they wouldn't have to haul water in the barrels to do the wash. Could they dig a well up here? They hadn't dug down very far for the outhouse when they hit solid rock. A well would surely do the same. Perhaps someday they needed to build a house down on the valley floor. Oh, the ideas that flowed through her head as she pulled on and laced her boots.

A breakfast of sliced, fried cornmeal and syrup, eggs, and chipped venison slid past. Cold weather aside, they were eating like royalty. This was delicious.

The men went out to work again on the corral, nailing long, thin poles to the posts and wrapping wire around the joints, lest rambunctious horses pull the rails down, nails and all. While Cassie cleared away the breakfast things, Runs Like a Deer added flour and water to the sourdough starter she had inherited from Mrs. Engstrom. Tomorrow they would have sourdough pancakes for breakfast. The leftover dough, with more flour added, became a combination between biscuits and buns, baked in a covered cast-iron pan, which Cassie learned was called a Dutch oven, on top of their stove. A stove with a real oven was already on her someday list.

While washing the dishes, she thought back to something the younger Mr. Engstrom had said. What kind of a plan was he envisioning? He'd mentioned talking to a man who might sponsor a shooting match. Was that a possibility? She *humph*ed to herself. She didn't even have the shells to practice with. While she had downed that elk, shooting falling objects rapidly was not the same. But if she couldn't enter shooting matches, how could she make the money to help them through the winter?

Othello barked, announcing visitors. Obviously he knew them, because there was no trace of menace in his tone. She went to the door to see Mrs. Engstrom driving the wagon and the others on horseback.

"Good morning." Her greeting brightened an already lovely morning, with frost etching each grass blade and the air nipping any exposed body parts. One no longer ran to the outhouse barefooted.

"Are you ready to pull trees?" Mavis called as she stepped to the ground.

Anything sounded better than cleaning intestines. Cassie snagged a flannel shirt off the peg and shrugged into it as she stepped outside.

"Mornin', little lady," Mr. Arnett said from horseback. "You might rather want to come look at trees with us instead. Pullin' 'em is hard work."

"Don't scare her away, Dan," Mrs. Engstrom scolded. "We need to get that garden plot ready."

Lucas had dismounted and was unhitching the team while

Ransom dragged the chains out of the wagon. Micah brought out the saws, axes, and some other tools.

"I will stay here," Micah said with a nod to Cassie. "They can go talk hunting and trees and who, or rather, whatever, lives up there."

Mr. Arnett gave a laugh that ended in a hoot. He sure seemed to be enjoying himself this morning.

He rode over to where Ransom was giving Micah advice. "I think you need to top those taller ones. If they land on those horses' rumps, they'll be down the hill and in the next county before you know it."

Ransom nodded and took one of the saws. "Lucas, you take the other one. Micah, go along and pull the tops away from the saw blade."

With a deft flick of the wrist, Lucas tossed a looped rope up over one of the larger trees.

"Weed trees," Mrs. Engstrom had called them. Trees? Mere weeds?

As nimbly as a ten-year-old, Lucas scrambled up the tree, the saw under his arm. When he got up to a skinny part of the trunk, he began sawing while Micah pulled on the rope. With a crack, the top broke over, although not all the way. It hung there, forlorn, almost like the hangdog look Othello offered when he knew he'd been a bad fellow.

Lucas clambered back down. "That'll do. Next one."

Ransom was not the tree-climbing squirrel that his brother was, but he got there. The top he sawed through fell to the ground.

Cassie watched carefully. If she was to become a rancher, she might be called upon one day to top trees. So far, it did not seem too onerous a task. As the tops fell, she and Mrs.

Engstrom gathered them into a pile. Some were surprisingly heavy.

Mrs. Engstrom pointed. "Let's put the pile nearer to the house, and it can dry for kindling. You can never have too much dry tinder."

Ransom cinched the chain around the nearest tree, snugging it about a foot up from the ground. "Micah, you take one of those axes, and as the roots start to break free, you can chop the big ones. We'll stack them over there to dry."

Micah nodded casually and stood near the tree of the moment. Cassie wondered what he was thinking. Micah had joined the show in his youth, and like Cassie, he had known no other world for many years. Now here he was on a hillside in the middle of nowhere, ripping trees out of the ground. What strange turns their lives were taking!

With the chain hooked over the whippletree, Mavis flicked the lines slightly and clucked the team ahead. The chain tightened down, the horses dug in and leaned into their chest collars. The tree shook but otherwise refused to budge. The trunk didn't even tilt.

"Back off and relax. Then try again."

"Okay, boys, let's get this done." Mavis flicked the lines again and kept encouraging the horses, calling them by name to "get up! Get up!" The ground quivered, buckled, and the tree gave a groan. "Come on, boys, keep it up."

Nothing moved.

The horses strained, one hoof slipped and regained footing. They lunged against their collars.

"Let's add a rope. Miss Lockwood, you want to ride and pull?" Ransom nodded toward his saddled horse. He retrieved a rope from the back of the wagon, cinched it around the tree just above the chain, and handed it to her to tie around the saddle horn. "Pull in tandem with the team. I think that should be just enough extra to make it work."

Cassie nodded and did as he said. Her saddle moved; the tree did not.

"Wait! I need to tighten the cinch." She dismounted and, lifting the stirrup, tightened the cinch and remounted. Again the team hit their collars and she nudged her horse forward. The rope lay across her leg. Her horse snorted and dug in, straining against the pull. With a mighty groan, the ground gave way, released the tree, and a mass of roots threw dirt to all sides. The tree came swishing down, missing the horses' rumps by inches. There it went, sliding after the team, dropping dirt and stones as it dragged across the smashed grass and weeds. The smell of fresh dirt filled the morning air.

"We did it!" She patted the horse's neck and unwrapped the rope from around the horn.

"You can go," Mavis said to Ransom as she and Micah prepared the next tree. "We'll do fine."

Ransom hesitated, but at his mother's insistence mounted his horse. "Fire your rifle if you need help."

"Yes, of course. Show Chief where the deer bed down in that copse over the hill. And look for those walnut trees up amongst the oaks in the coulee. I wish we could send the hogs up there to gorge on the acorns." She turned to Cassie. "Pigs love rooting around for acorns. Our oak tree by the house doesn't produce enough yet to keep them happy."

Pigs? She hadn't seen any pigs down at the house. "Where do you keep them?"

"Out behind the barn. They eat all our dinner scraps and turn them into bacon. Everybody needs a pig."

They watched the riders head on up the hill, Lucas's laughter ringing back behind them.

Mrs. Engstrom commented, "Lucas likes nothing more than riding up into the hills. I'm surprised he doesn't have his rifle along."

"He has a shotgun. I saw the scabbard on his saddle."

"Some birds would taste mighty good."

"I shot some grouse on the way down here. They'd roost in the trees. They weren't too hard to hit."

Othello whined at Cassie's side. "What is it, boy?" She looked up the hill to see what he was watching. "Ah, you wanted to go along. Sorry. You and I'll go another day."

"Well, we had a breather. Let's get on it."

By the fourth tree, patches of glistening sweat darkened the horses' flanks and shoulders, as they all stood breathing hard.

"I think the horses are due for a rest, and we are due for a cookie break." Mavis pulled a basket from the back of the wagon and opened the tin of ginger cookies, offering it to Micah first.

"Mrs. Engstrom?"

"Cassie, dear, let's drop the Mrs. Engstrom, please. My name is Mavis, and I'd like for you to call me that."

Cassie swallowed. "Ah, all right. Do you know what the younger Mr. Engstrom is trying to make happen?"

Mavis rolled her eyes. "Lucas is hoping to get Josiah Porter, who owns Hill City Hotel, to sponsor a shooting match so you can compete."

"I see. There is a problem, however." Cassie could feel her face growing hot. "Uh, I . . ." She heaved a sigh. "This is embarrassing."

"Spit it out, girl."

"I don't have enough shells to practice with. I'm rusty. Shooting grouse is easy. A contest isn't. I can't go into a match without practicing. So he probably better reconsider," she finished with a rush.

"We can buy shells at the store in town."

"I can't." *Go ahead and tell her why; you're in this far.*

"You don't have the money to buy shells?"

Cassie nodded.

"You can put the shells on our account at the store. We'll be your sponsors."

"But . . ."

"No *buts*. You can pay it back from your winnings if you feel the need. So don't worry about it. And until we get back into town, you can borrow a couple boxes. I'll set them out for you soon as I get back, so we don't forget."

But what if I don't win? You can't let yourself even think that. What would Father say? You have won many matches through the years; you're a show star. Not only one voice, but several. This was getting worse.

Othello yipped and looked up the hill, ears full up. At least the one that stood up did, and the other was at attention.

"They're coming back. Micah, let's get some more trees pulled out."

Lucas, leading the pack, loped his horse down to join them and made it dance a bit pulling up. *Showoff.*

"Hey, we thought you'd be done by now," he said with a grin.

"No you didn't. You knew the horses would need a rest. And so did we. How about you all work on the fence and we'll finish the trees?"

"I'm going to Hill City. I'll stop by Arnett's on the way home. Gotta feed his dog."

"I should really head on home," Dan Arnett said with a nod. "You've all been so kind to me."

"That's what neighbors are for, but if you plan to be here tomorrow, why not stay?" Mavis smiled, offering the invitation. "I mean, it's no trouble and we'd love to have you."

"Besides, I have a lot of questions for you." Ransom added his plea. "I want to know more about using wood, and maybe take a look at dragging over some of those downed trees we looked at."

Cassie watched the exchange. How could the Engstroms be so generous? It seemed they truly cared for the old man. But why? She realized his wife had died and he lived alone. Still . . . they must have been friends for a long time was all she could think.

But they were offering her that same kind of caring. Why? Sure, she had a piece of paper that gave her title to half the land. But ever since she walked through that door, Mrs. Engstrom, er, Mavis, had offered her nothing but welcome and a feeling that she belonged to the family. A long-lost relative, perhaps. If she allowed herself to think on it further, would her father, or her mother and father, have been as welcoming if one of the sons had shown up at the show?

She had no answer. And did it really matter? After all, one couldn't change the past. Her mother had said that often enough. You couldn't change the past, you couldn't live in the future. You could only live in the day, the right now.

They were still cleaning up the garden area when Gretchen came riding up the trail, just home from school.

Cassie saw Gretchen and groaned. She and Wind Dancer were supposed to put on a show today. At least Jenna wasn't along.

More apologies needed. She dragged another bush she'd pulled out over to one of the brush piles. But instead of Wind Dancer, she was riding one of the Engstroms' horses while hers was happily grazing in the far pasture.

Gretchen waved and stopped her horse to look around. "This sure looks different."

Mavis nodded. "We're pretty close to finished with both the corral and the garden. There are a few cookies left in the tin."

"Thanks. I hurried home."

Cassie lifted her hands, a gesture of contrition. "I'm sorry we're not ready, but I can ride back down with you and whistle for Wind Dancer. He'll meet us at the barn."

"You would do that?"

"I said I would, but this all took longer than we thought it would." *Not that I had any idea how long anything would take. Or what we were going to do, for that matter.*

"Maybe tomorrow would be better," Mavis said as she joined them.

"Well, Jenna can come then, and her little brother really wants to watch too."

"Are you sure?"

Gretchen nodded with a grin. "That would be better. May I see what the cabin looks like now?"

"Of course." Cassie dismounted and dropped the reins. Ground tying was new to her, but she couldn't wait to train Wind Dancer to it. All the Engstrom horses were trained that way. "Come on." She opened the door and ushered Gretchen in.

"It looks nice. The last time I was here, rats and squirrels had made it their home. Did Mor show you where Pa carved their initials?" She crossed the room to the kitchen and pointed at the small carving under the shelf. "Their initials and the year. He did it again down at the ranch house when they moved there." She traced the letters with one finger. "Sometimes I really miss him."

"I feel the same for my father. When he died I thought the world would stop."

"But it didn't."

"No. It didn't. I know he would have loved it here. He talked about the valley a lot before my mother died but after that not so much. I wish he could have been buried here, at least."

"Well, I'm glad you came." Gretchen walked back outside with Cassie. "Where's Lucas?"

"Gone to Hill City. He left a couple of hours ago."

What if he returns with a match all set up? When could she go to town to buy more shells? Putting the shells on the Engstrom account did not sit well with her at all. When she won a match, she would pay them back with interest.

Perhaps she could find some more information in the wagon. She still had some drawers to go through again. Maybe she should just take some of those names she had and send a letter to say she was available and interested. Her father had always been a stickler for doing things in advance and keeping careful records. That was something she would have to start doing. All those years she could have been learning things like this. But it never entered her mind that the show would fold and she'd be looking for work. If she ever got a hold of Jason Talbot . . . Here they were with nothing and no idea how much money he had taken with him. What a scoundrel. What would it be like to get some of that money? Even more delicious, to get even? How would one ever go about that? What would God think if she prayed for a way to get even?

16

"My, that felt good today." Mavis squirmed back into the most comfortable position on her rocker and pulled her shawl in around close. Her rocker creaked; that old familiar sound made the day complete.

"What?" Ransom looked up from the ledger in front of him.

"Pulling those trees out, getting that garden plot back toward planting condition felt really good. That Micah is really a worker."

"Yes, he is. He's so quiet I wondered about him, but when he has something to offer, he says it. Up there with the sawmill, he would see what needed doing next and go do it."

"And John Birdwing." She pushed back in her rocking chair and let it carry her back and forth, as it did when her babies were tiny. "I remember him as a young brave who sometimes got frustrated with the two white men he had taken on. But if they had not listened to him, none of this would be here now. When he left with Talbot and Lockwood, your pa lost his two best friends."

"Then how come no one ever talked about those early days?" Ransom's voice was sharp, accusing. "We used to ask questions about the mine and the ranch, and no one ever mentioned a man named Lockwood or an Indian named John Birdwing. Like they didn't exist."

"I think . . ." Mavis rocked for a bit, staring into the fire. "I think your pa had a hard time forgiving them for leaving. In fact, it may well be that he never did, at least not completely. He and Adam had such big dreams for this place, for parlaying their land purchase into a prime property, run Appaloosas—oh, the dreams. And then John and Adam left, just like that, and as far as your father could see, they took his dream with them. He was afraid it wouldn't happen without the others."

"How did they meet Talbot?"

"Over a card game at the saloon one night."

Ransom's mouth dropped open. "Pa gambled at cards?"

"No. He'd sometimes go into town with Adam, but he never gambled, never bet on anything. Said he just couldn't see throwing money out on the table and watching someone else scoop it up. But with Lockwood, it was different. He loved the challenge, the adventure, the risk of winning big or losing big. So when Talbot bet half his Wild West Show and lost, Adam found himself the half owner of the show."

"Half owner of a four-hundred-acre piece of land and half owner of a Wild West show. Some businessman. What made him leave with the show?"

"The adventure of it, I suppose. A chance to see the country and meet new people. Maybe the risk too. A Wild West show is far riskier than a solid ranch on your own land. Yes, as I look back, I think the risk was a big draw to him. And he'd always loved to shoot. He would bet on himself to win. So to hear he had a shooting act was no surprise."

Ransom quietly closed the ledger. "You all kept in contact?"

"We'd hear from him sporadically. Your father and I were married by then and living in the cabin. Ivar felt driven to build us a bigger house, especially when you were coming along. We were running a few cows; buying a good bull was a major investment. But as long as we could live off the land, we plowed every penny back into the place. We logged all the trees to build this house, including milling the timbers for the roof. Neighbors came and helped build the first section of the house. We had it roofed and windows in by that winter. Ivar hauled all the rock for the fireplace. Your pa excelled at anything that had to do with building. That winter he worked on the inside of the house, and when he finished that, he started on the furniture."

"He excelled at everything. He's a hard act to follow."

She smiled and patted the rocking chair she was sitting in. "This was the first piece he made. He surprised me with it for Christmas, and you were born in February."

She glanced up at the carved walnut clock on the mantel, a work of art, really, something Ivar had made in the later years. "I thought sure Lucas would be back by now. He said he'd stop by Arnett's to feed the dog and make sure the chickens are locked up. I wish Arnett would let me buy those chickens from him. We could put them in with what we have and make it easier for him."

"Maybe going out to do his few chores is what is keeping him going."

"Hmm. Maybe." Mavis's eldest son never ceased to amaze

her; he was often quiet, keeping his own counsel, and then he'd come up with something deep. "You have a good point. I thought of offering him the bunkhouse for the winter. I worry about him over there all by himself."

"There's my mother, taking in strays again." He cocked his head to listen. "Lucas is home. Wonder what amazing story he'll have concocted this time."

"One never knows." Mavis breathed a prayer of thanks. Her son being gone like this was too reminiscent of the years when Ivar was drinking, and these last few years Lucas liked to spend an evening at the saloon. Sometimes he slept in the bunkhouse, and she figured it was because he knew how adamant her rule of no drinking was. Ivar nearly lost his family, his ranch, and everything else before he stopped. She hated liquor and what it did to men. And thus to their families.

Philosophizing was enjoyable, in a way, but it accomplished nothing practical. Speaking of practical, "Those elk haunches we have left, do you think we should cut them up tomorrow?"

"I'd like to let them hang at least one more day."

She nodded. "It's up to you. I think I'll take Cassie into town with me tomorrow, then. I have a list for at the store, and I thought to go visit with the Brandenburgs a bit."

"You think she'll want to go?"

How should she phrase this? "I know she wants to get shells and some other things. It never hurts to ask. Too, she really likes the Brandenburgs. And I'd like her to get to meet more of our friends, become part of the community."

"Remember she promised Gretchen she'd do her tricks with Wind Dancer after school."

"I know. We'll be back by then. What are you going to do tomorrow? Do you want to come into town also?"

He shook his head. "Thought I'd take Arnett back up to the big trees again. Let him help me choose which ones to take out. He sure knows his trees and how to run that sawmill. Any idea how many head of cattle he still has?"

"No, we've not talked about things like that. He misses Hazel so much, he seems lost. So do I at times. Not like him, of course, but Hazel was a good friend."

"I wonder if he'd be of a mind to trade that sawmill for a cow or two."

"Why buy it when he said you could use it all you wanted?"

"Well, Lucas and I could maybe turn that into a winter business. Let folks know we'll come with the sawmill and cut up their trees for them. Easier than hauling the trees to the lumber mill."

Mavis pondered that idea a while. "What about the mine?"

"That can be a job for later this winter, shoring up that cave-in. I don't plan on living under the ground, you know."

Mavis's breastbone gave a tiny shudder; it happened whenever he talked about the mine. "I want you to promise me one thing."

"What's that?"

"You'll never go down in that mine by yourself, and you'll always tell someone else too that you're going in there. Also, I want you to make a diagram of the mine tunnels, so if someone has to come looking for you, they'll have an idea of where to begin."

"All right. I promise. Not sure what drives me to thinking there might still be some gold in there. Guess that's my idea of a gamble, or maybe an adventure." He looked at his mother when he heard the back door open and close.

"We're in here," Mavis called. "Your supper is in the warming oven."

"Thanks. Sorry I'm late."

They heard Lucas banging around in the kitchen, and pretty soon he came into the big room in his stockinged feet and carrying a full plate. "All was well at Arnett's. I picked the eggs and fed the dog and the chickens." He sat down on the other side of the fireplace from his mother and stretched out his feet to the heat. "It's getting real cold out there. Probably could have watched the thermometer falling. It's close to freezing already."

"So how did your meeting go with Mr. Porter?"

"Fine. Chamberlain, the head cook, would like another elk. Actually, he'd like one every week. I told him it wasn't like raising cattle; they're wild and sometimes can't be found."

Leave it to Lucas to decide to tell the story in his own time, when she wanted him to get straight to the part about the shooting match.

She picked up the mending basket and set it on her lap, taking out one of the men's socks that needed darning. She slid the sock over the darning egg that Ivar had carved for her so many years ago. Egg-shaped but with a handle and worn smooth through his careful sanding and her using it all these years, the piece of oak aged golden. She unwound the fine wool yarn she'd saved from a hand-knitted sock that was too worn out to mend anymore. Threading the big-eyed darning needle, she slipped her thimble on her finger and stretched the sock over the egg so the hole was on top.

She first worked around the hole with small running stitches, then began the weaving pattern that blended right in with the sock so as to never cause blisters from long use. She'd been darning socks and mending other clothes ever since her grandmother taught her how when she was around ten.

Darning was the kind of thing one could do on a winter's eve when the family was gathered in this room and visiting or each working on their own project.

Ransom was often working at the books or reading, Gretchen doing her homework, and Lucas turning antlers into buttons for a customer he'd had for years. And Jesse always had his nose buried in a science book or any medical book he could find. He'd be so absorbed, he never heard anyone, even if they called his name. Touch him and he'd smile that gentle smile of his. Often he would have whatever wounded animal he was doctoring, if small enough, tucked into his shirt. The animals always knew they could trust him.

Fine memories.

If she wasn't darning, she was often quilting or knitting. Or her favorite—tatting. But she needed better light for tatting than for the other things.

"Mr. Porter is real excited about setting up a shooting match. He wants to come out here and talk to Miss Lockwood about it, so I invited him for dinner on Sunday. I figured that would be as good a time as any."

Mavis nodded. "Good idea. We can roast one of the elk haunches that day. It's a shame we couldn't have a smoked one to serve, but that won't be done yet. I'll tell Cassie tomorrow." She paused. "Maybe we should invite some others. A good time for people around here to know Cassie better too."

"When I told him about her acts, he got an idea to put on a Wild West show in Hill City during the summer to entertain the summer folk. He wants to talk to her about that too."

"Where could they do something like that?"

"I don't know, but knowing him, he'll come up with something. Maybe have some steer wrestling and calf roping. That kind of thing. I thought I'd ask around and see what else might be included."

"Be good to have a big barbecue too. Like we do here." Ransom joined in the conversation.

"And a dance in the evening?" Lucas set his plate down. "We just might have all kinds of good ideas for him." He turned to look at his mother. "Do you think Miss Lockwood might loan out George for something like that? He'd be quite a draw."

"Especially if folks saw George taking a carrot from Gretchen or someone young like that." Mavis laid her darning down. "Oh, Lucas, maybe this could be a real help for them."

"It can't hurt to try. Of course, Mr. Porter is trying to bring more customers in for his hotel. That's why he's doing it, but something like this could be good for a lot of people."

Mavis wove the last of the yarn through a couple of stitches and pulled the needle free. She put the needle away in the needle holder and the sock and egg back in the mending basket. "Anyone want anything before I go to bed?"

Each of her sons shook his head. "'Night, Mor," they chorused like they had as children. Mavis made her way to her bedroom, with a kerosene lamp in hand and set it on the dresser by her bed.

While Ransom didn't say much, she knew he still resented Cassie's arrival, but the way she and the others had all pitched in and helped with the sawmill and the elk butchering might have made a difference. The stars in Lucas's eyes grew brighter whenever he spoke of her. And here she thought he was in love with Betsy and they would be hearing of coming nuptials at any time. *Please, Lord, I don't want anyone getting hurt.*

17

Ah, morning. Each the same, each so different. This one Lucas would probably call crisp. Mavis's footsteps, usually silent, had crunched this morning, the hoarfrost thick and hard on the grass behind the house. Now down at the barn for a few moments she watched the hogs grunting and rooting through the slops. She always took time to watch the livestock. You could almost always tell their condition just by watching. There was certainly nothing wrong with the hogs.

Lucas came riding into the yard and tied up by the door.

Mavis walked out to meet him. "Did you talk to her or just leave the note?"

"She was out feeding her horse, so I didn't need the note. She said she'd be delighted to go along into town with you this morning."

A sudden thought caught her short. "Oh, I should have suggested she wear a skirt or dress, not pants."

Lucas chuckled and strolled with her to the door. "I think she'll figure that out. Chief caught several rabbits in his snares. You should see the vest Runs Like a Deer is making for Miss Lockwood. She's made mittens too."

"I wonder if she has ever made deerskin gloves. If she has, she might have some good suggestions for me."

When Cassie drove her rickety old wagon into the yard a short time later, Mavis smiled, for the girl was dressed in the same lace-trimmed waist and black skirt. Mavis wondered if that was the girl's only go-to-town outfit.

Lucas was hooking in the last of the tugs on Mavis's wagon. He grinned, whipped off his hat, and executed a sweeping bow. "Miss Lockwood!"

Cassie tittered. "Mr. Engstrom. Good morning, Mrs. En— Mavis." She climbed down from her wagon as Lucas tied her horses to the rail. When she clambered up into Mavis's wagon, it was apparent she was not accustomed to clambering in skirts.

And off they went, Mavis and Cassie, to go shopping in Argus. "I'm so glad you could come." Mavis flicked the lines for the team to pick up their pace. Why did she so enjoy this girl's company? Cassie was charming in her own right, of course. She radiated sweetness, tenderness. But was the deeper reason simply that Cassie was Adam's?

They talked of light things for a few minutes—the weather, the hard frost, the ice on the water barrel that morning. Quiet.

Then Cassie turned to look at her. "Something is bothering me."

Mavis nodded. "Go ahead."

"The thought of charging my shells on your account at the store. Do you suppose the owner will allow me to open an account? I can pay him the five dollars that I have and promise the remainder after the shoot. I have never had to borrow money or supplies from anyone before. It goes against all I believe."

"I'm sure he will when he knows you own half the ranch."

"Do we have to tell people that?"

"Why not? That is something to be proud of."

"I know. I mean I am, but then they'll want to know the whole story, and not only do I not know the whole story, I don't think it is any of their business."

"I can understand your feelings. But one thing you'll learn about living out here is that in a small town everyone seems to know everyone else's business. That's just the way life is."

"But you never even told your family about the contract."

"And as I said, I'll be paying for that decision for a long time. I won't tell anyone your story. I'll leave it up to you and how much you want to share. Is that okay?"

"But Lucas, I mean Mr. Engstrom—"

Mavis interrupted. "Just call them Lucas and Ransom, please. This Mr. and Mrs. manners business is getting ungainly."

"All right. But what if Lucas already told that man in Hill City about the deed?"

"Well, in that case, your owning half the ranch will get out, but no one need know the rest of the story."

Cassie nodded but Mavis could still see the worry lines on her forehead. "Cassie, this will be all right. You have a home on the ranch, and that means you are entitled to all the ranch has to offer, be it food for humans and animals, shelter, a place to put down roots. There is plenty of work for all of us, and we can trade for the things we need to buy. God has provided for us all these years. Why would He quit now?"

"My mother would say something like that too, but . . ."

"But what?"

"I don't see that the show going bankrupt was taking care of us. So many people were suddenly without a job or knowing where their next meal was coming from. The debt to the banks not repaid."

"They repossessed the show?"

"I guess. We didn't stay around to find out."

"But God provided for you all the way south. At least that's what it seemed like to me when you told me what happened. Yes, things were rough, but you got here. You found us, and now you have a real home." *Please, Lord, help me help her. Trusting you is never easy, but it's sure worth the effort.*

Cassie sent her a shy smile. "Thanks to you."

"No, well, yes and no. Thanks be to Him, for He so wonderfully supplies our needs."

The silence between the two lasted a good mile or so, supported by the rattle of the wagon and the singing of the wheels. The jingle of the harness sang counterpoint and the horses' hooves kept the beat.

When she stopped the wagon next to the store, Mavis turned to Cassie. "Jason Daniel McKittrick owns this store; he's been around ten or fifteen years. Everyone calls him JD. He knows more about what's going on in Argus and the surrounding area than anyone. Sheriff Edgar McDougal runs a close second. They are both good men who are worth getting to know. I'll introduce you. Oh, and if you need something he doesn't have, if it can be gotten anywhere, JD will find a way."

"Good to know." Cassie had no better grace getting down from a wagon in skirts than she had climbing up. But she managed a full measure of modesty. Mavis led the way inside.

"Well, what a nice surprise." The clean-shaven man with a shiny pate smiled wide, revealing a missing tooth on the lower jaw. "How you been, Mrs. Engstrom? You got time for a cup of coffee? I'll tell Gertie to put on the coffeepot."

"Thanks, JD, but we need to go see the Brandenburgs, too. I brought my order, and I have someone I want you to meet." She turned to Cassie. "Miss Lockwood, meet Mr. McKittrick."

"How do you do." She smiled shyly.

He extended his hand, so she shook it. "Good to meet you, miss. Lockwood. Lockwood. Why does that name sound familiar?"

Mavis answered. "Her father, Adam Lockwood, used to live here, dug that mine in our hills with Ivar. He became world renowned as a shooter in one of the big Wild West shows."

"And a wagon that came through town said Lockwood on the side. That's where I've seen it recently. Was that you?"

Cassie nodded. "We camped one night over by the church."

"I heard you had some big old buffalo."

"We have three. The biggest one is George."

"You don't say!"

Mavis said, "Cassie's father bought our ranchland with Ivar. Partners they were."

"Then you should feel right at home here. What can I get for you?"

Mavis stepped in again. "Miss Lockwood would like to set up an account here, if you don't mind, JD."

"Why, of course." He flipped open a ledger on the counter and turned to a new page. "Now, tell me how to spell your name. I like this book to be accurate."

Cassie spelled it out. "Do you need my signature or anything?" When he shook his head, she added, "I can pay five dollars on it now. I need shells for my guns."

"Right over here. You pick out what you need and I'll write it up. No need to pay in advance. I know where you live." His grin brought forth one from her.

Cassie chose what she needed and carried the boxes to the counter. "I need to practice for a shooting match coming up."

"A shooting match? When? Where?" He turned to Mavis. "Why, this could be the best thing that happened to Argus since the railroad came through." He paused a moment. "Don't shooters usually have sponsors?"

"Some do."

"Well, little lady, I'd be right proud to be one of your sponsors. I'll give you half price on all your shells."

Mavis turned to see Cassie's mouth drop open. She couldn't stop the chuckle. "Thanks, JD. We'll make sure she takes you up on it. Come on, Cassie. If we're going to be home before Gretchen, we need to get moving." She turned back to the proprietor. "We're having an informal demonstration at the ranch on Sunday. Why don't you and Gertie come for dinner and our entertainment?"

"Why, thank you, Mrs. Engstrom. I'll tell Gertie about your invitation. And I'll have your order ready in about half an hour."

Cassie led the way out. "We could just leave the horses tied up and walk over there. It's not far."

"Not carrying the squash I brought for them."

Cassie glanced in the back of the wagon at the crate of squash in huge pieces. "That's all from one squash?"

"No. I canned some and I'm drying some in the oven. It's

hard to keep the oven from getting too hot. I'll send some up to Runs Like a Deer. The Indians used to dry squash and pumpkin too."

Cassie untied the horses as Mavis climbed in, but she walked alongside. Was the girl self-conscious about wearing skirts? It would seem so.

The Brandenburgs were overjoyed to see them and laughed at the chunks of squash.

"Well, I never saw one that big," Mrs. Brandenburg said. "Ours were teeny and only a couple made it. It could have been the time those cows got out at the stockyard and ate all the squash near to the ground. I suppose that could have caused our lack." The two chuckled. "It's a good thing they didn't get all the corn and the potatoes. Those came back just fine."

Mavis led as they followed the couple into the kitchen. Cassie was grinning like a little girl at her first tea party.

Mrs. Brandenburg turned and gave Cassie a hug. "I am just so happy you live near us. God answered our prayers for your safety, and now I get to teach you to cook, like I said I would."

"Mavis is helping me too. She showed me how to clean out elk intestines to make sausage a couple of days ago. I figure if someone can do that, they can do anything."

"Sit down, sit down. These cookies just came out of the oven. The coffee will be ready in two shakes of a lamb's tail."

Mavis sat, but she perched on the edge of the chair. "We can't stay long. Cassie promised Gretchen she'd show off Wind Dancer's tricks this afternoon."

"Why, you know she did some of those right out in the church field. Little Lisbet is still talking about it. She pointed you out at church last Sunday as that pretty lady who made her beautiful horse bow. I think she spoke to you, Cassie. The little girl with the lisp."

"Oh dear!" Cassie groaned. "I was looking for her, but I didn't see her."

"They had to leave early." She set a plate of cookies on the table. "Help yourselves. The coffee is almost hot."

Mrs. Brandenburg did love to talk, so Mavis sat back and let her. Mostly she just watched, rather bemused. Cassie had cast upon Mrs. Brandenburg the same spell she had cast upon Mavis, and Mrs. Brandenburg had never loved Adam the way Mavis had. So her instincts were good; Cassie was indeed a sweet and sensitive child, along with being a gutsy young woman.

By the time they left, Cassie had a basket with two dish towels, two jars of jam, a loaf of bread, and a small crock of butter. And more potatoes. The Brandenburgs accepted an invitation to dinner and the entertainment on Sunday.

"This is turning into quite a party," Mavis announced after they had loaded all their supplies, picked up the mail, and left the store. "What a great time we will have." A cloud crossed her thoughts, literally and figuratively. "I do hope it doesn't rain."

After supper Mavis read Jesse's letter to her family.

"Dear Mor,

Well, that was a shock. How did you and Pa ever keep something like that a secret? I don't ever remember any mention of an Adam Lockwood when Pa would talk about the early days, but then, when I thought about it, most of his stories didn't go back that far. Other than he found the land and gold. I wish he were still here so I could ask him questions. I am sure the others are feeling the same way. I have a feeling, though you didn't say so, that Ransom and Lucas are really upset, are angry over this. Like everything else, this too shall pass. No matter. I am glad and grateful this seems to be working out. God has amazing ways of making that happen, has He not?

I will write more at another time. Please tell everyone that I love them and look forward to seeing you all again.

Your happily beleaguered son,
Jesse"

Mavis finished the letter with a smile. Leave it to Jesse, her lover of words and ideas son. Beleaguered was an excellent word for them all. Or maybe not.

"Goes to prove he's forgotten this ranch is part his too."

"Come on, Ransom, all Jesse thinks about is being a doctor. He doesn't care about living here again."

"That's enough. You both have to admit things are going well here. The work is getting done." Would Ransom ever give in?

18

She tapped Wind Dancer's knee.

"Oh, look." Gretchen turned to her mother. "Isn't he just the prettiest horse you ever saw? And so smart."

The Engstroms were lined up along the rail of the small corral, watching Wind Dancer go through his paces. No one was laughing harder or grinning more broadly than Gretchen's friend Jenna, who was perched with Gretchen and Mavis on the top rail. Lucas and Ransom were leaning against the rails, their elbows draped over. At least on the Engstrom ranch, Wind Dancer was a big hit.

Cassie laughed along with Gretchen. "He's pretty smart, all right. Wind Dancer, how many legs do you have?"

The horse nodded one, two, three, and paused. He shook his head and nodded one more time.

"He's teasing you." Jenna's eyes sparkled.

"That he is." Cassie rubbed his neck, right behind his ears.

She whistled for Othello, who came bounding across the corral and leaped up onto the horse's rump. Wind Dancer cantered around the circle, stopped next to Cassie, and bowed again. Othello barked twice and leaped to the ground.

She debated saddling him up for trick riding and decided not to. Instead, she sent him cantering around the ring again, signaled for him to turn and go back, stop, back up, and go forward at a trot. When he returned to her side, she gave him a chunk of carrot and more pats. "Gretchen, do you want to come help me, please?"

Gretchen scrambled down from the top rail and walked to the center. "Wind Dancer, this is Gretchen. How do you greet cute little girls?" Wind Dancer nuzzled her cheek and then licked it. Gretchen giggled. "Do you like to be kissed by cute girls?" Wind Dancer nodded and stuck out his nose. Gretchen kissed the soft spot right between his nostrils, and the horse shook all over.

Mavis almost fell off the fence laughing. Jenna clapped and laughed and hooted along with Lucas.

"You are quite the dandy, aren't you?"

He shook his head and turned his neck to look the other way.

"I'm sorry. Did I insult you?"

He nodded and continued to look the other way.

"Will you forgive me?"

He nodded and wuffled her cheek, then blew, spitting all over her.

Cassie mopped her face. "Well, I guess I deserved that."

Wind Dancer nodded, put his head down so she could rub the top of his head, and then leaned closer to her.

"All is forgiven?"

Another nod.

"Shall we say good-bye?"

He nodded and the two of them bowed together, Othello joining in to do the same.

The applause and laughter made her feel better than she had for a long time. At least she didn't have to shoot the apple off Othello's head. If she had her way, she'd never do that part of the act again. She and her horse strolled over to the fence.

"Does he do more tricks?"

"Yes, but he needs to be saddled for the riding exhibition, and I've not practiced for so long that I won't do it now." Wind Dancer draped his head over her shoulder, and she stroked his cheek.

Gretchen patted his shoulder. "That's the first time I've been kissed by a horse." She grinned at Lucas. "Remember when I taught my pony to shake hands?" The others nodded. "I didn't think he was ever going to figure it out."

"He figured it out all right; he just kept waiting for more sugar. About rotted his teeth out."

Cassie leaned against her horse's shoulder. Ever since the journey began, she'd not had the time to spend with him, or George, like she did before. *Before*. Such a simple word that had grown complex beyond understanding.

The new corral up at the cabin was quite small. Wind Dancer would have trouble hitting his stride, but she could probably practice their riding routine there, away from curious eyes. Eyes that might set her on edge. *Now, that was stupid,* she told herself. All those years in front of audiences, some of whom were not overly receptive or friendly. When the unusual happened and she didn't hit her mark, sometimes she received groans, and other times some mean-spirited person would boo and yell catcalls. Her father always laughed and said, "*Poor sucker, doesn't know quality when he sees it.*" Then he'd get Cassie laughing too and all would be right with her world.

If only her father were there to enjoy his dream land. She turned when Mavis said something, making sure her face wore a smile. "Sorry, I missed that."

"How could you do this in a big arena? No one would be able to hear you."

"We did this only for smaller audiences. Sometimes a person or organization would hire us for an afternoon party or an evening event."

"Us, meaning you and your father, not the whole cast?" Lucas asked.

"Right. He and my mother used to do a routine but without horses. When we realized Wind Dancer would pick up tricks so quickly, we added the other things. He's kissed lots of pretty ladies and been a clown for little children.

"After my father died, I added to the routine and someone from the show would go with me. I had an assistant for my shooting act, and he would go along for other events." *I wonder if Joe got another job in a Wild West show or had to find something else.* She thought of some of her friends from the show every once in a while—so many good people cast adrift. If only there were a way to contact some of them.

"Well, what were Chief and Micah doing today?" Mavis asked.

"Sawing and splitting wood. Chief found a dead tree dry enough to burn, and they dragged that in. I'm sure Runs Like a Deer is softening that deer hide. And she will probably get working on the elk hides too. I never realized before that soft leather takes a lot of work."

"Did you know that Indian squaws used to chew the hides to soften them?" Lucas added.

Cassie made a face. "That would be far worse than cleaning intestines." She shuddered. "I don't see how they could do that."

"Speaking of which," Mavis said, "tomorrow we'll be cutting up the elk, and grinding sausage is part of that. Would you and Runs Like a Deer like to come down to help?"

"Of course. Well, the show is over. Say good-bye, Wind Dancer."

He extended one front leg and lowered his head, nose nearly touching the ground. When he straightened he shook his head, setting his mane and forelock to flying. Cassie led him out of the corral past Ransom, who almost nodded but never cracked a smile. *Oh well*, she thought, *can't win 'em all*. She ignored the little needle of sadness that tried to pierce her joy.

The next morning after breakfast the men headed out to the log they were sawing into stove or fireplace lengths, and the two women walked down the hill. Cassie stopped to scratch George's ears. Most places on his body were covered with such a dense coat that he'd never feel the pleasure. Ears and nose were about it. He rumbled deep in his throat, his thank-you sign. When Wind Dancer trotted up, she patted him a bit and then backed away.

"Sorry, no treats. As soon as we have some extra money, I'll buy you some sugar cubes, but now there's nothing." She was hoarding the bit of grain they had left for when the cold hit. At least her animals would have hay through the winter, and for that she was deeply grateful.

After making a detour to check on some plants she had seen, Runs Like a Deer came striding down the track, so Cassie walked out to join her. "Your leg seems to be working better all the time."

The woman smiled. "Doesn't hurt much either."

They strolled over to the back door. Cassie was learning that with all the work around the ranch, she couldn't start out like a house afire, for by day's end she'd be weary, weary, weary. Runs Like a Deer had already mastered the art of pacing herself.

"Good morning," Mavis called when they knocked. "My goodness, just come on in; you needn't knock."

"Are we early?"

"No, the men are already cutting up the larger elk. We have tubs to brine the cuts we'll be smoking. Lucas will bring up the meat that needs to be ground up for sausage." She nodded toward a row of tins on the table. "Those are the spices and herbs we add, along with lard from the hogs. Elk have so little fat in the meat that we have to add some for good sausage."

Cassie took it all in, not really understanding what all was meant, but by later that afternoon, with the sausage ropes hanging in the smokehouse, she knew one thing for sure. Her arms and shoulders were on fire. When the sausages were done, they'd ground still more meat, seasoned it, and formed it into elk patties that were now layered in a crock and covered with lard.

Runs Like a Deer paused to hone the big knife and then sliced yet more elk meat into thin strips. Some of it they would take to the cabin to dry at the campfire in front of the wagon and in front of their fireplace. Mavis set up racks in her fireplace to do the same. An elk provided an awful lot of jerked meat, along with all that was smoked or eaten fresh. The weather wasn't quite cold enough to freeze more of the fresh meat.

They sat down around the table for a cup of coffee before leaving for the cabin. Mavis served them each a piece of apple cake with applesauce over it, while Runs Like a Deer poured the coffee.

"We'll do this again tomorrow for the other elk. I know you don't have a cellar to store food, so we'll put it all out in ours and you help yourself."

"So that is something else we'll need to build?"

"Before we built this house, I planned to dig a cave back into the hill for a cellar. Ivar said maybe he could loosen things up with just a teeny touch of dynamite. Ivar and Adam had to use dynamite in the mine. That used to frighten me to pieces to hear they'd been blasting. They would just laugh it off and say, 'That's part of mining.' They claimed they used only small charges, but how small is small?" She stirred some cream into her coffee. "I never trusted that mine, and then when part of it caved in, I was grateful beyond belief when they said they weren't going back in."

Cassie listened, fascinated by this glimpse into her father's life. "Did they tell you about being trapped?"

"No, not until much later. One night after Ivar had had too much to drink, he told me the story. This was before Gretchen was born. By then Lockwood and Birdwing had been gone for years. When I questioned him later—he was sober by then—he barely answered my questions and said we'd never talk of it again. He told the children from the time they could ride that the mine was off limits and going in there or even near it would bring on a whipping like they'd never seen. They believed him until one day they brought in a gold nugget that they said they'd found in the creek near the mine, but I have a feeling they'd been playing in the mouth of the mine. They couldn't go far in because Ivar had walled it off. He never tried to clean out the shaft and rebuild the supports, and now that's what Ransom wants to do."

"But Lucas and everyone else say there's no gold left. Who's right?"

"Apparently sometimes a vein is broken off by a fault, and part of it gets shifted over. The idea, they said, was to find where the vein picked up again. So they hired specialists to come and inspect the mine after their vein ran out, to learn where the rest of the vein had shifted to, and their reports all said the vein petered out. There would be no more gold coming from that mine." Mavis took a sip of her coffee. "I wish Ivar had blown up the entrance like he so often threatened to do. I have no idea why he didn't."

"Will we have to blast a hole for a cellar?"

"Probably. But it would be worth it if you decide to continue to live up there. Get through this winter first, and then we'll see what God has in mind."

Cassie nodded, her mind a tornado of unanswered questions. One kept coming to the forefront. "I remember you said my father won part of the show. What did you mean by that?"

"It's one of those hard-to-believe stories, but I'll gladly tell you. Your father loved adventure. You should have heard some of his stories, and he wasn't that old yet. One thing he enjoyed was playing cards."

"For money?"

"Oh yes. There was more risk in that, you see. He and Ivar would stop by the saloon, and they'd both play for a while, but when the stakes got too high, Ivar would lay down his cards and turn into an onlooker. One night there was a new man in town. They got into a game and managed to come out even that night. That man's name was Jason Talbot, and over a couple nights' playing, the three of them got to be friends. In fact, they took Mr. Talbot out to the mine to look around. They'd already lost the vein, but the accident had yet to happen."

Mavis took a bite of cake and then sat back. "For some reason, during the next game Talbot kept on drinking. And Adam kept on winning. Ivar backed out and the other player finally did too. Adam said they should quit, but Talbot would have none of that. He'd gotten a bit on the mean side, didn't like losing all his money, but he was so sure his luck was going to turn that he insisted the game continue. He finally wrote a note offering half of his Wild West Show as his bid.

"Adam won. I don't recall what the hand was, but I know Ivar had his gun at the ready. Talbot leaned over the table. 'Well, now you're my partner,' he said and shook Adam's hand. So Adam now owned half the show. After spending some time with the cast and crew and making sure he could have an act of his own, Adam agreed to go on the road with the Wild West Show. They changed the name to the Lockwood and Talbot Wild West Show and headed east."

"Mr. Engstrom must have been really angry."

"He was, for a while. We were married shortly after that."

"And my father never returned?"

"Nope, never. We corresponded for a few years, and he'd

send us posters or newspaper articles, but when Ivar would ask when Adam was coming back, he'd say, 'Someday. When I get this show out of my system.'"

"I thought he might quit when my mother died," Cassie said, "but then he got to working up some changes to the routine, and away we went again." She heaved a sigh. "I still miss him some days something fierce. Thank you for telling me."

"You are welcome. I have a feeling Chief has plenty of stories he could tell."

"If only he would. I better get up to the cabin. May I please take a couple of carrots for Wind Dancer and George?"

"Of course. Help yourself to whatever you'd like out there. You'll take one of the livers, right?"

Runs Like a Deer nodded. "Fry it for supper. Do you know where any wild onions grow around here?"

"I'm not sure. When you go out foraging, I'd like to go along. I've always been interested in using wild greens and things. We could ride up or walk, whatever would be best. Meanwhile, you're welcome to take some of our onions. We still have quite a few left from the garden."

Runs Like a Deer hesitated then nodded. "I'll take one today. And let's look before the snow comes."

"All right. Perhaps a day next week." Mavis smiled at the nod. "Good. Oh, and do you want to dry some of the squash? There's no hurry on that. It'll keep for a while before it goes moldy."

Cassie and Runs Like a Deer took their leave and started the pleasant walk back home. Home.

"What will we keep the dried meat in and the squash once they are dry?" Cassie asked on the walk back up the hill to the cabin.

"Burlap bags work well. We used to weave loose baskets to keep things like that."

"So you know how to make baskets too?" When the woman nodded, Cassie paused before asking, "Is there anything you don't know how to do?"

"I don't know how to knit or train a horse or trick shoot and ride. Or keep books. I can read some but not well."

Cassie looked at her in astonishment. Never had Runs Like a Deer talked so freely. Maybe one of these days she'd be able to ask her questions about the woman's life before they found her lying in that hollow with her leg at an impossible angle. She knew Chief had learned more of the story, but he wouldn't say anything. Sometimes the two of them talked in Sioux, making Cassie wish she could speak that language they were so comfortable in.

She whistled for Wind Dancer, and when he trotted over to the fence, George came too, just like they used to in the corral at the show. She broke the carrots into smaller pieces to make them last longer and fed both of them. When they finished, she swung aboard Wind Dancer.

"Hand me those two baskets, and I'll meet you at the gate." Riding her horse without saddle or bridle was nothing new, but riding in an open pasture like this was. There were still traces of red and gold in the trees going up the hill behind the cabin. Smoke trailed out of the cabin chimney, and the ring of an ax told her the fellows were there. She dismounted at the gate by swinging one leg over her horse's neck and shoulders and sliding to the ground with a basket in each hand.

Wind Dancer sniffed the basket contents while she opened the gate. "Hey, get out of there."

But he raised his head and backed off at the smell of the

liver and raw meat. He did manage to grab a potato and stood crunching that while they waited for Runs Like a Deer, and then he followed them up the trail to the cabin.

Cassie led him to the corral gate. "Brand new corral, just for you, Wind Dancer." The gate was made of three parallel poles that were slid back to create the opening. Cassie closed the poles again and watched her horse for a few moments. He trotted around the newly built enclosure, snuffling the posts and spooking sideways at whatever he noticed that he didn't like.

Cassie picked up her baskets again and set them on the table inside the cabin.

"Have fried potatoes with the liver?"

"And the onion and squash."

Cassie pulled out a string of sausages and held them up. "For breakfast tomorrow?"

Runs Like a Deer nodded. "We have eggs."

"And some of that bread that Mrs. Brandenburg sent." Seeing all the food they had reminded Cassie of the times on the road when they had beans—beans with roasted rabbit, beans with wild onions, and the rare treat of biscuits. Now they had good choices, and none of them had to be beans.

"I'm going to practice with Wind Dancer. Do you need me to do anything?" When the other woman shook her head, Cassie hoisted her saddle off the rack by the door and the bridle from a peg and carried them out to the corral. Once she had him ready to go, she did a few stretches, using the post and rails of the fence.

"Tight. My word, I'm tighter than a fiddle." How would she ever be able to do all those things she did before? One practice would not be nearly enough. She needed to work on this every day if she was going to be able to perform again. And if she was out of shape, so was her horse. She mounted and rode around the corral a few times before turning tighter circles and backing. When she finally tried spinning in place, she got dizzy before she stopped. She'd not been dizzy in these routines for years. When they were both warmed up, she started her simplest routine of swinging off, hitting the ground, and swinging back into the saddle. Then the side to side act.

The sun was getting low and the pine trees were throwing long shadows across the valley before she slowed down and walked her horse around the corral nice and easy. She whistled for Othello, and he leaped up behind her, a happy bark making her smile. Wind Dancer no longer tugged at the bit or danced along. "I know, you're tired too. When you cool down I'll take you back to the pasture. We're going to be doing this every day. Sunday is only three days away. This isn't going to be much of an exhibition."

Tomorrow they'd be cutting up the other elk. She'd just have to quit earlier. Of course she could take horse and gear over to the corral by the barn and practice there, but here no one was watching.

"Will you do any of the shooting stunts?" Micah asked from the other side of the fence.

She shook her head. "I don't think so. Surely not the fancy stuff. We're not ready for that. We'll throw things in the air to shoot down, shoot at targets, and things like that. If I can't outshoot the locals, I surely can't handle a real match."

"What guns will you need?"

"Pistols, shotgun for clay pigeons, or something like that, and the Winchester for distance targets. Maybe tomorrow we can set up something here to practice with, now that I have shells again."

"We will. They felled some trees up the hill today, but Ransom said they would do more tomorrow. Next week we might be working at the sawmill again. Drag the trees down first."

Cassie dismounted and uncinched the saddle. Her tack needed a good cleaning, and polishing too. Micah carried the gear into the cabin, and she swung aboard Wind Dancer again and rode down to let him loose in the pasture. He trotted out, lay down, and rolled, kicking his feet in the air and grunting in pleasure. When he stood and shook himself all over, she smiled. What a sight to see her animals loose on acres of pasture, with room to roam, plenty to eat, and water available when they wanted it.

A far cry from life on the Wild West show circuit. All their lives had changed, and it was up to her to provide the wherewithal to keep them alive and healthy. Impressing that man from Hill City might well be the first step on a new journey. But she was nowhere near ready. What would it take?

19

Taking time out of preparing for the party in order to go to church on Sunday set Ransom's teeth to clenching. However, the inviolable rule was, come hell or high water, one attends church every Sunday. So there he sat in their usual pew. Of course he understood his mother, and of course he understood God's Word, but . . . He kept a sort of smile in place with difficulty.

He glanced down the row. Oh-oh. Trouble ahead. Lucas was again sitting next to Miss Lockwood, smiling at her, gesturing at the hymnal. Sometimes his brother displayed a decided lack of common sense, or else he was so sure he was right that he wasn't thinking of anyone else. Ransom had already looked around the congregation before he took his seat. The Hudsons were all in their usual pew, but Betsy was not present. Her brother Harry, Lucas's best friend, looked like a statue carved in stone. Granite. Unless there was some kind of stone even harder than granite, then it was that kind of stone. Betsy's younger sister's eyes sent out sparks. She often overdramatized a situation, but this hostility didn't look like that. This was real. The amazing thing was that, so far as Ransom knew, the tinderbox, if there was one, was still being kept under wraps.

The organ music swelled and the congregation stood for the opening hymn. *Pay attention,* he ordered himself. *There's nothing more you can do at home anyway. But what about the Hudsons? This would not be a problem if Miss Lockwood had not arrived with her wild tale and my mother had not instantly taken her in like a long-lost daughter. If Lucas had not decided this young woman was destined to be his wife, they could have worked through the rest of it without causing problems for other people—people who now were beginning to look not like friends but like former friends.*

When Pastor Brandenburg pronounced the benediction and they stood for the closing hymn, Ransom realized he had not heard any of the service. Surely the pastor had delivered a sermon, but it had whistled right past him. His mind, his thoughts, his dreads had wandered down all manner of bumpy trails. And nothing had come of those excursions. The only thing he could think of to do to diffuse the situation was to hustle the family out and get home as quickly as possible. Perhaps they should leave through the back. But Mor was already headed out the front door, chatting with friends, shaking the pastor's hand.

When Lucas and Ransom stepped out the front door, Harry Hudson was waiting at the bottom of the steps. From the look on his face, this was not going to be a friendly discussion.

"Good morning," Mor greeted them with her normal good manners as she descended the steps. "Have you met—?"

Ransom clutched her elbow, a no-nonsense grip, and almost dragged her forward. "Sorry, Mor, but we have to get home before—"

Harry grabbed Lucas by the arm and turned him. "We need to talk, my friend." The last was more a snarl than the beginning of a conversation with a friend.

Here we go. Ransom hated this hostility, hated that it was his friend.

"Mor, please take Miss Lockwood and wait in the wagon." It was more an order than a request. Ransom turned back toward those two just in time to see Harry slug Lucas and both of them stagger backwards. Good grief! Hostility, yes, but he hadn't expected this. He grabbed Harry's shoulders from behind and dragged him back. "That's enough! Come on, boys. You're supposed to be friends."

Lucas wagged his head. Blood, lots of blood, spattered from his nose in red spots all down the front of him. "Harry, are you crazy?"

"I'm not the one leading your sister on. Some friend you are!"

"I never promised Betsy anything!"

"You led her on. She was true to you, and she was expecting you to be true to her!"

Half the congregation stood around, staring at the ruckus, murmuring. The women looked shocked, and the men—did the men appear bemused, some almost smiling?

"That's enough, boys." Reverend Brandenburg stepped in beside Ransom. "Go on home and cool off." He turned to his flock. "All right, folks. Show's over. Let's go on home and forget this ever happened."

Ransom grabbed his brother's arm and half pushed, half

dragged him to his horse. "Can you ride, or should we tie your horse to the wagon?"

"I can ride. What got into him?" Lucas crawled up into the saddle, a lot shakier than he pretended to be.

"Your sitting in church with Miss Lockwood." In his mind he called his brother several uncomplimentary names, but in a beautiful gesture of restraint that his brother was never going to notice as a good example, he did not say them out loud. He climbed up into the wagon seat and flicked the lines. The wagon lurched forward toward home, away from the mayhem.

"Hand him this to stop the bleeding." Mavis pressed a dish towel from the basket behind the seat into Ransom's hand.

"Here." Ransom gathered his lines into one hand and held out the cloth. Was his voice sounding terse? A little angry? So be it.

Lucas leaned over to get it. "I can't believe he did this." The cloth muffled the words, but Ransom heard. He felt like finishing off the job that Harry had started, but instead, he clucked the team to a trot. They didn't seem to mind. They were always happier to break into a trot going toward home than going away from it.

Was there any way he could get out of town faster than the rumors flew? Hardly.

By halfway home, the nosebleed had dried up, but the swelling and the dark purple mouse under his eye announced to the world that Lucas had been in a fight.

Mor looked at Cassie and rolled her eyes. "Sometimes I wonder . . ."

"It's all my fault," Cassie whispered.

"No, this is all to be laid at Lucas's doorstep. He often

forgets to take other people's feelings into consideration at times. Too often."

"But if I weren't here . . ."

"Then none of us would know the joys we've had the last few days. We can flow with God's plans, or we can go out on our own and reap the harvest of what we sowed. This too shall pass."

"Is that why you can remain so calm?"

"It is. Takes years of practice but it's well worth the time and effort."

Ransom knew what Mor had dealt with. So many years enduring his father's drinking, his anger, but he could see that her endurance was paying off. And as he knew Mor, he realized she would be thanking the Lord now for the wisdom and steadfastness she had prayed for then.

They were lessons he too would have to learn, and he had not really done so yet. Learning such lessons was not easy.

Gretchen hopped down and swung the gate open wide. They rolled into the yard and up to the door.

Cassie announced, "I need to go up to the cabin and change clothes before that man from Hill City arrives. I'm going to wear one of the outfits I used to wear for the shows."

Mor nodded as she climbed down. "Good idea. I have a big pot of beans in the oven, and I'll warm up the roast I fixed yesterday. Others will be bringing food too. That's the way we do things around here."

"I don't have anything to bring."

"No, you're a guest."

Cassie slanted her a look of disbelief.

Mor chuckled. "Just you wait. You'll get the hang of socializing in the Black Hills soon enough."

"I hope so."

"Here. You take the wagon up and bring down the others too. If they try to beg off, tell them we are counting on them. It is important for them to be part of this. Just leave the gate open."

"All right." Cassie climbed up and picked up the lines. Ransom noticed she was being careful not to meet his gaze. She knew his disapproval; she had to.

Dark clouds were scudding across the sky, the fitful wind nipping noses.

"We might want to see her riding exhibit before serving the food," Ransom suggested, looking skyward. "We can shoot from the back porch if the rain doesn't hold off, but the riding has to be out in the corral."

Mor looked up at Cassie. "Would that be all right with you?"

"But the man from Hill City isn't here yet."

"He'll be coming up the road any time now. We'll start people toward the corral. Is Wind Dancer all ready?"

"Yes. He's saddled and waiting in the barn. Maybe we should bring the guns up to the house?"

"Good idea. Yes."

Gretchen asked, "Are you going to bring Othello along with you?"

"Oh yes! He's part of it."

Cassie steered the wagon back out the lane.

Mor paused before going to the house. Her voice had its scolding tone. "This isn't her fault, you know, so you both be very careful not to lay the blame on her. That's the sad side of carelessness. Innocent bystanders get hurt." She looked at each of them directly. "Lucas, if I were you, I'd just ignore it when someone comments."

"Easier said than done." He rode toward the barn to put his horse away.

"Maybe he should just stay in his room or the bunkhouse." Gretchen shook her head. "This makes me so sad."

"Me too." Mor heaved a sigh. "Let's go get the food together. We'll set the table for fourteen. Any others will have to hold their plates." The women headed for the back door.

"Gretchen?" Ransom called. "Can you take a clean shirt down to Lucas?"

She nodded and disappeared around the corner of the house.

A low cloud of dust out by the road told Ransom that at least one buggy was coming. More people would soon arrive. He brushed the dust off his coat and checked the water in the trough by the rail. Two thirds full; that would be plenty.

And then Ransom went out front to greet their guests.

20

Cassie blew out a breath. She needed to provide an excellent performance, but she'd not been able to practice enough to feel really secure about some of the tricks. Better to leave them out rather than fall.

She climbed down out of the wagon box, and Micah led the horses away.

Ransom beckoned to her from the front door. "Let me introduce you before you go get your horse."

Cassie made sure her public smile was in place and joined him on the front porch. Several other folks were milling about, chatting with each other.

"Miss Lockwood, I want you to meet Josiah Porter, owner of the world-famous Hill City Hotel. Mr. Porter, this is the renowned Cassie Lockwood."

"Miss Lockwood, I remember seeing your father's act one time. It is my pleasure to meet his daughter, since I didn't get to meet him." With dark hair dusted in silver at the temples and a charming smile, the tall man, dressed in a black suit with a silver-flecked vest, would catch the eye of anyone who saw him. While he could have been thought of as a dandy, she got the distinct impression that he was an astute businessman who enjoyed his work.

Cassie nodded and shook his extended hand. "Thank you. I've heard good things about your hotel and Hill City."

"You must come and have dinner with us sometime soon. This is my wife, Abigail. I think the two of you have a lot in common."

Ransom interrupted. "Since the weather looks like it may become uncooperative fairly soon, we thought to have Miss Lockwood ride now, and we'll have the shooting match after we eat."

"Good, good. Just show us the way." The man was beaming proudly, as if he had actually just met an important person.

"We're going to use our large corral for the show. Shame we didn't build some raised stands." Ransom nodded for her to go ahead. "I'll be announcing when you are ready."

Cassie blinked in the dimness of the barn and found Chief wiping down Wind Dancer with a cloth. They'd polished the silver on her saddle, and now it winked in the light from the door.

"He's ready but walk him around a bit."

"I will. Any other suggestions?"

"Go easy. No hurry."

"Go tell Mr. Ransom that we'll be right there."

Cassie rode Wind Dancer out of the barn and looked out to the corral. It appeared that all the guests were gathered, but she couldn't be certain. She trotted her horse around in a small circle that expanded as she went around again. *Please, Lord, please Lord, let this be good.*

When she nodded, Ransom swung open the gate to the corral and stepped inside. "Ladies and gentlemen, for your entertainment this afternoon, I present Miss Cassie Lockwood, her horse Wind Dancer, and Othello, her faithful hound." He extended an arm toward her in the best ringmaster tradition.

"Okay, boys, let's go." The three of them burst in through the entrance at a fast clip, circled the corral, and slowed a bit, and then Cassie went into her routine. Flying dismounts and mounts, over and under his neck, front to back, back to front, a vaulting dismount, hands in the air. Wind Dancer turned and tore back to slide to a stop right beside her, Othello on the other side.

At the applause, the horse took off again, turned, and this time Cassie mounted on the run, swung over and did the legs-around, switching with her hands on the saddle. Back straight, canter back, and Othello jumped aboard to ride around with them again, and then jumped to the ground. Dead run, plowing stop, spin in place with back feet hardly moving, spin the other direction, and bow. Cassie stayed in the saddle, and from the bow she signaled him to a right turn and pulled a tight circle, and when she waved her hat, Wind Dancer reared and pawed the air. This time she dismounted close to the spectators and asked Wind Dancer, "Did you enjoy the show?"

The audience certainly did; they were applauding enthusiastically.

He nodded and then shook his head.

"Oh, what didn't you like?"

He walked over and tipped Micah's hat off before trotting back.

"You didn't like his hat?" Wind Dancer pawed the ground.

"That's a shame. What was wrong with it?" She gestured subtly, telling him exactly whom to approach.

The horse trotted over to the fence, lifted the reverend's hat off his head, and carried it over to Micah.

Reverend Brandenburg hooted. "He stole my hat. Stealing is a sin, you know." Everyone laughed and clapped some more.

"Ah, you like that one better?"

The horse nodded.

"Do you think Micah might like that one better too?" Another nod.

She had him count and act sad and then kiss the pretty lady but not blow on her. When her hat blew off, he backed up as if frightened, then trotted over and hid behind Cassie, looking over her shoulder.

"Were you bad?" she asked. He shook his head and turned away as if she'd hurt his feelings. When they all laughed, he turned his back and switched his tail. "I'm sorry. Did we hurt your feelings?" A nod. "Would a carrot help?" Another nod. He turned back around and trotted over to Gretchen, who handed him a piece of carrot.

Cassie faced the group and turned on her fill-the-arena voice. "Now that we got that worked out, we want to thank you for coming and hope you enjoy the shooting a bit later." The three of them bowed again to enthusiastic applause. Cassie swung aboard Wind Dancer, Othello leaped up behind her, and they loped out the gate, applause echoing behind them.

"Hey, Miss Cassie, that was some show," JD McKittrick from the general store shouted.

She waved to him and rode back around to where the guests

were gathered. For some reason she looked to Ransom. He almost smiled, and gave a brief nod. It was the most positive gesture he'd ever made toward her. Gretchen bubbled, a totally happy young lady, and gave both horse and dog bits of carrot.

"Miss Lockwood, that was an excellent show." Mr. Porter was beaming, as brightly as ever. "From something I read I understand you shoot from horseback too?"

"I do, but we don't have all the supplies here to do that well. I also have more riding routines, but I've been without a show for long enough to make me rusty. I didn't think you all wanted to see an accident out there. Getting back up to my show days' expertise will take some doing, but we can adjust."

"Well, I think we will have to do some real serious planning. We'll talk after the shooting match."

Mavis stepped in beside Cassie. "Dinner will be ready as soon as we can dish it up, so let's go on up to the house." She smiled. "And Reverend Brandenburg, would you please say grace for us? Oh, and you don't need a hat to do that."

With a public smile, Micah returned his hat to him.

Cassie followed Mavis to the house, amazed at the way the lady so smoothly brought the jovial crowd from the corral to her table. Talking excitedly, they streamed into the ranch house and, at Mavis's direction, settled themselves both around the table and on other chairs. Cassie found herself seated directly across the table from Mr. Porter and his Abigail.

The chatter ceased and the Reverend Brandenburg offered a brief grace. When all had filled their plates and those not at the table found a place to sit, the conversations picked up again.

Mrs. Porter seemed nearly as excited as Gretchen. "How you ever got that horse to do those things, I'll never know."

"And I'm sure she'll never tell," Mr. Porter assured his wife. "But it sure looked like he could read your mind."

"Sometimes he gets contrary, and then he can be even funnier. I have a hard time keeping a straight face." Cassie paused to savor Mavis's splendid cooking. Perhaps someday she would prepare food like this.

Mr. Porter sobered. "Your father died a few years ago?"

Cassie nodded. "Five years ago. I think his heart broke when my mother died, but it took a few years for it to catch up with him."

"I'm sorry to hear that. I believe I read that you and he were a superb shooting team too."

"He was the best." She made herself smile, as much as she could manage. "He always dreamed of coming back here to this ranch to raise Appaloosa horses and beef cattle."

"Well, we welcome you to the Black Hills, Miss Lockwood, and look forward to working with you."

After they'd finished eating, they all headed outside behind the house to where Lucas and Ransom had set up the targets. Cassie unpacked her guns and filled her pockets with shells. She and some of the men who wanted to pit their skills against hers shot with shotguns first, knocking spinning plates out of the sky. Cassie didn't miss a one.

"I sure would like to see you shooting pigeons," Mr. Porter said after she put her shotgun aside.

"I have many times. Live ones are harder than the clay—less predictable."

Since no one else had pistols, she demonstrated her ease with them on tin cans and bottles lined up on the fence. One of the men tried using his rifle on the bottles but missed. When they switched to the targets, several of the shooters, including

Mr. Porter, kept right up with her, hitting the bull's-eye even as they moved the targets farther away. When she put three bullets into nearly the same hole, the others groaned. No one could match that.

Cassie turned to Ransom. "How about pounding a spike a little way into that post. We can take turns hitting it to drive it home."

"With a bullet, right?" Mr. Porter drawled.

"Yes, sir. You can set the distance. Or we can do separate targets."

"Separate might be better."

She nodded.

"They can't do that," someone muttered.

"I can't do any of it," another answered.

Cassie loaded her rifle, watching as Chief helped set up the first target.

Mavis raised her voice. "All right, so who's going to challenge her on this one?"

"I was going to, but I can't see well enough," Lucas said, making everyone laugh. His story that he'd walked into a barn door made some laugh and some shake their heads, but no one pushed him on it, not even those who knew the truth. "Ransom?"

"I already missed on the three-in-one. I'm not wasting my shells on this one."

Mr. Porter rolled his eyes. "Am I the only taker?"

"Looks like it." Mavis glanced around again, just to be sure. "Who's shooting first?"

"He can." Cassie stepped aside.

"After you, Miss Lockwood."

Cassie grinned at him. "Flip a coin?"

Lucas pulled out a nickel. "You call it, Mr. Porter."

"Heads." The coin flipped. Heads. The man would shoot first.

The group quieted, watching intently. Mr. Porter took in a deep breath, let it all out, sighted, and fired three times in rapid succession.

"One hit." Ransom called after inspecting the target. "Bent the nail." He got well out of the way. "Ready."

Cassie breathed a sigh of relief. At least he didn't hit all three so they would have to shoot another round. She could hear her father's voice.

"Breathe and let yourself relax. If you tighten up you'll miss every time."

Ransom stepped away. Cassie shrugged her shoulders, let out a breath, and raised her rifle. The first shot missed, but the next two drove the nail deep into the wood. The spectators broke into applause.

"That was some shooting," someone called.

"One more would have finished the job." Lucas studied the target. "Sure was close." He grinned at Cassie. "Some shooting is right."

"Congratulations, Miss Lockwood. That was mighty fine shooting." Porter shook her hand. "I'm sure we'll be able to work out something for you. I'm thinking perhaps to star you in Hill City's first annual Wild West Days come summer. Draw in a crowd, get some merchants to offer food booths, sales booths—it can be big. In the meantime, let's talk about an early December match for perhaps a Saturday? That gives me some time to set it up. It's kind of late in the year, but I'm pretty sure we can draw a crowd."

"I'd be delighted." Cassie hoped she sounded more certain

than she felt. Hitting that nail had been a real gamble, as out of practice as she still was. Good thing it had a big head.

With daylight waning, the guests began gathering their things to head home. Runs Like a Deer had spent the shooting match in the kitchen washing dishes along with a couple of the other ladies.

"Good for you," she told Cassie when she came into the kitchen.

"I just hope I can earn us some money to help get through the winter." She dipped herself a cup of water and drank it down, then joined the others to say their good-byes.

Mr. Porter again shook her hand. "It's been quite a pleasure to get to know you, Miss Lockwood. I look forward to sponsoring this match, but chiefly I'm looking to other events in the future. I suspect they will be profitable to us both. We will have to talk."

"Thank you. I'm looking forward to it." *At least I hope I am.* Suddenly so much was riding on skills that had grown rusty, an aim that was no longer perfect. She should have hit the nail with all three shots. She waved good-bye wearing her public smile.

But she was only smiling on the outside. What would it take to get ready for trick riding again, riding and shooting, and competition quality marksmanship?

And, the real problem to solve: Could she make enough money at it to pay her family's expenses? Especially when she had no idea what they might be.

21

The lovely golden leaves were dancing to their death, the trees that used to glow so brightly now becoming skeletons. And they'd had no more snow after that first blizzard. It seemed ages ago now, but it was shortly before Cassie arrived in her valley of dreams. And that was not long ago at all.

She made certain that she spent part of every afternoon working with Wind Dancer in the corral, adding her shooting tricks to the riding routine. Their act smoothed out again, and her confidence returned, but she realized she also needed more shooting time. And the practice she needed most was with live birds. That didn't seem possible. The game birds she did get to hunt weren't released like those in a shooting match, so she made do with Micah throwing things into the air. But a can or a wood chunk arced cleanly in a smooth line, and she needed practice with the unpredictable track of an actively flying target.

That Wednesday after the Sunday match, as she referred to the exhibition for Mr. Porter of the Hill City Hotel, she rode into Argus with Mavis for more shells.

"I never paid attention to how many boxes of shells I went through before. Practicing can go through a box in no time. Do you think Mr. McKittrick was serious when he said he would like to be my sponsor?"

"JD has a reputation for picking winners, so I'd say he was very serious. All you can do is ask. I know he was mighty impressed on Sunday. He took Ransom aside and tried to find out more of your story, but Ransom never volunteers information, as you might have figured out by now."

Cassie smiled. Wasn't that the truth! "He should have asked Lucas."

"If you remember, Lucas was keeping himself in the background on Sunday."

"He still doesn't look too good." Cassie had seen Lucas the other morning when all the men went up to cut more trees and start lopping off branches. Mr. Arnett had gone home to his own ranch but promised to return when they were ready to mill the next trees. Cassie paused before continuing. Should she ask, or should she not? She took a deep breath of the air that was beyond crisp now and well on the way to cold. The robe they had over their legs was mighty welcome.

"How soon, I mean, ah . . ." She caught her breath and started again. "I am concerned about meeting with Mr. Porter, and yet I think we need to talk sooner rather than later. Does that make any sense?"

"Talk about what?"

"The December event he said he was setting up. I guess I want to know what kinds of events he is going to stage. Will it be strictly shooting contests? More than two entrants? Will there be live birds, and if so, where will he get them? I haven't shot live birds for quite a while, and I would sure love a chance to do that before the competition."

"Those are good questions, and I have absolutely no answers. I guess we just have to take a day and go into Hill City to talk with him."

"What if we go all that way and he isn't there, or doesn't have time, or . . ." Cassie stopped, made fists, and scrunched her eyes. "I'm worrying, aren't I?"

"In a word, yes. You have no control over any of it, so you just pray and ask God to show you, to tell you what to do."

"*Just* is a mighty big word."

"I know. If we had those newfangled telephones out here like they do in some other places, this would be easy. But we don't, so we'll ride into Hill City. If we pray about it and God doesn't put up any roadblocks or give either one of us a feeling of danger or His saying no, then we go."

"Do you really believe God will do that?"

"Oh, Cassie." She grabbed Cassie's left hand with her free one. "I do so believe that, and I've seen it happen over and over. We can pray for that together, right now, if you want to."

"But you're driving the team."

"Do you think God can't hear above the clatter of the wheels?" Her grin told Cassie she was teasing.

"I . . . I'm just not used to this kind of praying." *Actually, if I were to be honest, I'm not real comfortable with any kind of prayer any longer. Is prayer something like a habit that needs building?*

"What kind?"

"Well, out loud and with someone else."

"Then now is as good a time as any. If you like we can stop the wagon, pray, and then continue."

"All right." Cassie released a breath that felt as if it had been trapped down around her knees.

"Whoa." Mavis eased back on the lines. The horses stopped, steam rising from their breathing like a cloud around their heads. "I'll start, and then your turn, and I'll close. Okay?"

Cassie couldn't talk around the lump in her throat, so she nodded. In a way, this felt so disturbing. And yet it seemed not the least bit wrong.

Mavis took Cassie's hands in her own. "Heavenly Father, you said that wherever two or three are gathered together in your name, you would be right there with them. So we know you are right here in this wagon with us and you want us to talk with you. I know you've been listening to this discussion, so we needn't tell you again what's been said so far. So, Lord of heaven and earth, please let us know if you want us to go to Hill City tomorrow. Or if another day would be better. We know you will make the path level and clear for us, because you promised that." She squeezed Cassie's hands to let her know it was her turn.

Cassie struggled to find words. She cleared her throat and then needed to do so again. Why was this so hard? "Uh, God, this is so strange to me but yet exciting too. Will you really give me an answer? I truly want to do your will. I want you to guide me because I know you are smarter than I am. Thank you in advance. Oh, and please make your answer *real* clear."

"Dear Father, we, your daughters, will watch for and listen for the answer. Thank you for all you do for us, all the time, whether we are aware or not. In Jesus' name, amen."

"Amen."

"Now, you have a Bible, right?"

"Yes, my mother's."

"Good. Tonight I want you to read some of the Psalms and see if God speaks to you through them. Okay?"

"I will."

Mavis hupped the horses and they continued on into Argus to stop at the general store. Mr. McKittrick greeted them with a huge smile when they entered. Several men were gathered around the potbellied stove set in an open area off from the counter. The coffeepot steamed on the stove, and smoke rose from the pipes and cigars clenched between teeth. They'd been laughing when the door opened but stopped to see who was there.

"Well, Miz Engstrom, good to see you," one man said as he teetered back on the chair legs.

"Good to see you, Mr. Emmons. If your wife saw you treating the chair that way she'd—"

"She'd let me know, all right. But you wouldn't tell on me, now would you?"

"I don't know," Mavis said. "Depends on what you're offering."

The overall-clad man slapped his knee and hooted. "Can't never get one up on you, that's for sure." The chair legs resumed their rightful angle—straight up.

"Hey, how's Lucas's nose? That blood sure spurted." This was a different speaker. A sheepskin hat was parked on his bent knee.

"He'll live. Hopefully they both learned their lesson."

"Not a good thing to go trifling with a Hudson girl. That Harry's got a hot temper."

Cassie could feel her face start to heat up, possibly from the warmth of the stove but probably from the topic of discussion. She smiled in the general direction of the three fellows and continued to the counter.

"Don't pay attention to those guys," JD told her. "They got too much time on their hands, you ask me."

Cassie smiled. "Thanks. Could I talk to you for a minute?"

"Sure. Come on back by the dry goods." He led the way to the aisle with bolts of fabric on both sides. "Now, how can I help you?"

Cassie wiggled her fingers and nibbled her lip. "Well, the other day you said you'd like to be a sponsor for . . . for my act."

"You're right. I did say that."

"Were you serious? I mean, I'm going through shells like . . . well, too fast, but if I don't practice, I'll never win that match. We need some other things too, and while it bothers me to put things on credit, I know I need to for those supplies." She grimaced and looked away. This was terrible. She should never have come begging. Nothing was more humiliating than begging.

"Tell you what. The missus and I talked this over, and she's as excited about this as I am. We'll pay for all your shells up to the match, and after that we'll look at the plan and maybe renegotiate. And maybe there is someone else who would like to share in the sponsorship. I mean, none of us ever did anything like this before."

"How will you make anything on this deal?"

"Well, let's say you give us ten percent of your take, at least at first, and perhaps we can talk about that at a later date too. I mean, if you make a lot of prize money, maybe you'd like to share more with us. You know, we scratch your back, you scratch ours. And we put up a sign that says the Argus General Store is a sponsor. That way we'll get some advertising too. What do you say?"

"I'd say you are being very generous."

"So how much do you need?"

"Say, ten boxes."

"That'll last you what, a week?"

"Maybe I should start refilling my own."

"It's hard to be perfectly accurate with handloads. You go along with this for right now. I think I have about fifteen boxes left. I'll order again. You leave me a box and take the rest. These are for your rifle, right? Do you need shotgun and pistol rounds too?"

She nodded. This was awful, and yet he was trying to make things easy for her. "All I can say is thank you, and I will do my best."

"What more can we ask for? Now, if you and Mrs. Engstrom have other errands to run, you go do that, and I'll get your orders ready. Do you need anything else beside shells?"

"Yes." She dug the list of three things out of her pocket. "And you'll put those on my account?" She returned his nod and went to find Mavis.

She was at the other end, looking at kitchen utensils. "Let's leave the wagon here for JD to load, and we'll walk over to Brandenburgs'."

"Fine with me." They set out and Mavis moved to the other side of the street when they passed the saloon.

"It wouldn't break my heart any if they drove that business not only right out of town but right out of business."

"I wonder if that was where my father won half interest in the Wild West Show."

"Doubtful. I don't think they were in business yet. I think from something Ivar said, the saloon was in Rapid City."

"That's quite a ways from here."

"It was even farther then, as the roads were almost nonexistent. If it hadn't been for John Birdwing, they never would have found the valley. I think his tribe was really put out with his showing those two white men where the gold was. Perhaps that was why he never went back, or at least never stayed there again."

"Did he have family there?"

"Must have." They climbed the porch steps of the Brandenburg manse and banged the knocker against the plate.

Mrs. Brandenburg opened the door and burst into a broad, warm smile. "Mavis and Cassie, what a nice surprise! Why, I just took an egg cake out of the oven, too hot to frost even. Come in, come in. Reverend Brandenburg, look who we have for company." She turned back to them. "He gets into the books in his office, and a big wind could blow the front door right off and he'd never notice."

"Now, don't go telling on me like that." He extended both of his hands, one for each of them. "Welcome, welcome. Oh, what a treat this is."

Mavis laughed. "You two." She shook her head. "We can't stay long. JD is gathering our order."

Husband and wife exchanged a serious look, and then he nodded. "I think since you are here, that is an answer to one of my prayers. Come into the kitchen, where we can be comfortable. I've been hearing some strange rumors, nasty ones, and much as I hate to think I might be gossiping, I think you need to hear them too."

Mavis and Cassie now exchanged a startled look. They

took the chairs offered around the table, and the three of them sat down while Mrs. Brandenburg cut the cake and poured Juneberry syrup over it. Once cake and coffee were on the table, Reverend Brandenburg stared at his dessert before looking at Mavis.

"There is a rumor going around town about some folks muttering about them Injun lovers out to the Engstrom place. I just ignored it until a third person warned me about it."

"Do you know who it is?"

"Not for sure, but I could make a good guess."

Mavis nodded. "I could too. So do you think we need to be afraid?"

"I don't know. We're praying God's protection for you, and I'm sure Edgar is aware of it too. He always keeps his finger on the pulse of the town."

"We'll keep a watch out. But, Reverend, you know those loudmouths. Get them liquored up and they'll say anything. All they need is one troublemaker to stir the pot."

"That's what concerns me." He paused. "There's more."

"More? Isn't this enough?"

"Well, on this one we know the source for certain. The younger Hudson daughter is threatening to get even with Lucas for leading her sister on. She says Betsy's heart is broken, and she had to go away to visit her aunt, because she can't get over the heartache. So the whole family should do something. That Lucas must pay."

"He insists he's never mentioned marriage to Betsy."

"But he rode her home a lot, and they seemed pretty cozy at that last party. I'm sure that where there is smoke there is fire. And the wind seems to be blowing it Lucas's way."

"Pay. How?"

"I've no idea."

Mavis finished her coffee, shaking her head every other sip or bite of cake.

"You never had any trouble like this until I arrived, did you?" Cassie blinked away any possible tears. This was not the time for crying but for action. Other than leaving, what could they do?

"Cassie, Miss Lockwood . . ." Reverend Brandenburg leaned across the table, reaching for her hand. His wife took her other. "The people we are referring to have frequently transgressed the law but have steered clear of actual injury. They are mostly mouthy, they disturb the peace, and sometimes they have to spend a night or two in a jail cell. Our sheriff is watching them, but most importantly, our God is watching over you."

The warmth of his hand and his gaze nearly undid her. "Th-thank you." She swallowed hard and blinked several times, not bearing to look into his face any longer, for she would surely melt into a puddle of tears. Instead of saying anything more, she nodded.

Mrs. Brandenburg hugged her as they prepared to leave. "You are always welcome here, you and your show friends."

"They've become my family, strange as it may seem."

"It's not strange at all. You've known each other for a long time and been through a lot together. God has a plan, you know."

Cassie tried to smile, but for some reason her public smile refused to stay in place, wobbling into more tears. "Thank you for the coffee and cake."

In spite of what they'd said, her mind sought answers to the questions that refused to stay down. Perhaps she did need to leave and take her people somewhere else, where being an Indian or having Indians for friends didn't matter.

Was there such a place? Or were they right where God wanted them to be? That thought required prayer and pondering. If she were to really believe that God had brought her to this place, that she didn't just come on a fluke because the show closed, a desperate run into the unknown, then . . . Then what would life be like if she truly believed? Would she ever be like Mavis, who believed that God was her heavenly father, that He loved her beyond measure, and she trusted He would guide in things like when to go to Hill City? Did God really care about such trivial things when He had to run the world too?

22

The ride back to the Bar E was silent most of the way. A heavy chill settled in Cassie's middle and stayed there. What if . . . ?

Mavis glanced toward Cassie. "You needn't worry about them, you know. I'm fairly certain those who the pastor was referring to are a bunch of blowhards—at least one is, and the others tag along with him. They've not done any real damage in all the years I've known them. Liquor is their backbone, and after they sleep it off—sometimes Edgar throws them in jail for twenty-four hours—they either forget about it or think the better of it."

"But what if this time it doesn't work that way?"

"If someone strange comes on the ranch at night, our dog will announce it to the world. And Ransom and Lucas trust his bark. Besides, you have Othello. When he barks, he sounds like a huge dog. And Dog too. Barking dogs scare drunks."

"But what if someone were to injure or even kill the dogs?"

The thought of Othello being wounded or killed made her want to cry already, with just the fear of it. "If something happens it'll be all my fault."

"Cassie, no! Try to grasp that you are not responsible for the actions of others. Your only control is through prayer, and that is in God's hands, not yours. It is not your fault that you have a heart big enough to love your friends no matter the color of their skin or what they do for a living. Would you feel better if we went back and talked with Edgar? The sheriff? Asked him to keep an eye out for them? It always starts at the saloon. The final test, Cassie, is that we've asked God for protection, and He is far stronger, wiser than anything we have."

"This is a test, then?" *Why would a test have to come so soon? I don't know enough yet.* Mor would have said the same. But there were questions bubbling in her mind that seemed to have no answers. Questions like why did God allow the show to die like that. So many people there trusted Him. What happened to them?

Cassie inhaled a deep breath of the chilly air and forced herself to answer Mavis with a nod. "If you think there is no danger, then I will believe that. You know the people here. I don't. But if the dogs start barking—I know Othello's danger bark—I will be grabbing the rifle. And I will teach Micah to fire the shotgun."

"What about Chief?"

"He doesn't want anyone to know, but his eyes are not like they used to be. He can see things but not really detailed. That's why he taught me to hunt. Before our trip south, the only live things I had ever shot were birds released in a shooting match. Mostly pigeons."

"I see. How close must something be for him to see it well?"

"I'm not sure. I hate to make him feel bad, so I've never asked. But I know he would shoot to protect me, to protect all of us."

When they reached the ranch, Mavis drove up to the cabin to unload the boxes for Cassie.

Micah greeted them. "Where do you want this?"

"Inside by the chifforobe." Cassie climbed over the wheel and stepped to the ground. Othello instantly attached himself to her side, as though she'd been gone for days rather than hours.

Mavis gathered up her lines. "You know you are welcome to use the corrals at the barn for practice, if you want."

"Thanks, but this is working well."

"I'll be baking bread in the morning." She smiled at Micah when he returned. "What are the men doing tomorrow?"

"We'll be back up with the trees. Some of those oak branches are the size of trees, so they take time. Ransom is bringing up another saw tomorrow."

"I see. Oh, Cassie, if God says tomorrow is our day to drive to Hill City, we'll leave early. I think we'll ride in rather than use the wagon. If Runs Like a Deer would like to come along, there are plenty of saddle horses."

"I'll tell her. Maybe the sooner I get this over with, the better I'll feel." Cassie patted Othello's head. "How will I know that we're to go tomorrow?" To go into Hill City and get the discussion with Mr. Porter over with or to wait? All these decisions that she had to make now when the main one used to be whether to eat a meal in the dining tent or go without.

"One way is to make plans to do something and ask God to block those plans if we are not in tune with Him."

Cassie gave a short nod. "If nothing happens to stop us, let's do it tomorrow and get it over with. Can you bake bread the next day? If so, can you teach me? Someday we are going to have a stove with an oven, and I want to know how to bake bread and a lot of other things."

"Yes, I'll bake the next day. I'll be ready to leave whenever you come to the house." Mavis waved and turned the team in a tight circle to head back down the hill. Since they all kept using the same tracks, it was now beginning to look like more than a trail up to the cabin. The almost-road now continued up the hill too, to where the trees had been felled.

"Supper nearly ready," Runs Like a Deer said after the greeting. "I found wild turnips today. Good patch. Also a walnut tree, the only one I found around here. I filled my basket. We can shell them in the evenings."

That night after supper, all four of them sat shelling and husking the walnuts. Another skill Cassie had never learned and Runs Like a Deer had mastered. Cracking the hard shells was difficult enough; breaking away the tough husks was more difficult. They left dark brown stains on Cassie's hands.

"Does this stuff come off?"

Runs Like a Deer grunted. "Someday."

Cassie grinned. It was the closest Runs Like a Deer had come so far to joking.

She was joking, wasn't she?

When the basket was empty, the men headed outside to the wagon, taking a kerosene lamp with them. Since they'd not started the stove out there, they didn't have matches to light the lamp.

Cassie asked, "What will you do with the nuts?"

"Mix with dried chopped up elk, fat of some kind, and

would add dried fruit if we had some. Berries, apples, pears. Whatever we can find. And give some to the missus."

"They have apples in the cellar down at the ranch house. They came from the trees up here. Mavis said they planted those trees while they were building the cabin."

"Long time ago."

"Do you want me to ask for some apples? How will you dry them?"

"Next year."

Before Cassie blew out the lamp, she checked to make sure Othello was lying on his bed by the door. She'd brought him in when it started freezing harder at night. Besides, she felt more secure with him nearby. Dog didn't like it in the house.

She fell asleep thinking on the conversation with Reverend Brandenburg. She was almost asleep when she remembered. She'd not read those Psalms like she told Mavis she would. And her Bible was still out in the wagon.

Tomorrow, she would bring it in first thing.

She was all saddled and ready to go in the morning when she thought of the Bible again. The men had already gone up the hill, so she climbed into the Wild West wagon and found it in the cupboard where she had put it. One of these days she would need to get all the paper work into the cabin too, but all these drawers and cubbyholes made sorting things so much easier out here. The locket lay in a drawer too, but it seemed safer there. Pausing a moment, she thought back to the conversation with Mavis. Was this what was meant when she said God would guide? Did He sometimes guide by just staying quiet, letting you use common sense and what you thought best? Would she always have more questions like now?

"You sure you don't want to go along?" she asked Runs Like a Deer when she put her Bible on the shelf by the bed.

"No. Better for me to stay here."

Cassie stopped. "Why?"

"Just better."

Cassie knew better than to push when Runs Like a Deer made up her mind. Trying to get information from Chief wasn't much easier, but somehow they needed to have a talk.

As she promised, Mavis was ready with a saddled horse. "Runs Like a Deer isn't coming?"

"She said no." And away they went down the now-familiar road. Cassie decided she'd liked the trees much better as gold than as skeletons.

Riding Wind Dancer was so much more pleasurable than riding in the bumpety wagon, even when she had skirts to fight with like today. Riding a sidesaddle, as her mother often had, was out of the question. Not only did she not have one, she could not remember what had happened to her mother's. Had they sold it when her mother died?

She'd hated it when her mother wanted her to learn how to use it. Thinking of the sidesaddle made her remember other times with her mother, like one of the many times she fell off her pony and her mother comforted her, holding her close before putting her back on the pony. Always she heard, "*When you fall off, you get right back on. When you fall down, you get right back up. If you are bleeding, we'll put a bandage on it, and you go right back to what you were doing. There will be no quitting.*"

She waved an arm. "My mother would have loved it here.

She loved shows in the cities, but she loved the country more. She always wanted to see what was beyond the next bend or across the next hill."

"I can understand that. But I never wanted to leave this land once I came here. These mountains and hills are home to me, not the flat plains that really aren't very far away. On the eastern side of Rapid City, the hills get smaller and then flatten out. There are more farmers there than ranchers. We grow some crops, like oats, for feeding our animals, but mostly grow hay. Plus our garden and orchards, of course. We are pretty self-sufficient. One has to be in this day and age."

"I am learning so much here—things I never thought about, like where food comes from, how to fix it, how to be prepared for winter. We never really had winter, at least not like that blizzard we encountered on our way south. According to Chief, there will be many more like that. Hopefully we will be more prepared."

"The best preparations are to have a huge woodpile close by and plenty of food to eat for us and for our animals."

The ride into Hill City took longer than Cassie had expected. They tied their horses at the hitching rail to the side of the hotel. Such an elegant place! A wide porch fronted the second story of the building, with stairs leading up to it with the first story built into the hill behind it. Velvet draped the tall windows, and elaborate woodcarving graced the eaves clear to the roof peak and around the windows and porch. The hotel sat like a grand dowager lording it over the squat buildings on both sides.

"Grand, isn't it?" Cassie said with a smile. She'd seen big fancy houses, including castles in Europe, but there was something about this one that caught her fancy. Maybe because she was living here and not just passing through.

A bespectacled, rather rounded man greeted them from behind the reception desk. "Good morning, ladies. Welcome to the Hill City Hotel. How may I help you?"

"We'd like to speak with Mr. Porter. I am Mavis Engstrom and this is Cassie Lockwood."

"The shooter?"

"Yes, she is."

"I'll get Mr. Porter. I'll be right back. Don't go away." He wagged a forefinger at them and hustled off to turn aside at a heavily carved door.

Cassie and Mavis exchanged grins. Obviously Mr. Porter had talked with his staff about the shooting match in rather glowing terms.

The dapper Mr. Porter came bustling out, smiling broadly. "Well, Mrs. Engstrom, Miss Lockwood, welcome to my hotel. Now I know why I didn't go to Rapid City this morning. Have you had dinner yet? No? Oh good! Then let me entertain you this time. I have been bragging about our time at your ranch. You made quite an impression on both my wife and on me. I've thought of nothing but the shooting match and the idea of a regional Wild West show this summer." He showed them to a table in the dining room, seated them, and promised to be right back.

Cassie watched him push through the swinging doors to what was most likely the kitchen, since she had seen waiters bringing food out from there. "Have you eaten here before?"

Mavis shook her head. "I wasn't planning on eating here today. I know of a small café down the street. If we don't bring our own food, we eat there. This restaurant is a bit pricey. But we do most of our business in Argus. Once in a great while we come to Rapid City. Lucas has been supplying this hotel with elk meat, so he comes here most often. In the past we've sold them beef and pork too."

"Do they have a lot of guests here?"

"I believe so. People come on the train from the East to spend summers in the Black Hills, so Mr. Porter caters to them. He provides tours and camping trips into the interior. You should ask Lucas. He could tell you more than I can."

Cassie watched the proprietor make his way back to their table, stopping to greet people on the way or say something to a waiter, all the while scanning the room to make sure all was in order.

"Sorry for the delay. They will be bringing our meal out shortly. While elk is on our menu for today, I thought you might enjoy something else. I hope I was correct?"

"Everything smells so delicious that we will be pleased with the surprise." Cassie smiled at him as he took his chair.

"Since I know how long the ride is back to your ranch, I'll be right up front. May we talk business during the meal, or would you rather wait until after?"

"The sooner the better. I'm excited to hear what you have planned for the shooting match in December."

"Good. We have sent out invitations to five competitive shooters besides you. Two others have responded in the affirmative. We have three yet to hear from. I thought a field that size might be more exciting. What do you think?"

"This will be a one-day event?"

"Yes. And I have invited all the contestants to stay the night before and the night after here at the hotel at my expense. For this first time of what I hope becomes an annual event, I will use it as a promotion for the hotel, with your name as a draw. This should help you get known more in this western region, and hopefully those who attend will choose to stay here also. We'll have a special banquet that night, after the match. I'm thinking formal, but I wanted to ask you how you would feel about that."

A waiter arrived at their table, pushing a white-clothed serving cart that held plates with silver-domed covers, crystal glasses, and a silver woven basket of bread covered with a napkin. If this was a simple meal, what in heaven's name did "formal" mean?

"I kept this simple, since you haven't all afternoon to try various courses. Our chef here, Mr. Chamberlain—Henri—is famous for his seven-course suppers and five-course dinners." Mr. Porter dropped his voice to a murmur. "The man's name was Hank when he first hired on, but now he insists on Henri." His voice returned to normal. "By the way, Mrs. Engstrom, he said to tell you that the last elk your son brought in was superb. We are still serving the sausages for breakfast. He's hoping another will be coming soon."

While Mr. Porter talked, the waiter lifted off the domes and placed their plates in front of them. He passed the bread basket and then the butter, which was cut into small squares.

Cassie inhaled the aromas that rose from her plate. Slices of some kind of meat, with gravy, mashed potatoes, shredded beets in some kind of sauce, a small shallow bowl of perhaps baked squash, a thick pat of butter melting in the center. The rolls were obviously freshly baked, and a flat dish held several kinds of pickles.

The waiter announced each dish as he placed it. In French. The names he gave the items made no sense to Cassie, but then French had never been a favorite language. Her mother had spoken Norwegian, French, German, and English. Cassie remembered some Norwegian and just a few words of French and German, but her English was proper. She would have had an even better education had her mother lived longer.

"Thank you. Now would you translate?" Mavis gestured to her plate.

"Of course. Pork tenderloin, mashed potatoes, beets in sweet vinegar sauce, baked squash, and fresh rolls. Henri believes that even clear out here in the wilderness, the proper French and German food names are important. I believe taste is even more important. So please, let's enjoy our meal."

When they finished their plates, he asked what kind of dessert they would like. "I won't offer you apple pie; coals to Newcastle, you know. However, if you ever want to come here and bake apple pies, you are more than welcome. We do have custard pie, chocolate cream pie, chocolate mousse with raspberry sauce, or three-layer lemon cream cake. Which would you prefer?"

Cassie chose the mousse and Mavis the three-layer cake. "This way," Mavis said, "we can share and taste them both."

Never had mousse been served in the show's meal tent. Or a three-layer anything, for that matter.

"Do you have any questions regarding the shooting match?" Mr. Porter asked.

"Yes, several. Will you be doing a live bird release?"

"No."

"Clay pigeons?"

"Yes. We'll have stationary targets of different types, moving targets, the usual sort of thing. Do you have any suggestions for more?"

"Not for this one. My father and I participated in matches that had some rather creative setups. But that was some time ago, and I've not done nearly as many since he died."

"I have a list to give you with all the times and events on it. I will mail you more as, or if, they change. I also wrote the first three prizes on the list. That too may change."

"This will not be a winner take all, then?"

"No. I considered that but decided we need to build a reputation of excellence first, which will draw more contestants. Perhaps someday we will have several shooting matches here. One during the summer Wild West Days and others on various occasions. I have a place lined up to hold the shoot indoors if the weather turns bad on us."

"The show this summer—have you decided on a date yet?"

"Since that will be a community-sponsored event, I am working with the other business leaders in our town to set the date and plan the events. I was hoping we could discuss that further after the match in December and before the gala evening. Or perhaps the day after."

He turned to Mavis. "Will you and your sons be in attendance? I will need to put your name on the list so we have a place for you. This will also be part of my promotion expenditures, since I am hoping you will all play a part in the summer event."

"I will talk with them, and Lucas will let you know when he delivers another elk. He is planning for one yet this week."

"Good, good."

Cassie now brought up her most important question. "Mr. Porter, I have a further question regarding the Wild West show."

"Of course."

"Are you planning to have Indian events? Perhaps invite the local tribe to participate? That became a big draw for the Lockwood and Talbot Wild West Show. We had a mock battle between the bluecoats and the Indians, an Indian attack on a settler's cabin, and a grouping of teepees that visitors could tour and observe our Indians cooking and making things, some of which were for sale. My friend, John Birdwing, who was titled Chief in our show, might have some good suggestions about this."

Mr. Porter nodded thoughtfully. "We will take that into consideration, Miss Lockwood. Thank you for the ideas."

Mavis asked, "Have you ever been to a Wild West show?"

"Yes, many years ago, but I imagine they have changed somewhat through the years. Everything else has."

Cassie nodded. "Yes, they did and have. We were beginning to notice that rodeos were becoming competition for the Wild West shows, especially out here in the West."

Mr. Porter was nodding. "We're considering that. It may be that a combination of the two events might be a way to proceed."

So this is chocolate mousse. And the cake was superb as well.

When finally they rose to leave the dining room, Cassie turned to their host. "Thank you for the delicious dinner and the opportunity to shoot in a match again. It is exciting to talk with someone who is so excited about doing something that will benefit not only his own business but his town and region too. Being in on the planning portion of an event is a new experience for me. I'll do my best to help you succeed."

"Thank you, Miss Lockwood. And Mrs. Engstrom. As soon as we have definite commitments from others here in town, I will let you know, and we'll proceed full steam ahead. Keep late June or early July in mind."

"The fourth of July might be a good time for an event of

this type, although I hear that most rodeos are early in the fall, when the summer work is completed." Mavis nodded as she spoke, obviously thinking hard. "Spring roundup is what led to many of the rodeo events, like bulldogging and calf roping, penning cattle and separating cows from their calves. You might come out to the ranch this spring and watch the weaning and the branding. That will give you more ideas. We have a big barbecue after the work is done, a kind of community celebration. You're welcome to come and spend the night or nights."

"You are most generous. I'm looking forward to further discussions." He waited and waved them off as they mounted their horses and rode away down the street.

Cassie could feel excitement bubbling deep inside her. "This is exciting and scary, and I sure wish my father were here to enjoy it all. He would have been boiling over with ideas."

"Adam Lockwood was definitely an idea man, and while he wasn't afraid of hard work, he usually found a way to get someone else to do the labor end. I think he passed that gift on to you."

"I sure wish you would tell me more about life when he lived here. He never really talked about it, other than dreaming of returning."

"Someday we will talk more. For right now, let's set these boys into a lope so we get home before dark."

The lamps were already lit when they rode into the Bar E and the temperature was dropping. Mavis said good-bye at the barn, and Cassie hightailed it across the valley and up the hill. She had some definite questions about her past, about shows, about what Indians might do in shows. She wanted to ask Chief now, if she could get him in a talkative mood.

23

"Isn't she a fine young woman?"

Ransom stared at his brother. "I take it you mean Miss Lockwood, not Betsy Hudson?"

"Now, boys." Mavis's mouth went straight as she shook her head.

Ransom raised his eyebrows, letting his mother know he was not going to pursue this. He'd never understood the term *besotted* before he'd witnessed his brother watching Miss Lockwood. Granted, he was supposed to call her Cassie, but for some reason he knew beyond a doubt that he better keep his distance. Most of the young women in the area would go into the flirty giggles when Lucas turned his warm smile on them. But Miss Lockwood seemed unaware—not rude, but unresponsive to his brother's charms.

"You better do something about the Hudson family before you follow your heart after this one."

"Leave it to you, Ransom, to hit the nail on the head. When

she drove that nail into the post, I could hardly believe my eyes. That was some shooting."

Ransom snorted under his breath. Like he'd said, *besotted*.

As they banked the fires and made their way to bed, he turned his thoughts to the morning. Perhaps this was the day they could finish dragging those hardwood trees down to the sawmill. Beautiful wood had a grace all its own.

Just starting to fall comfortably asleep, Ransom wanted to ignore the barking dog, but the bark said something bad was happening. What could be wrong now?

He slammed his feet into his boots and headed for the front door, grabbing a robe as he left his room. Lucas met him in the hallway.

"You check the back. I'll get the front." Stepping out the front door, Ransom searched for the barking dog. With a moonless night like this one, the animal blended into the shadows. But he didn't stop barking. "Okay, Benny, what is it?" He went down the steps and into the front yard, searching for a skunk, deer, anything out of the ordinary. Benny must be down by the barn; he wasn't right at the porch as he usually would have been. He slept in a doghouse kept by the front door, with a pile of blankets to keep him warm.

"Don't shoot. It's me." Calling the warning, Lucas came around the end of the house. "Listen! Isn't that Othello barking now?"

"Get dressed and get the horses. Good thing they're by the barn." Within minutes both men were in the saddle, rifles in their scabbards, and racing full tilt across the valley.

"What is it, Othello?" Cassie's feet hit the floor as she heard her dog slam against the door. "I'm coming." Shoving her arms into her robe, she crossed to the door and let the dog go tearing out, then grabbed her rifle from the rack by the door. Instead of charging out like her instincts screamed, she stepped out onto the stoop, rifle at the ready, ears straining for sounds of whatever was alerting the dogs, for she could hear the Engstroms' dog barking down at the ranch house too.

The thunder of horses' hooves, a spine-chilling shriek, and riders broke into the clearing. "Injun lovers! No Injuns wanted here! Go back where you come from!" Rifle shots and curses rent the air. Riders circled around the cabin.

With no idea how many were there, Cassie clung to the building. She aimed and shot to where the sounds were coming from. Insane laughter, curses, more shots rang out.

Chief and Micah erupted from the wagon. "Where are you, Cassie?"

A low growl from Chief. "Don't shoot us."

Cassie could see nothing on this hazy, moonless night. She fired again in the direction of the horses' hooves and crazy screaming. "Get down!" What was out there? By ear she could tell they had at least two rifles and a .44. Slugs slammed into the wagon and the cabin. She returned fire. Chief fired. In this blackness his failing eyesight was as good as hers. Both he and Micah hit the ground and bellied under the wagon as more bullets thudded into its wood. One shot must have entered the wagon through the open door, for Cassie heard the shattering of glass. What could that be? Something was hit for sure.

The smell of burning kerosene drifted to her. Now what? The riders came around again. More firing.

"Hey, lookee there. Fire!"

"The wagon's on fire!"

"More riders coming." Cassie fired in the direction of the latest ringing curse, heard a yelp, and turned her fire at the riders coming in.

"Don't shoot!" Was that Ransom's voice?

At that moment she found herself slammed against the logs at her back. Her right arm went slack. Grabbing her rifle with her left hand, she fired off a couple more rounds before the burning made her catch her breath. Was something burning? She turned to look.

"Save the wagon!" Lucas and Ransom shouted again as they skidded their horses to a stop and hit the ground running.

"Chief? Micah?"

"Wagon's burning!"

She could hear them off to the left, muffled. Where was Runs Like a Deer? Why couldn't she move her arm? Pushing against the house, she inched herself back up on her feet, her rifle clenched in her left hand.

"Pull it out. Get it away from the cabin!"

The men grabbed the wagon tongue to pull, but nothing happened.

"The wheels are chocked." Micah ran to one front wheel and pulled away the block while someone else did the others. With arms and shoulders and grunts, they got the wagon moving and pulled it away from the cabin. They kept pulling until twenty feet or more stretched between the cabin and the burning wagon. Someone jumped through the open door to fight the fire inside.

"Get back!"

"Water bucket! More water!"

"Open the long window!" The shouts rang out.

"Runs Like a Deer!" Cassie screamed this time.

"I'm here" came the answer from somewhere outside the cabin.

Othello's bark now came from down the hill. Was he following the attackers? "Othello!" she screamed. The wagon was fully ablaze now, its light casting a flickering orange glow. The wagon . . . her only home of so many years. The final contact with her mother and father. Tears leaked down her face while a fierce burning started in her arm. Her locket and the papers were still in there.

The four men stood back. A groan came from somewhere beyond the cabin.

"Cassie! Where are you?" Lucas's voice this time.

"Here, by the cabin." In the dancing light she looked down to see a dark patch staining her robe. No wonder her hand had quit working. She'd been hit.

Runs Like a Deer knelt beside her. "You're hurt."

"I know but not bad, I think." *Please, Lord, I'll need this arm for the shoot.* The burning intensified, pierced. Othello plowed to a stop in front of her and whimpered. "Okay boy. Good boy."

"I think one of them is wounded," Ransom called.

"How do you know?"

"Othello, go get him." Chief waved the dog outward again.

Othello whined, his tail low but wagging. He edged closer to Cassie, sniffing her hand. "Go get him, Othello, go." He did as she told him, but obviously he was reluctant to leave her.

"Ow." Cassie muffled a scream and jerked away from Runs Like a Deer's probing fingers.

"Let's get you into the house." Lucas put his arm around her waist and half lifted her. "Can we get some light in there?"

"I'll get the lamp." Runs Like a Deer lurched to her feet and hurried inside.

"You better go see what Othello has." Cassie let herself be lifted but groaned when the action moved her arm.

Micah left. Runs Like a Deer helped hold Cassie's arm to her chest while Lucas tried moving her again. "No, stop."

"Chief, come help me!" Micah called from the lower edge of the clearing.

Cassie closed her eyes as the world tilted. *I've never been shot before. How bad is it? What if I can't trick ride or shoot again?*

"She needs to see a doctor."

"No, just . . ." But she had no more energy to speak.

"We've got to stop the bleeding."

"Here, wrap this tight around it. Can we get her down to Mor?"

The words and sentences ran together. They were doing things to her arm, mostly intensifying the pain. Then the pain eased a bit. Surely it couldn't be too serious. She just had to tough it out to get into the cabin. With a man on each side of her, they tried again. Cassie clamped her teeth against the piercing pain that burned all the way down to her fingertips. Never before had she felt such pain. One of them banged against the doorframe, and she bit back a shriek.

"Set me on the chair by the fire." She remembered her manners belatedly. "Please."

"The fire's gone out."

"I'll start it. Put her there." Runs Like a Deer's voice.

She felt herself lowered to the chair and gratefully leaned against the back of it. When the world stopped spinning, she turned to the ruckus at the door.

"Just knock him out." Chief sounded furious. "Ain't good for nothin' anyway."

"Is he hurt?" From the disgust in their voices, Cassie perceived they were talking about one of the raiders. "How bad is he hurt?"

"Not bad enough." Chief and Micah dumped the man on the bench by the door. Thumps and flops told her he missed the bench and landed on the floor.

"Where's he hit?"

"Grazed his head. Knocked him off the horse. His friends left him behind."

Ransom raised the lamp to see the man's face. "Well, that figures! Dooger, you worthless piece of trash, do I need three guesses to figure who started this?"

"Ain't got nothin' to say."

Ransom snorted and stood up. "Good. Just go dump him back outside. Pull his boots off. It'll slow up his walking. Mighty cold out there tonight. Maybe he'll be dead by morning. Save Edgar a passel of work."

Cassie tried to smile. That sure didn't sound like the man she sort of knew. "Who is it?"

"Crazy Jud Dooger, one of Beckwith's no-good cohorts. If there's trouble in Argus, you can pretty much lay it at their doors."

Lucas squatted in front of her so he could look her in the eye. "Cassie, looks like we stopped the bleeding, but we need to get you to a doctor. You don't need infection to set in. We can ride in or put you in the back of the wagon. Riding would be faster, but we could put a pile of bedding down in the wagon, where you might be more comfortable."

She could still smell burning wood. "Our wagon. What about our wagon?"

Lucas wagged his head. "It's still burning. There's no way to stop it. Some of the frame is left, and the wheels, but the inside is basically gutted. It was old and dry and went up fast."

"How do you think it started?"

"Bullet exploded the kerosene lamp and started the fire—burning coal oil spattered all over," Chief told her. "We couldn't catch it fast enough. Too much caught too quick."

She could feel her pulse in her arm, in her whole arm. She should ask them to loosen her bandages a little. "How many of them were there? I think I heard at least two rifles and a pistol."

Ransom knelt beside Lucas. "Three for sure, maybe four. Guess we'll have to haul Crazy Jud in too."

"His horse still out there?" Lucas asked.

"Haven't seen it. Probably left with the others."

Cassie still couldn't believe all this, even with her arm as a constant reminder. "Can we prove who did it?"

"Oh, I have a feeling that when Edgar is done with Dooger here, he'll know who to arrest. Maybe they won't get away with it this time."

"You know . . ." Ransom paused. "From how the dogs were barking, and they didn't come in the lane, these yahoos knew to go around the fences and come up the west side along the hill. How did they know that? I mean, it's not like they've been out here visiting or helping."

"What are you thinking, brother?"

"I'm thinking that maybe these three are the rustlers too."

"Surely Edgar investigated them." Lucas frowned.

"Can't say, but . . ."

Runs Like a Deer brought Cassie's coat and helped her shove her good arm into the sleeve.

She sat erect. "I need to get dressed first."

Ransom said, "You're decent. Let's get going."

"What about him?" Chief waved a hand toward their crumpled raider.

"Is his head still bleeding?"

"Oozing some."

"Tie him on a horse, and we'll take him in too. I'd rather leave him in the barn, but Mor would rip us apart."

The two helped Cassie stand again and half carried her out the door. Micah had brought the horses around. Lucas swung aboard and scooted back over his cantle to sit behind his saddle. Micah and Ransom lifted Cassie in front of him and settled her into his saddle.

"I can ride Wind Dancer," she protested.

"You could, but this way we can make sure you get there in one piece," Lucas murmured in her ear.

The warmth of his arms around her seeped through her coat, and Cassie let herself lean against his chest. They started down the hill, but Lucas stopped. "Othello, go home."

But the dog just hung back and continued after them.

"Cassie, tell him to go home. We don't want to have to worry about the dog too."

"Othello, g-go home." She tried to speak sternly but stuttered instead. "Is he obeying?"

"He sat down." Lucas turned the horse and stopped by the dog. "Tell him again."

"Othello, good boy. Now go home. I'm okay. Go home. Now!" She threw all her energy into the command. Othello waited, turned, and started back up the hill.

"He's minding." They continued down the hill and across the valley.

They stopped at the ranch house to let Mavis know what had transpired before heading into town.

"Oh, Cassie, I'm so sorry. I never dreamed they'd really follow through on their threats."

"Didn't mean to hurt nobody," Crazy Jud mumbled. "Jest scare 'em off."

"Well, *mean to* and *are* are two different things. I hope Edgar throws away the jail key after he locks all of you up." Mavis stopped by Ransom's stirrup. "I could come along, you know."

"You could, but this will work the best. We'll be back as soon as possible."

The ride passed in a blur of pain and motion, cold and freezing tears. This was too much. They'd not done anything to deserve this. The jeers and curses, the laughter and obscenities pounded along with the rhythms in her head. Would this bad nightmare ever be done and gone?

Did they dare stay here, or would it be better for all concerned if they moved on? Leave behind the only real home she'd ever known and go to who knows where next?

God, if this is an example of your kind of protection, I think you didn't live up to your word.

24

Ransom pounded on the door of the doctor's house in Argus. "Wake up, Doc! We've got some injured people here." He pounded again. "Come on, Doc."

From behind the door came "Hold your horses. I'm coming." Doctor Barnett opened the door. "Ransom Engstrom. What's wrong?"

Ransom turned around. "Bring her in, Lucas."

"What about that guy?" Lucas called.

"I'll be right there. We have two for you, Doc. Take the girl first."

Doc held the door open, and Lucas carried a mumbling Cassie inside, swinging around to keep from banging her feet or head on the doorjamb.

"Put her over there on the table." Doc waved an arm. "What happened?"

"Three, four of the town riffraff shot up our cabin tonight where Miss Lockwood and her friends are staying. Case

Beckwith and his bunch didn't like the color of our new neighbors' skins." Ransom left. He heard the doctor saying, "Right here. Careful."

Ransom pushed through the front door, half dragging, half carrying the wounded man. "Where do you want him?"

"Is the bleeding stopped?"

"Pretty much. Bullet creased his head."

"That chair by the door will be fine. If he can't sit in it, drop him on the floor."

Lucas had set Cassie on the examination table, keeping an arm around her to hold her upright. "Would it be better if she were lying down?"

"Yes. Let me call the missus to come help us." He stepped into the hall, hollered up the stairs, and returned.

Lucas carefully laid her back, and Ransom swung her legs up onto the examining table. How could she suddenly be so small? Her face like alabaster, so white and still. She'd taken a bullet. Could it possibly have been from one of *their* guns rather than the screaming maniacs'? The thought made swallowing difficult. When in all the fracas had she been hit?

Doc placed his hands to either side of Cassie's head and raised one of her eyelids with a thumb. Ransom was going to protest that it was her arm, not her eye, but the doctor was saying, "Lost a fair amount of blood, looks like; pallid under her eyelid where it ought to be pink."

"We think the bullet went right on through. Don't know if it nicked the bone or not."

Mrs. Barnett bustled in, still tying her wrapper. "Why, this is that young lady from the Wild West Show. I've heard such good things about her." She leaned over so Cassie would hear her. "We're going to get your wrapper off so we can see the damage. It's going to hurt, but I'll be careful as I can."

Cassie mumbled a reply.

"Ransom, light those lamps and set them on the shelves over here so we can see better."

Ransom did as told. A thunk from the front room took Ransom back out the door. Their prisoner lay in a heap on the floor. "Well, you fool, trying to run away, were you? I do hope you saw stars and plenty of them."

The doctor waved Ransom away. "You want to go get the sheriff? I'm sure he'll be so delighted to be gettin' up at this hour that he'll thank you kindly."

"Thanks heaps. Give me the fun jobs." Ransom headed out the front door, out from the yellow light of the doctor's examining room into chill blackness, away from the bloody wound of a young woman trying to protect her friends. Seeing a gunshot wound on a man was difficult, but this . . . this was unconscionable.

Hauling Edgar out of bed was not something that was about to make Ransom popular. Pounding on the sheriff's door got three dogs barking and the lights on in the house next to the sheriff's.

"I'm coming. I'm coming. Keep yer hat on." Edgar swung open the door with a growl. "Just got to bed, so this better be important. Ransom, what brings you to town at this time of night?"

"We have a candidate for your jail over at Doc's. Beckwith and his cronies came calling tonight, shooting up the cabin and wounding Miss Lockwood. Burnt up their wagon. We got Jud but not Beckwith. Hurt him but not bad enough."

"Oh, for . . ." Edgar shut the door and called, "I'll be right there." He opened the door again. "You go on back and make sure he doesn't crawl away from there. Low-down, good-for-nothing varmint."

Ransom made his way back through the cold heavy darkness to Doc Barnett's house, setting more dogs to barking. He wanted to shout, "Shut up!" but knew it would only make things worse. Right about now, he was close to not caring whom he offended. Had Edgar been on the ball, this might not have happened. They'd warned the sheriff there was trouble afoot. Apparently Edgar had done nothing about it.

Ransom stomped back up on the porch and opened the door. Glaring at the bundle on the floor who was still muttering, he crossed to the room where Cassie now lay on the examining table with a blanket tucked around her and Lucas holding her hand. The doctor was threading a needle with what looked like a very fine guitar string.

"How bad is it?" Ransom asked. Here he was, wanting to light into the sheriff, and he himself had not taken the threats too seriously either. He should have known better. They could tell Cassie had been on edge over the threats, and basically they had made light of her fears. And now she was lying on Doc's table, the lamplight showing her pale skin and closed eyes. Shot in the arm. Her wagon, the last link with her life in the Wild West Show, burned to the frame. Terrorized by a night attack.

They were guests on his ranch and, according to his mother, closer than friends. And he had let them down. She—they—could have been killed. Were it not for the dogs barking, things could have been so much worse. As his mor would say, the barking dogs were indeed something to be thankful for. But being thankful took some real doing, for he was in a mood ready to kill.

Barnett looked up from his examination. "I'm going to knock her out a bit. This is going to hurt."

"How bad is it?" Ransom repeated.

"Looks like it ripped through clean, like you said. In and out, exit wound, so no slug still in her. I'll disinfect it good. It didn't hit bone, which is a miracle, so tiny her arm is. She should be right as rain in a few weeks."

Lucas looked up at him. "Mor is going to have our hides."

"We should have known better."

The doctor snorted. "Would you two quit yammering and tell me what really happened?"

"Our dog was barking fit to raise the dead, so we went out to see what was going on. Couldn't see anything. Then Cassie's dog started barking, and we heard yelling and gunfire, so we saddled up and charged up the hill." Ransom raked his fingers through his hair.

"You know that cabin is about a quarter of a mile from the ranch house. The raiders didn't come through the home yard. They rode out around the fence line and sneaked up on the cabin that way. But Othello, her dog, roused the house and wagon, and when the shooting began, Miss Lockwood and the others shot back. By the time we got up there, the lowlifes were hightailing it out of there. Left behind that pile of garbage out there on the floor.

"The wagon was parked right next to the cabin and somehow caught on fire. I don't know if they threw a brand in or what. Come to think on it, Micah or Chief mentioned a battered kerosene lamp. We pulled the wagon away from the cabin before it could catch too. Wagon's pretty much destroyed, but the cabin is okay. We found Cassie slumped against the corner of the cabin. No idea who hit her. When we heard the firing we opened fire too. Found Jud on the ground about a hundred yards from the cabin, moaning and bleeding. Loaded them both up, stopped to let our mother know what had happened, and brought them in here. That's about all I can tell you." *Other than that we let her down. We all did.*

"Well, if that ain't the strangest story. I know I'd heard the rumors too, but you know Argus, rife with rumors. Guess we took 'em too much for granted. You sure it was Beckwith and his cronies?"

"You ever see Jud in there hanging out with anyone else?"

"No, can't say as I have." He nodded to his wife, who laid a packet of sterile bandages on Cassie's chest. "Let's wrap this up. She'll start to come around any minute."

Cassie moaned as he tied the final knot in the bandage.

"Lucas, you carry her into the other room, and the missus will take over then. I want to keep her here for the rest of the night, at least, see how she does. The real danger is if infection sets in."

"You want help?" Ransom asked.

"No, thanks." Lucas sounded just plain smug. "I can manage."

He slid his arms under her knees and shoulders and lifted her gently. Mrs. Barnett led the way as they left the room. Ransom watched them go. Surely that look on Lucas's face was more than just concern for a neighbor. And here he'd thought—hoped—Lucas would lose interest like he usually did. Life would never be the same again. That was for sure.

The doctor cleaned off the table that Cassie had vacated. "Can you bring him in here by yourself, or do you need a hand?"

"I can drag him real easy."

"Now, Ransom, whatever happened to 'Love your enemies'?"

Ransom started to jump down the doctor's throat when he caught the glint of amusement in the man's eyes. He was teasing. Good thing he'd not lashed back like he wanted. "You might have to help get him up on the table."

"A jab with a hot poker might work."

Feeling a mite lighter, Ransom stopped beside the man on the floor. "You know, Jud, you're not such a bad one until you let Beckwith get you in trouble. What is your wife going to say to this?" He leaned over and started to hoist the man up, but the fumes from the booze Jud had consumed stopped him. "Uff da. Saturated your worthless hide. Don't know how your missus can stand to have you around."

"Let me help you," Sheriff McDougal said as he stepped through the front door. Together they got the man up and supported him, stumbling, toward the examination room. A yelp accompanied a string of curses, but he kept his feet moving.

"Might be easier to treat if you put him in that chair. Looks like the bullet gave him a new part in his hair."

The man slumped to the side, still muttering.

The sheriff pulled him upright. "Who else was with you?"

"Let me at him first, then you can start." Doc Barnett swabbed the four-inch groove about halfway up the man's head, wiping the dried blood away and causing new to well. "I'm going to have to stitch this too. Hand me that tray from over there." He pointed to an enamel tray on the shelf.

Ransom did as asked.

"You two are going to have to help me. Hold him steady."

With the wound cleaned, the doctor laid in a row of stitches, ignoring the muttering punctuated by a yelp now and then. With the bleeding stopped, he took a pan of water and cleaned the blood from the man's neck and ear. "I can care for him here, or you can let him sleep it off in a cell. I take it you won't be releasing him immediately."

"Not by a long shot. I'll notify his wife. Poor woman probably will be glad she doesn't have to clean him up. We'll get to the bottom of this. With a wounded victim, it won't be just to sleep it off in jail and go home in the morning. The judge will have his say, for sure."

"You going to arrest Beckwith?"

"I can't. No proof unless someone says he was out there. So far all you told me is hearsay."

"I'm sure I could convince Jud to tell us the truth." The doctor rubbed his hands together.

"Yes, well that's vigilante law, and you know I don't hold with that." Edgar looked to Ransom. "And son, I know you don't either."

Maybe not usually, but the attack hasn't been on my land before. Nor were people I know and am concerned about wounded before. Ransom narrowed his eyes. "There better be justice in this—and soon."

"You just do your job, and I'll do mine. Help me drag him back to the jail."

"Just a minute." Ransom went to find Lucas. His little brother was sitting on one side of the bed Miss Lockwood lay sleeping in, and Mrs. Barnett sat on the other.

Lucas announced, "Once we're married, she'll be out of harm's way." The matter-of-fact tone of his voice startled Ransom.

"Don't go jumping ahead of things. Like Mor says, one day at a time. I'm helping Edgar get Jud over to the jail, and then we'll head on home."

"I could stay here."

Mrs. Barnett sniffed. "I don't think that's proper, you keeping watch in a young lady's bedroom. I'll be here. You go on home. You can come back in the morning to check on her."

"But—"

"Don't go giving me no *buts*, young man. You go help Ransom and the sheriff. You've done all you can around here." She made shooing motions with her hands. "She's safe here."

"We thought she was safe in the cabin too, and look what happened."

Mrs. Barnett stood and planted both fists firmly on her ample hips. "Now, Lucas Engstrom, I've known you since you was no bigger'n a leapfrog. When I say git, you git."

Ransom heard the exchange and swallowed a grin. Mrs. Barnett was not one to fool with. She'd been known to stop a pack of twelve-year-old boys in their tracks when they were snitching apples from her tree. Not that he knew anything about that, of course. He grabbed Jud by one arm, the sheriff took the other, and Lucas held the door open. If Jud tried to walk at all, it was a useless effort as they dragged him down the steps and the two blocks to the sheriff's office, where Lucas took the sheriff's place and Edgar swung open the cell door.

He airily waved a hand. "Throw him on the cot and drag that blanket over him. I'll go see his wife in the morning."

They did as instructed and returned to the doctor's house to get their horses. Neither one had anything to say on the ride home.

Mavis woke and met them in the hall on their way to bed. "How is she?"

"Sleeping off the sedative at the Doc's. Mrs. Barnett is

happy; she has someone to fuss over. We'll go back in the morning."

"Which isn't terribly far away. You two sleep in and I'll get Gretchen off to school. She's going to be real upset that she missed all the action."

"Someone needs to ride up to the cabin and tell them what happened. I'm sure they're worried about her." Ransom stopped in his doorway. "I'll take care of that when I get up."

Mavis watched her eldest son disappear into the room and close the door. His shoulders sagged. He looked weary, as well he ought. She still couldn't grasp it all—raiders, fire, poor little Cassie injured. She would ride up to the cabin first thing, for sure.

But Mavis found Micah waiting on her doorstep when she started the morning fire in her kitchen stove. "Come in, please. Don't stay out there freezing."

"Where is Cassie?"

"In Argus yet. The doctor kept her at his house, just to watch her. We're going in to see how she is first thing this morning."

"The bleeding stopped? She was bleeding a lot."

"Yes. Ransom says it was a clean wound, but she lost enough blood to make her weak." Mavis filled the coffeepot with water and added the ground coffee before setting it on the quickly heating stove. "Hopefully we'll bring her back home, and she can stay here until she gets back on her feet."

She looked to Micah. "The wagon burned completely?" At his nod she continued, "You and Chief can sleep in the bunkhouse. It's better than the floor."

"Cassie and Runs Like a Deer up there by themselves?" He was shaking his head as he answered. "No. Wouldn't work."

Mavis could see the concern in his face. Or was it fear?

"Our sheriff will take care of that gang of ruffians. They won't be bothering anyone from jail."

"Are they in jail now?"

"One is. The one that was knocked off his horse."

"And the others?"

"Micah, I will find all that out when I go to town. And then we'll come tell you."

Gretchen wandered into the kitchen, rubbing her eyes. "How come Ransom and Lucas are still sleeping? Mr. Micah, good morning." She looked from her mother to their guest. "Something has happened."

Mavis told her in a couple of sentences.

"So I missed it all?" Gretchen moaned. "How could I sleep through all that?"

"Because all the noise and the shooting were up at the cabin. But Cassie will be all right."

"What if she can't shoot for the shooting match? Then what?"

Mavis stood like someone had struck her.

For sure. What then? As soon as Cassie realized this, she would be frantic.

25

"I should have known better than to trust anyone concerning that riffraff."

"But, Mor, you can't blame yourself. That's what you'd tell me."

"Gretchen, eat your eggs or you'll be late."

Seated at the table, Gretchen whined, "But I want to be here when they come back."

"Who knows? You might be. We have no idea how long Dr. Barnett will keep her there." For the millionth time Mavis's thoughts turned to town and what might be happening there.

"How come no one woke me up?" Gretchen glared at her plate. "I can't believe I didn't hear the dog barking. I always hear him before anyone else."

Mavis ignored her daughter's grumbling and handed Gretchen her lunch pail. "You'll have to get your own horse this morning." Usually one of her brothers saddled her horse for her if they were already working outside.

"It's all right." She shrugged into her coat and looped her scarf around her neck. "I could go by and see Cassie before school starts. She might like company."

Mor shook her head. "She no doubt is sleeping. Her body needs rest to heal quickly. Besides, you're going to be late if you don't get a move on."

"Are you riding into town or taking the wagon?"

"Quit stalling. You'll have to lope all the way as it is. And don't slam the door as you go out. That will wake up your brothers for sure."

Gretchen closed the door with exaggerated care, making Mavis smile for the first time that morning. She poured herself a cup of coffee and took the cinnamon roll she'd been heating out of the oven. While she rarely had breakfast alone and would normally treasure the time, today having someone to discuss the matter with would have helped keep her mind reined in. Instead, it went shooting off in all directions, all of which were unhappy possibilities.

Finally, she got up and fetched her Bible from beside her rocking chair in the big room, as she so often referred to what others might call a parlor. Since she'd not started the fire in the fireplace yet, the room still wore the chill of the night, so she settled at the table in the nice warm kitchen. She flipped pages until she located Jeremiah. *I know the thoughts that I think toward you . . . thoughts of peace, and not of evil. . . .* Surely these verses were for Cassie, who if she was awake, was most likely worrying about how she would take care of them all through the winter.

Lord God, how do I convince her that she is welcome to whatever we have, that she is not alone in this, that we are here, and as far as I'm concerned, she is a member of our family? Forgive us for letting her down like this.

And even more, help my boys to forgive themselves. I know Ransom, and he blames himself. I've never seen Lucas so visibly concerned about another person. Maybe he is coming to love Cassie, and maybe his desire to marry her is true, not just some dream. Lord, you know my mother's heart.

She turned from studying that passage and heard Gretchen loping out of the yard. Did the child remember to pick up her lunch pail when she saddled up? She'd be mighty hungry come dinnertime if she didn't.

She heard stirring from the bedrooms, mostly boot soles slamming on the floor.

Mavis got up and moved the coffeepot to the front of the stove, the frying pan to the hottest spot, and scooped bacon grease out of the can and into the pan. Giving the oatmeal a stir to keep it from burning on the bottom, she dished up two bowls and set them on the table just as Ransom wandered into the kitchen.

"Gretchen already gone?"

"Yes, but running late. You'll probably hear from her how disgusted she is to not have wakened with the dog barking."

"I'm glad she didn't. Good thing someone got some sleep. How long until you'll be ready to go?"

"Give me half an hour?"

Ransom poured cream on his steaming oatmeal and added brown sugar. "I'll go on up to the cabin before we go."

"No need. Micah was waiting on the back porch when I came into the kitchen."

"They are all right?"

"He didn't say not."

Lucas came meandering into the kitchen looking more asleep than awake. So far today, he'd forgotten to shave and comb his hair. She handed him a dish as he shuffled by and plunked into his chair. She pulled the plate of warming rolls out of the oven and set it on the table.

"I'll get dressed and ready while you two eat. We better take the wagon with bedding in it in case we can bring her home." They both nodded and kept on eating.

In less than the half hour she'd said, she was stepping into the wagon. Ransom clucked the team forward. Mavis forced her mind to keep praying for Cassie, for her friends, and for the sheriff, that he would have all those involved in jail.

"What do you mean, you couldn't find him?" Ransom leaned rigid arms on the sheriff's desk, almost nose to nose.

"You're saying Beckwith got away?" Lucas joined his brother.

"I'm saying he never came back to town. No one has seen hide nor hair of those two. Like they disappeared off the face of the earth." Edgar sat up straighter, leaning toward the two confronting him. "Now all that means is—"

"What did you find out from Jud?"

"All their names. Exactly the ones we suspected. He don't know where they went either. But then, he's not feeling too good himself. Says he has a terrible bad headache."

"He can be grateful he still has a head that hurts."

"Lucas, Ransom, give the man a chance to answer you." Mavis turned to the sheriff. "So what do you plan to do?"

"Well, nothing right now. They'll come sneaking back into town, and I'll throw them in there." He nodded toward the cells, where Jud lay softly snoring.

"Has Doc been over to see him?"

"Yep. 'Bout an hour ago. He said Miss Lockwood slept through the night, and depending on how her arm looks this morning, she can probably go on home."

Mavis nodded. "I know. He told us the same. But I said let her sleep as long as she can. It'll hurt less that way."

The sheriff looked rather put upon, and with good cause. "You got any other suggestions regarding the troublemakers?"

"Track 'em."

"Now, how can we do that? This ain't some Wild West show, you know."

Ransom straightened. "You don't mind if we go looking? I hear Chief used to be a mighty good tracker. We can hope he's not lost his touch."

"Now, Ransom, let's hang on here. You know I don't abide vigilante law."

"Oh, if we find 'em, we'll bring 'em in all nice and proper." He leaned forward again. "But you swore to protect the citizens of Argus, and from what I can see, you failed in this case."

The sheriff planted his hands on the desk and rose to his feet. His voice softened, something like a hissing snake. "Ransom, let me give you a warning. You don't want to go too far here and step over the bounds. Granted, I miscalculated, but I will catch them, and they will be punished."

"Miscalculated? *Miscalculated!*" Lucas clamped his teeth. "That young woman has a hole clean through her arm and her personal possessions up in flames because you miscalculated?"

Mor chimed in. "Lucas, Ransom, so did we. Keep that in mind."

Lucas whirled on his mother but cut off whatever he was

going to say. Ransom huffed a sigh and took a step back, releasing his jaw and forcing his shoulders to relax a little. "But you are not telling us that we can't go looking for them?"

"No. I'm just trying to defuse worse trouble here. I don't believe they will return. They don't even know if Jud is still alive. I don't know if they realized Miss Lockwood had been hit. But you riding up there like avenging angels certainly put the fear into them." Edgar sat back down. "Now, tell me. Did you actually see these men, or were they already hightailing it when you arrived?"

The brothers looked at each other. Ransom shrugged. "I heard the shooting and the shouting coming up the hill, and we opened fire immediately."

"What were you aiming at?"

"Mostly shooting into the air to frighten the intruders away, I'd say." Lucas narrowed his eyes to remember better. "Nowhere toward the cabin. Probably a good thing no one else got shot in the mayhem."

"What started the fire?"

Ransom shrugged again, realizing how little they did know.

"Chief John Birdwing said that a bullet must have exploded the kerosene lamp and started the fire."

Edgar grunted, studied his desk blotter. "Jud says they didn't throw any burning brands or flaming arrows or anything."

Lucas snorted. "Oh sure. He's going to own up to that?"

"He said they just wanted to frighten the people away, get them out of the area here. Said they didn't intend to kill anybody. And it's for sure they were all drunk as skunks."

"And that's an excuse for this kind of behavior?" Mor raised her voice. "If they didn't intend to hurt anyone, why were they firing right into the wagon and cabin?"

"No excuse, Mavis. Just a fact."

"And why do you believe anything that Jud says? Do you mind if we ask him some questions?" she continued.

"No, but it won't do any good. Doubt he'll wake up, at least enough to think straight. He's sound asleep again, probably thanks to something the doctor gave him. Hear that snoring?"

"Have you talked with his wife?"

"Yep. She said good riddance or something to that effect. Miz Beckwith said he hadn't come home, and she didn't mind if he never did. Mayhap this will be a good thing for their families in the long run. Put some backbone in those women."

Mor snorted. "'Some backbone' isn't going to help much if the men come back and take out their anger on the wives."

"The word is out that we're watching for them."

Ransom was getting fed up with this whole business. "Be that as it may. Thank you, Sheriff. We'll be taking Miss Lockwood back to our house, and if Chief is willing to track them, well, we'll see what happens. By the way, did you ever question any of this group as to the beef rustling? Seems to me that anyone coward enough to get drunk and try to drive out law-abiding citizens might have needed some money and helped themselves to some of our pastures."

"Yes, I asked them, but there was never any indication that they were involved. I can't accuse anyone without some kind of evidence, you know."

"Good day, Sheriff." Mavis turned, marched toward the door, and looked at Ransom and Lucas. "You coming?"

"Yes." Both her sons followed her outside into the morning sun.

Ransom was boiling. Boiling! Here they had an innocent girl injured, her wagon lost, even the wives of these yahoos in danger from their men, but those men still ran at large, and their precious sheriff was sitting on his hands in the comfort of his office. Certainly Mor had preached to Ransom from infancy that God was in control, but he sure couldn't see it. He strode to the doctor's house with his thoughts so churned up he didn't even notice where they were until they got there.

Doctor Barnett greeted them at the door. "We saw you getting out of your wagon down at the sheriff's office. Come on in. Cassie's awake, and the missus is helping her get into some clothes the missus loaned her. They're too big on her, but that makes it easier to dress her."

"So she's going to be all right?" Lucas asked, worry in his voice, maybe even fear.

"There's no indication of infection so far," Dr. Barnett informed them. "But you'll need to watch for any signs of heat or swelling in the arm, or excessive redness. I'm putting her arm in a sling, and she's not to use it for at least a week. Then in about ten days bring her in so I can check it and remove the stitches."

Mrs. Barnett emerged from the back of the house. "Your timing is perfect. You may go to her if you wish."

Mor started toward the door to the hallway, Ransom and Lucas following. "We brought the wagon so she can lie down."

"Good. She's liable to be some woozy yet. And weak. Make sure she eats well. Oh, and keep the arm dry."

"We will," Mor said with a nod. "Does she need help walking?"

"Yes. You two strong bucks on either side of her will be good. I just gave her some more pain medicine to make the trip easier on her."

Strong buck, huh? *Angry buck*. But letting his burning

anger show wasn't going to help anyone just now, so Ransom banked his fires. With difficulty.

Miss Lockwood was sitting on the edge of the bed. Ransom could see why his brother might be smitten with her, as Lucas had been smitten so many times in the past. Viewed objectively, she was rather pretty, and she had a wispy, vulnerable quality about her that the pain medication was probably enhancing.

"Good morning, Cassie." Mor's voice was light, upbeat, so different from the tone of voice she'd used on the sheriff. And on her sons. "Are you ready to go home?"

Miss Lockwood smiled wanly and nodded. "Thank you." She was clutching her injured arm close to her with her other hand.

The doctor stepped up to her with a large white triangle, bedsheet material it looked like, muslin or something like that. Expertly, he laid it down across her chest, snugged her arm in it just so and drew it up, tying it behind her neck. He made it look so easy. She didn't even wince. The pallid sling nearly matched her pasty face.

She looked tired. Sad. "I guess I don't even have a coat here."

Mor smiled. "We have quilts and blankets aplenty. We'll get you in the wagon and wrapped up all snug."

"Did you tell the others that I'm all right? They'll worry."

"Micah was on my doorstep this morning, so they know."

When she started to stand, Lucas leapt to her left side, so Ransom, the other strong angry buck, moved in at her right. She was game; you had to give her that. Not deliberately frail and feeble, like so many girls her age acted, obviously acting too. She could have simply let them do the work, but she walked out on her own. And she didn't yammer. No talking at all. Ransom valued that in a girl, but rarely found it.

"I'll ride in back with Cassie," Mavis announced as they carefully hoisted her into the back of the wagon.

"I could do that," Lucas offered hopefully, but no one paid him any attention.

Ransom took it slow driving home, keeping the horses at a walk except over the really smooth places. Not many smooth stretches on that road, he noted ruefully. Still, a couple times when he looked over his shoulder, her teeth were clenched against the jolting. It was a long, long, long trip.

They finally rattled through the ranch gate and along to the house. She scooted to the end and crawled off the wagon by herself, the boys at her side as her feet hit the ground.

"Gretchen's room," Mor instructed. They tucked her into Gretchen's bed.

She sighed. "Thank you."

"I will have some hot soup ready for you in a bit."

"I'm not hungry."

"That's okay. Doc said you need to eat. Which do you want, scrambled eggs with cinnamon rolls or soup with bread and cheese?"

"I don't really care." Cassie's eyelids fluttered. "A cinnamon roll sounds good." Her voice faded off.

From the doorway Ransom watched her fall asleep almost instantly. She was weak, all right, like the doctor said. And pale. Really pale. He glanced down to see Lucas clenching and releasing his fists. Ransom's jaw was doing about the same.

Mor turned to her sons with a sigh. "I'll take care of her. You go see what you and Chief can find out."

"Thanks, Mor." The two grabbed their rifles off the rack by the front door as they left the house and headed for the barn.

26

Mavis stood a bit in the doorway to Gretchen's room watching Cassie but mostly thinking, or maybe it was dreaming. Long, long ago she had come so close to riding off with Adam Lockwood, but she had decided against seeking adventure. Now here was adventure seeking her out, whether she wanted it or not. This poor girl . . . her boys out in the hills courting danger . . . Where was all this leading? Thank God Gretchen was safe in school.

Please, God, let them find a trail. A verse floated through her mind. *"Vengeance is mine; I will repay, saith the Lord."* She understood that, but they could help find the men. Surely that would not be remiss. She waited, letting her mind rove through the Scriptures. Nothing else popped up. *Lord, if you have a plan for this, which I am sure you do, please show it to us. We don't want to run ahead of you.*

Since Cassie was now sound asleep, Mavis washed the breakfast dishes, all the while thanking God that the child was not hurt worse, that no one else was seriously wounded, and that God was indeed in control. She asked for Him to give her sons wisdom and sharp minds and eyes.

"And, please, Lord, forgive my vindictive attitude. I am so angry at those fools that I could spit. It's not the love of money that is the root of all evil; it's the love of liquor. Nothing else turns a man into such an idiot as that. It ruins homes and children and jobs and lives. How can I help those wives? You gave me wisdom in my situation, and I do indeed thank you that Ivar responded like he did. I can never thank you enough that he never drank again. Could I really have carried through on that threat to send him away?"

She stared out the window at the neat stacks of wood in the backyard and the pile yet to be split. "Oh, Lord, I am so blessed."

She dumped the dishwater out the back door, hung up the pan, and went to check on Cassie, who was sleeping soundly. A few more inches, and that slug would have pierced Cassie's heart. They could have been burying her today instead of watching her sleep and praying for healing.

But then, a few inches the other way would have missed her completely and she could have gone on living, learning, enjoying, training her beautiful horse, sharpening her shooting skills.

Cassie was so set on winning the shooting match coming up. Was there even a chance of that?

Cassie woke sometime later with a thirst that dried her throat, a burning pain in her arm, and no idea where she was. Last she remembered she was at the doctor's, and Mrs.

Barnett was helping her dress, or rather was dressing her. Cassie raised the arm not bound firmly to her chest and sort of recognized what she was wearing.

She moved her head enough to let her gaze wander around the room. Log walls. She must be at the Engstroms'. When she closed her eyes and thought hard through the fog in her mind, she remembered a ride lying down in a wagon. The memory was so hazy she wasn't sure it was real. Brief scenes flashed through her mind. Riding in front of a man—was it Lucas she'd leaned against or Ransom? Seeing the doctor and the smell of the cloth he'd put across her nose and mouth. She'd awakened in another bed, not this one. And then getting dressed.

She heard something, a chair scratching on the floor perhaps. Turning her head the other way, she saw Micah sitting in a chair, watching her. Her voice sounded more frog than human when she tried to say something to him.

"What can I get for you?"

"Water." Hopefully the croak was clear enough.

He nodded and crossed to her bedside, sliding one arm around her shoulders to lift her so she could drink from the cup he held with his other hand. After a couple of swallows, she nodded that she'd had enough. Never had cool water felt better sliding down her throat.

"Thank you."

Ever using as few words as possible, he laid her back down. "Anything else?"

"Did we have a fire and a shooting spree?" Her voice at least was better. "Or was that a terrible dream?"

"No dream."

She heaved a sigh, which made her wince. Her arm did not

care for that action. Not that it liked being moved when she drank, but the need for water overwhelmed even the pain.

"I am at the Engstroms'?"

"Mrs. Engstrom rode up to get clothes for you. She'll be back soon."

"Oh." *So how did you know to come?* She wanted to ask more questions, but her mind was slipping away again into some kind of fog, and . . .

"Cassie. Cassie." The words came from some far distant place.

I'm coming, I'm coming. But she blinked her eyes only thinking she had said something.

"Good. I need you to drink this. The painkiller is in the tea."

Cassie cleared her throat, swallowed, and shook her head the slightest. "Wait."

Mavis set the cup on the table beside the bed. "What can I get for you?"

"I need to use the outhouse."

"I have a pot in here for you. I'll help you, all right?"

With Mavis helping hold her upright, they managed to take care of that matter. Then Cassie sat up on the edge of the bed, with Mavis's arm propping her, and blew out a breath. "I don't remember ever feeling like this."

"You lost a lot of blood. That will make you weak, and the pain medication makes you woozy. We need to get some soup into you and another dose of medication before the pain gets extreme."

"I did get shot?"

"Yes."

"There were men shouting and shooting around the cabin.

A fire, I think, and I got slammed against the cabin wall. Or did I dream that?"

"No, no dream. Two of the men got away. Someone wounded one of the men, and he is in jail. My boys and Chief are out tracking those that escaped. Micah stayed to watch you while I brought your clothes back. Runs Like a Deer said for you not to worry about them."

"How bad is my arm?"

"The bullet went through the muscles in your upper arm but missed the bone. For which we are so grateful."

"Went through."

"Yes, leaving two holes. Doc Barnett says the biggest concern right now is infection. I can take better care of you here than up at the cabin, so we all want you to stay here."

"I see. What day is this?"

"November thirteenth. Friday."

"And the shooting match is December fifth?"

"Yes."

"I have three weeks to get this arm strong enough to get me through a shooting match." She flexed the fingers of her injured arm, but the pain shot up and exploded in her head. "Oh!" She struggled to catch her breath again.

"The less you move any part of that arm, the better. You should see a difference even in a couple of days. That's why Dr. Barnett sent more painkillers home with you."

"I see." Her head weighed fifty pounds or more. "I think I better lie down again." She slumped against Mavis's shoulder. Once eased back into a prone position, she let out the breath she'd been holding. "You better give me that stuff now, because the fog is coming back in."

Mavis held her up enough to drink the sweetened tea

mixture and laid her back down. "I'll have the soup ready next time you wake up."

"Thank . . ."

Mavis kept watching out the windows for the men returning, hopefully with the two on the lam in tow. She checked on Cassie, but the young woman slept on. "That's the best thing you can be doing," Mavis whispered as she returned to the kitchen. She fixed herself a bowl of soup and slices of bread, sat down to eat, and picked up her earlier conversation with her heavenly Father.

"I know you care about all of us, including Beckwith and his cohorts, but right now I am asking you, actually pleading with you, to help my boys find them and bring them back. If they get too far up in the hills, they can disappear into the rocks and keep on going clear into Wyoming. I believe Jud when he said they didn't really mean to shoot anyone, just scare them all away. But how did the fire in the wagon start? Micah said he smelled kerosene. Did the lamp get tipped over and the stove hot enough to burst into flame, or did the kerosene drip through onto the coals?"

She mulled that over, dunked her bread in the soup, and stared blankly at the cupboards above the counter on the north wall. "What about Cassie, her dream, or more her need to win this match? She's been through a lot, as you well know. Not having any cash is eating at her. How do I help her understand that you will provide? And if we are part of your provisions for her, for them, what is wrong with that?"

She poured herself a cup of coffee and reached to the center of the table to open her Bible again. "Where do I look?

What can I find to help her the most?" She flipped through pages, reading a verse here and a paragraph there, finally settling on Matthew and the Sermon on the Mount, where Jesus spoke of worrying about clothing and food and His care of the sparrows and the lilies of the field. She found a piece of paper in the drawer and copied the verses in a firm hand. *Your heavenly Father knoweth that ye have need of all these things.*

Heaving a sigh, she drained her cup and pushed herself back from the table to go check on Cassie again.

"Ah, you're back," Mavis said.

"I believe so. May I please have a drink of water?"

"Of course, right here." She helped Cassie sit up and held the cup for her. "I'll bring your soup right in. Would you like some bread too?"

"Yes, please. Am I in Gretchen's bed?"

"Yes. She'll sleep with me tonight so she doesn't bump you." Mavis hummed on her way back to the kitchen. Cassie had some color back in her face. Not much but she hadn't felt warm, as in infection.

"What time is it?" Cassie asked on her return.

"Time for Gretchen to come home any minute. She left in a huff this morning because she never heard the dog barking and missed out on all the excitement, as she called it."

The barking dog caught their attention. "That's her, all right."

"I wonder how Othello is."

"Why? Was he hurt during the fiasco?"

"I don't know. I don't remember some things. I don't remember him yelping, but I don't remember him by me when I was shot either."

"I'll ask Micah. He'll probably come by again."

"Thanks. I couldn't stay awake when he was here before."

"Good thing. Sleep is the best thing for a wounded body."

Gretchen burst through the door into the kitchen. "Are they back yet? The horses aren't here."

"We're here in your room," Mavis called to her.

Gretchen plowed to a stop in the bedroom. "Cassie, I'm so glad you're here."

"Thank you."

"Do you feel strong enough to sit up?"

"Yes. I think so."

Mavis propped several pillows behind her and helped her sit up.

Gretchen walked to the bed. "You don't look real good."

"Actually she looks better than she did this morning. I'll bring in a tray with two bowls, and the two of you can eat together while I have another cup of coffee." She left them and returned to the kitchen. Benny started barking again, another welcome bark rather than warning, so Mavis knew the men were back. She dished up the soup, set the bowls on the tray with spoons, along with a cup of coffee, and carried it into the sickroom.

"Look, Cassie, why don't I feed you since you look about done in again."

"I didn't know sitting up took so much energy."

Mavis set the tray on the end of the bed and, taking the bowl in hand, sat on the edge of the bed and spooned the soup into Cassie's mouth.

"How bad does it hurt?" Gretchen asked.

"Not so bad right now, but . . ." She took another spoonful.

Mavis sent Gretchen a "mother" look, and Gretchen didn't ask the next question that was obviously on the rim of her lips.

"No more, thanks." Cassie closed her eyes.

"I'll help you lie down. You did well." Mavis removed the pillows and helped Cassie lie flat again. She watched sleep claim the girl and picked up the tray with its untouched coffee.

"Come along, Gretchen. You can help me get supper on the table."

A few minutes later she heard the thud of boots on the back porch, and her sons filed in the door. "How'd it go?"

"Nothing. We lost them on the rocks. Chief tried to follow the trail further, but darkness was starting to set in, and it was senseless to go on. Besides, there was always the chance we would be riding into a trap if they knew we were tailing them."

"Was Chief able to track with his eyesight?"

"He says it's distance that is a problem. He'd get down on the ground to examine a track every once in a while, but as I said . . ." Ransom hung up his sheepskin coat and hat on the pegs on the wall by the door. "I tried to get him to come down here for supper, but he said they'd have supper for him up there."

"I guess Edgar was right. No sense trying to follow them." Lucas sat down at the table, his gear already on the pegs. "Probably a good thing we didn't catch 'em. I'd probably beat 'em within an inch of their lives. Stupid fools."

"Do you think they'll come back?" Mavis set soup bowls on plates in front of them.

"Not if they have any sense at all, but then, who knows about that? Case can be pretty wily when he's sober, so unless they have booze with them, they're stone cold sober and who knows what they will do." Lucas dug into his soup. "I think Edgar should have someone watching their houses."

Lucas thought a moment. "If I were Case, I'd sneak in during the night or through the woods, get what I need, and hightail it out of there."

Ransom nodded as he ate. "That would make good sense. Maybe we need to go talk with Edgar again. Tell him what we found, or didn't find, as the case may be."

"What direction were they heading?" Mavis asked as she poured the coffee.

"Northwest."

"He could telegraph the town sheriffs along the Spearfish River and the railroad tracks. If they're heading for Wyoming, that's the best way. Put out Wanted posters, at least."

They finished eating and shoved back their chairs. "We'll be back when we get back, Mor, but don't wait up for us."

"You be careful now. Remember, you always catch more flies with honey."

"Right. It would be fine if we wanted flies, but—" Lucas clamped his hat on his head. "Sorry, Mor, I know this is no joking matter, but we'll keep safe."

"And be polite when we talk with the sheriff. Maybe this time he'll be pleased to have someone offering to help him."

Together they left and Mavis added their protection to her list of petitions. She grabbed a shawl and wrapped it around her before stepping outside.

"Ransom!"

"Yeah."

"What if they circle back here?"

"They won't. But we'll go tell Chief and Micah what we're doing, so if the dogs start barking, everyone will be on guard."

"Thank you." She returned to the house and hung up her shawl. Gretchen was adding wood to the stove and turned to her.

"Mor, are you worried about them doubling back?"

"No, but the thought crossed my mind, so I told the men. The dogs warned us before, and they will again. I truly think those men are too smart to do that. An accidental shooting is one thing. Gunning for someone only happened in the old West, not in this day and age. I have a feeling those men are real sorry for what they did, and now they're scared of the law. I would be. But God is protecting us."

"How come He didn't protect Cassie and the others?"

"I think He did, or it might have been a whole lot worse. We'll keep praying and wait to see what God does next."

Lord, I believe; help thou mine unbelief.

27

At least it wasn't in the middle of the night.

Ransom and Lucas kept their horses at the steady ground-eating lope that was easy on both horse and rider, the lighter color of the road making it easy to follow. Back into town and another confrontation with the sheriff. Maybe they should have just stayed home and hoped for the best. But maybe the man needed all their information regarding where they had tracked. Maybe this, maybe that. There were no easy answers. That was for sure.

Ever since that young woman rode onto the ranch, things had been in an uproar.

"We never even asked Mor how Cassie was doing." Lucas broke the silence.

"If there was a problem, she'd have told us."

"The sight of her lying bleeding against that wall has seared my brain, I think. Along with the burning wagon. It sure did provide plenty of light."

"Do you think those three had already left by the time we got there, or did our coming scare them off?"

"I don't know. But Jud told us plenty."

"I didn't ask him that question. But if he was right, and they weren't supposed to be shooting at the cabin, how did the wagon catch on fire, and how did Cassie get shot?"

"He might not have been shooting at the cabin, but someone in that group was. Knowing those three men, the only one that is mean clear through is Beckwith himself. Maybe the others thought they were on a lark, but I can see him getting bloodthirsty."

"True." Ransom let his mind wander again. What if it was one of their own bullets that ripped into her arm? The wagon was already on fire when they crested the hill. "So did they run off because of Jud being wounded, the wagon burning, and Cassie was shooting at them?"

"Ransom, you're thinking on this too hard. No way to answer any of those questions, but all that is important is getting them behind bars. And if they get a split lip or black eye in the bargain, so much the better."

"Right, and someone else, like his wife, could get shot up or beat up or . . ." He paused. "Let's just keep this without violence as much as possible."

"That's fine with me, but if he swings at me, I'm going to hit back, preferably with something solid. He's bigger'n me."

When they reached the edge of town, they pulled the horses down to a sedate trot and tied up in front of the sheriff's office. A lighted window said that Edgar might be there rather than at home. They dismounted and climbed the step. A knock on the door announced their arrival.

"Come in." The sheriff didn't sound too hospitable.

"Good evening, Edgar. Thought we better catch you up on what we learned today," Ransom said as they entered.

"I thought you boys were going to let this thing go, let me handle it."

"Well, you didn't actually say we oughtn't to track them, so we picked up Chief and set out after we brought Miss Lockwood back out to the house."

The man looked weary. Or bored. "Go ahead. I take it you didn't catch them. Did you see 'em?"

"No. We lost them up in the rocks. They were heading northwest. We thought maybe you'd like to notify the law in the towns up the river and the railroad tracks to Wyoming."

"Yeah, well, I thought of that too."

"So did you?" Lucas stepped forward.

"Now, lookee here, boys. I told you to let me do my job, and I'll do what I think best."

Ransom clamped his jaw and inhaled a breath of patience. He turned to the sheriff and deliberately made his voice more pleasant, like honey for those flies. "We just thought you'd want to know what we found, is all. We're not trying to tell you how to do your job. The other thing we thought was maybe it'd be a good idea to watch their houses tonight and through tomorrow. If they don't have any supplies along, which Jud didn't mention, they might decide to come home and get what they need."

"Thought you said they were heading northwest, into the hills deeper."

"But what if—"

"Ransom, like I said earlier today, you boys watch your ranch and let me watch the town. We'll get these fellas one way or another."

Ransom forced himself to nod. "All right. That's what we'll do. Come on, Lucas, we did what we set out for." He stepped back and made sure Lucas was beside him as he headed for the door.

"Why, that . . ." Lucas hissed as they got to the horses. "I just lost all respect for the man. We offer to help, and he tells us to go home and see to the ranch." He mounted. "Like patting us on the head." He reined his horse around. "And you backed down."

"Remember what Mor said?"

"Yeah, you mean like flies and honey and—" Lucas stopped his horse. "All right, big brother, tell me what we are really going to do."

"I am going to take up watch on Beckwith's house. We know that one well, since we reroofed the thing for him."

"Yeah, and look how he shows his gratitude."

Ransom bobbed his head in agreement. "The man doesn't have one inch of gratitude in his entire body. I'm sure he won't come home through the front door, so I shall be sitting in the bushes out behind. You take the others' houses. They're near together, so maybe you can find a place to watch them both somehow. I'll bet they'll all come in together."

"I still don't understand Edgar. Why, we've even been deputized by him before, like when that bank robber on the run came through here. He knows we're not hotheads who go off half-cocked."

"And, of course, the way we acted yesterday probably reassured him of that." Ransom knew he was being sarcastic, but the thought of hunkering down in the cold and dark didn't really sound appealing at all.

They each went their separate ways at the cross streets, and

Ransom contemplated where specifically he could hide. He tied his horse behind the trees well to the west of the house and made his way along the edge of what could be called a yard, if one were feeling generous. When he was even with the house, he crossed the open area to plaster himself against the wall and peep through the window. The missus and all the children were gathered around the table in the kitchen, probably the only room in the house with heat. While it wasn't freezing yet, the thermometer must be inching down thataway. No sign of Beckwith, unless he was snoring in his bed. Good thing this wasn't a two-story house. Far as he could see with the light coming from the kitchen, no one was in the bedroom that had a bed. The other room had pallets on the floor. The man had never even made beds for his children. How that poor woman could put up with the likes of Case Beckwith was beyond him.

Good thing they didn't have a dog. He followed the path to the outhouse and hunkered down. On the upwind side. Obviously the man never dumped lime down the outhouse either.

Sometime later, wishing he had a cup of hot coffee, he heard a rustle in the bushes. A medium-sized man in a slouch hat eased his way back into the brush. It had to be Lansing from down at the lumberyard. No one else in town wore a hat like that. Well, I'll be . . . So did Edgar plan on a stakeout or call one up quick after their suggestion? Either way . . . Should he go and make his presence known? He had just about decided to do so when another body made its way through the undergrowth.

Ransom turned his head to catch the sense of a big man. Case was a big man. The shadow paused behind a tree, studying the house and area for long moments, and then slipped silently forward. He paused again behind another tree, and then stepped into the cleared area. It was Case, all right. Two rifles cocked at the same time.

Lansing called, "Stop right there, Case Beckwith. You are under arrest."

Case spun around, his pistol instantly in his hand, firing as he moved. At a yelp from Lansing's direction, Ransom raised his rifle, hoping for a flesh wound. He fired. His shot slammed Case against the porch post. The pistol went spinning, and Case growled cuss words black enough to hide the stars. He staggered, stumbling for the steps, lurching up to the door. Ransom leaped through the bushes and caught him in the back of the head with the rifle butt. Case crashed to the porch, moaning invectives.

"You hurt bad, Lansing?" Ransom called.

"Naw, but it burns like fire. I'm coming out."

"Case is down."

The door opened a crack, and Mrs. Beckwith stared at Ransom, then down at her husband. Nodding, she stepped back and closed the door with a solid click. Ransom could hear the children crying inside and the mother shushing them.

"Case Beckwith, I hope the judge throws you in jail and they throw away the key. You don't deserve to live."

"Lansing, you all right enough to go get Edgar?"

"I'm right here, son." The sheriff came walking across the yard. "I thought I told you to go on home."

"You did, and I started to, and then I just kind of veered off to the side and decided to sit a spell. See if there was any action. You better see how bad Lansing is hurt. Case shot him too."

"And I'm sure your brother went on home without you?"

"Well, can't rightly answer that. Last I saw him he was heading out of town."

Edgar chuckled, "Yeah, well he and Mac managed to nab their assignment. Without any shooting, I might add."

Lansing joined them at the porch, one arm holding the other. "Case shot first. He never did have too much sense. Thanks to Engstrom here, he got him before he got into the house and used his wife and kids as a barricade. Wouldn't surprise me none if he'd use them as hostages even."

Edgar leaned down and hauled the livid man to his feet. "Where you hit?"

"'Bout blew my hand off," Case complained.

"Be glad it wasn't your head." He shoved the staggering man ahead of him. "Hate to waste the doc's time on offal such as you, but the law is the law. You boys come with me, make sure he don't try to take off. There'll be no more shooting unless absolutely necessary." He held out his hand. "Thanks, Ransom."

Ransom shook the hand. "You're welcome, Sheriff. Figure we all guessed right." He nudged Case with the rifle barrel. "Let's get going."

The sheriff paused. "I'm going to stop and let his missus know what's going on."

"Oh, she knows. She opened the door, took one look at him on the porch floor, and shut the door real quick."

"Then I'll come back later."

Ransom left the others at the doctor's house and strode back to the sheriff's office, where Lucas and the men from his side of town were sipping coffee and in general warming up.

"I take it you got him?" Lucas raised his coffee cup in a cheery salute.

"We did. He and Lansing are over being stitched up. Case got a lucky shot off and winged Lansing."

"Coffee?" the man nearest the stove asked.

Ransom nodded. He'd actually shot a man. The thought made his stomach clench. He never thought he'd be able to do such a thing, but when he heard Lansing yelp, it was all he could do to not aim for a body shot. For the sake of the wife and children, he was grateful for the way it had turned out. All because some men got liquored and hated up. Four people wounded, two innocents, the wagon burned, and Argus, South Dakota, turned into an old West range town. On the other hand, maybe this would be enough to shake some sense into at least Beckwith's buddies. Serve them all right if their families never took them back. He planned on talking to Mor about how they could help Mrs. Beckwith and her children to free them from Case's abuse.

"So you're the hero of the night?" one of the other men said to Ransom.

"No, looks to me like we all just did our job of keeping our families safe. You tell Edgar that we headed on home."

The door opened and the sheriff stepped in. He paused at the door. "Just want to tell all of you thanks from me and from the town, actually from our whole area. I'm sure you'll be called as witnesses when the judge sentences these so-called men."

"How's Lansing?"

"I've seen knife cuts worse'n that. Doc was just bandaging him. He got off easy. I knew Beckwith was mean, but I thought he'd respect the law. I learned a lesson here too. Good night to all of you. Oh, the doc gave Beckwith a shot and knocked him out cold. Don't need to worry about him trying to get away. Said he'd keep him doped up until morning. Then we'll bring him over here." He shook hands with each of the men, and they filed outside.

Ransom said his good-nights and swung up behind Lucas. "My horse is in the trees west of the house." Lucas headed that direction and then stopped so Ransom could swing down and mount his own horse.

Halfway home he felt as if someone had let his air out, like a collapsing balloon. Good thing he didn't have to walk. He'd never have made it. The ranch house was dark as they rode by it but for a candle in the front window, something his mother always lit. She'd started the practice years earlier, she said, to guide their father home.

No wonder she had such a hatred for booze. Their life could have been similar to the Beckwiths'. *Thank you, God, for the strong mother you gave us. And a father who put his family before the booze when the line was finally drawn.*

"You know . . ." He paused as he pulled the saddle off his horse.

"What?" Lucas was doing the same.

"I sure wish Pa was still alive, so I could tell him thank-you."

"Thank-you for what?"

"For choosing us and Mor and the ranch over the booze."

Lucas stood silently for a long moment. "Yep, our lives could have been so different." He took the reins of both horses and led them off to the corral to let them go while Ransom slung the saddles on the racks their father had built in the barn.

Ransom stared up at the Milky Way arched across their ranch like a heavenly benediction. "You tell him for us, Jesus, will you please?" He slung his arm around his brother's shoulders, and the two of them strode up the rise to the ranch house with the light waiting in the window.

28

Did he actually say that, or was I dreaming?

Cassie stared up at the ceiling. Dawn was sneaking in, the room lit by the pearly pink of a near-to-rising sun. For the first time since the shooting, her head felt almost clear. She let her mind rove back. "*When we are married.*" Was that what he'd said? Or was it "*After we are married?*" Not that one word was so important, but why would Lucas even think something like that? Sure he was being attentive, with special smiles and little glances. Perhaps they were courting, but she'd never thought of it in that way, and they'd never even had any time alone together. Sure he was handsome. Any girl would be delighted with his attentions. Take that Betsy Hudson—she was desperately in love with him, and up to now had been confident that he returned her affection. And it sounded like he had.

So why the switch? She had pushed the thought away until now, but here in the quiet of the early morning, maybe she needed to think about it. The only answer she came up with was the ranch. If she married Lucas, the ranch would all be under the Engstrom name again. What a vile thought! Marrying her because he loved the ranch. Would he love the ranch more than her?

When she thought of marriage, she dreamed of having one like her mother and father's. They had truly loved each other and loved being together. Which was a good thing, since they were together all the time. She'd seen other marriages that were not like that. Husband and wife screaming at each other, or ignoring each other or in some cases displaying physical violence. She remembered how her mother said she took one look at Adam Lockwood and knew that he was the man for her. She gave up a whole life in the upper crust of Norway to follow him into the world of Wild West shows. She said her heart went into triple time, and tingles ran up and down her spine when she was finally introduced to him, after begging her maid to make the meeting possible.

If that is what love starts out like, I've not felt any such things. Never in my life but especially not when I met Lucas, or sat next to him in church, or when he handed me in and out of the wagon. He is very nice, but no sparks. She enjoyed being with him, he made her laugh, and she appreciated all he had done for her, but friend or brother closer described her feelings for him.

Turn your mind to think about something else. The heat of the fire flared into her mind. No, not that. All the things that were in the wagon were now gone. All the contacts with people who'd sponsored shooting matches and other Wild West shows. All the paperwork from the years of running the Wild West Show, her father's journals of the finances. The bills of sale of all but the deed to the ranch. That she had folded and tucked away in the pages of her mother's Bible, which was in the cabin by her bed. And the locket. Her mother's and now gone again.

Trying to be thankful was not easy. Why had all this happened? She knew why. All because some people lived to hate other people. The fragrance of breakfast cooking wafted into her room. Her stomach rumbled and her arm ached. Especially if she moved. Could she manage to use the chamber pot by herself without calling for help? Using her good arm, she pushed herself upright and waited for her head to stop spinning. If she fell and smashed her arm against something, she would be in worse shape than she was at the moment.

A gentle knock at the door.

"I'm awake, come on in."

Gretchen peeked around the door. "Good morning. I hope you slept well."

"I did better. Could you ask your mother to come here, please?"

"Sure." The head disappeared.

Cassie inched her legs over to the side of the bed, crabbing her rear so she was sitting on the edge with her feet dangling. She blew out a breath. She must still be terribly weak if that little effort made her head swim and her heart pound. Bracing with her good arm, she breathed slowly and deeply, feeling her body start to relax. She knew the value of relaxing.

"Good morning, Cassie. Hey, you sat up by yourself. Did it hurt bad?"

"Some, but I need to use the necessary."

Mavis braced her and helped her stand again. "How's the head?"

"Woozy."

"Not surprising. That will pass. We need to get more food and drink into you to help your body rebuild. Gretchen will bring your breakfast. Do you think you can feed yourself?"

"Yes. I just have a hard time believing how weak I am. It isn't like this is a major wound."

"No. The blood loss is contributing to that. You have a guest waiting as soon as you're tucked back in bed."

"Micah?"

Mavis nodded. "And friend."

Cassie smiled. "Othello? I'm sure he wouldn't try bringing Wind Dancer in."

"No, but that dog has been pacing." Once Cassie finished her business, Mavis stacked the pillows behind her and settled her against them. "Maybe they'll come eat with you too." As she left the room, she said, "Go on in."

Micah stopped in the doorway, but Othello bounded across the room and leaped up on the bed, wriggling all over. He sniffed her hair, her arm, and her hands, and cleaned her face.

"I know. I've missed you too." She smiled up at her friend. "Thank you, Micah, you made this day perfect."

"Today you are much better."

"I am." She wrapped her good arm around Othello and hugged him to her side. "I kept thinking he had been injured too."

"I think he was knocked out for a time. He had a big bump on his head." Micah sat down in the chair she pointed to. "I know they are taking good care of you."

"I want to come back to the cabin."

"Soon. They caught those men. Ransom and Lucas helped the sheriff and his men in town last night."

"Beckwith's men weren't too smart to go back to town."

"I think they needed supplies. Two of them have been injured. You shot one, Jud, and Ransom shot another trying to get back into his house." He stood when Gretchen came in with a tray and helped her set it across Cassie's legs.

Gretchen smiled at him. "There's coffee for you too, Mr. Micah, and Mor said if you haven't eaten breakfast yet to come out and join them."

"Coffee will be fine." He took a cup and sat back in the chair.

Gretchen took her bowl and sat on the edge of the bed. "Hey, Othello. You look mighty happy. Look, he's smiling."

Cassie reached over to pet her dog. "Good boy, but I'm sure you are not supposed to be on the bed." His tail thumped on the quilt, and he licked Cassie's hand.

"Aren't you going to school today?"

"Today is Saturday. Mor says I should keep watch on you to make sure you're all right."

"You don't need to do that. I'll be fine. The way I feel, I'll probably be back to sleep as soon as I finish eating." She spooned her oatmeal into her mouth and broke off a piece of toast to chew.

"You can take that up with her. If you like, when you're awake again, I could bring the checkerboard in here, and we could play a few games."

"I've not played checkers for years. That would be great." Cassie laid her spoon back down, suddenly too weak to hold it.

Micah came to her side. "Do you need help?"

"I need to lie down again." Even her voice sounded weak in her ears.

Gretchen removed the tray and set it on the chest of drawers. "I'll take the pillows out."

Between the three of them, with Othello whimpering his concern, Cassie slid back to a flat position. Sitting up she felt like she was tipping to the side. Lying flat made the world stop tipping. "Thank you."

Micah picked up the tray and started for the door. "Othello."

The dog tried to disappear into the bedding, not looking toward Micah, instead imploring Cassie with his eyes to let him stay. "Sorry, my friend, you go take care of Micah and the others. Go, Othello."

He slunk off the bed, ears and tail down, and sending pitiful looks over his shoulder, he followed Micah out the door.

"Can I get you anything else?" Gretchen asked. "Water? Coffee? Anything?"

"No thanks. I'll see you later." Cassie quit fighting to keep her eyes open and let sleep claim her.

Later in the afternoon she muttered, "Now, this is getting disgusting," for she was right in the middle of a checkers game with Gretchen and the same thing was happening again.

"King! Crown me." Gretchen looked up at her. "Oh-oh." She picked up the checkerboard and set it on the chest of drawers. "Here, let me help you. And just when I was winning too."

"Later."

How much later? She could not tell. She knew only that this was later and Gretchen was elsewhere. She managed to stand on her own two feet with no one holding her up. But crossing to the chair made her huff and puff.

Mavis stuck her head in the door, one of the many times she would look in, just checking. "Are you all right?"

"I thought maybe I could walk out to the kitchen for supper."

"Not to worry. We'll all bring ours in here and have a party." Mavis smiled as she left.

And so they did, with plates on laps and drinks on any available surface. Cassie kept a watch on Lucas. Did she feel any differently about him? Not that she could discern. Ransom never caught her eye or smiled like Lucas did. One had to admit he had a winning smile.

Ransom drifted away after they finished eating, but Lucas told them all what had happened the night before. "Lansing said that Ransom shot so fast that Beckwith never had a chance. Good thing, or we might have lost a brother."

"Don't make it worse than it was," Ransom called from the other room.

"If you don't like the way I tell it, you get back in here and do it yourself."

Gretchen looked to Cassie and giggled. She poked Lucas. "Keep going. What happened next?"

"Lansing wasn't sure exactly, but the next thing he knew, Ransom had knocked Case down with the butt of his gun."

"Better than shooting him again, I suppose. Maybe. He was trying to get into the house."

This made Cassie chuckle too. She looked up to see Mavis grinning and shaking her head. How could something that could have been so bad be so funny? She thought a moment. "Can I ask about what happened the night before last? There's a lot I don't remember."

Ransom returned and leaned against the doorjamb, contributing when the tale needed more. After they finished, Cassie lay back against her pillows. "I have a hard time understanding what would make men do such a stupid fool thing."

Mavis leaned back in her rocking chair, which they'd brought in. "Greed, hatred, foolishness. I know Case seems mean clear through, but I have seen him carrying one of his children around on his shoulders and laughing with him. Now, someone who can do that can't be all bad. Sometimes I wonder if losing his job at the stockyard didn't contribute to his drinking; it's the drinking that makes him mean. Some men, well, women too, can hold their liquor. Some get funny and then sleepy, some maudlin, and then there are the mean ones. They're the dangerous kind, and Case seems to be just that."

"Well, he won't have to worry about getting mean drunk for a long time. They don't serve booze in jail or at the state prison."

"But what will Molly do to feed her children?" Mavis shook her head. "She hates taking charity, but there just aren't many jobs for women in Argus."

"Not for men either." Sitting on the floor, Lucas bent one knee and wrapped his arms around it. "Short of roundup and harvest. If we could get that sawmill going, we might be able to hire someone on once in a while."

Cassie listened to the conversation. The Wild West Show had hired a lot of people. She'd never thought of it that way before. Including Indians, which certainly didn't happen a lot. One thing for certain, she had to get this arm well enough for the shooting match coming up on December fifth. The day that had seemed so far in the distance was now almost breathing down her neck, and she was too weak to move out of the way.

A big concern was where would the men sleep now? If folks in town heard that two men and two women, none of them married, were sharing a house, they'd have a field day with the gossip. Add the fact that two were Indian, and the gossips would make sure she and the others heard about it.

"Time to clean up. Tomorrow will be here soon enough. Cassie, let me check your bandaging before I go to bed. The rest of you, pick things up. Gretchen, you start the dishes and Lucas can dry. I sure will be glad when we have a milk cow again. How soon do you think Rosy will calve?"

"Maybe as early as next week. For sure by the end of the month." Ransom picked up his mother's rocking chair and carried it out.

"It's cold enough now we can butcher those hogs," Lucas called after him. "How about tomorrow?"

"Tuesday. We need to get things ready."

Mavis rolled her eyes. "We need to do it, but what a chore." She checked Cassie's bandages and felt the skin around the wound. "No blood, no heat. I'll make you some more of the echinacea tea. It helps fight against infection. I read the other day that honey on a wound would help it heal faster. I think we'll do that when we change the bandage."

Cassie licked her lips. "I have a big favor to ask."

"What's that?"

"Is there any chance I could have a bath, a real bath? I saw you have a tub."

"That we do. But I think we should wait a day or two. You're still weak. We need to keep that wound dry, but I can help you wash around it. Do you want your hair washed too?"

"Oh, it would feel so heavenly. That was one thing my mother insisted on—a copper bathtub that she could sink down into. It had a high back to lean against. My father teased her about her traveling bathtub."

Mavis laid the back of her hand on Cassie's forehead. "You're not feverish at all. Thank the good Lord for that."

Cassie nodded, screwed up her courage, and asked, "I have another question."

"And?"

"Now that the wagon is burned up, where will Chief and Micah sleep?"

"I suggested before that they move into the bunkhouse, but after this attack they don't want to leave the two of you women up there alone."

"Surely women have lived alone out here before."

"Oh, I'm sure they have, but . . ." She heaved a sigh. "We'll have to think on this and pray about it. Just adding on another room wouldn't solve the situation either. Unless you and Runs Like a Deer moved down to the bunkhouse and the men stayed up there." She patted Cassie's good shoulder. "You just get some rest. God has a plan here, and we just have to wait for him to show us."

Cassie swallowed a humph. It looked to her like God hadn't been listening too well lately. And if all this was a sign of His protection, something had sure messed that up. Right now she was having a real hard time believing that she could trust God with much of anything.

Of course, this all could have been a whole lot worse. There was that voice inside her head again. She thought for a while that perhaps the holes in her arm had silenced it. She was fairly certain that was what Mavis would say. And most likely her mother would have agreed. But right now . . . Right now the pain was catching up with her again, and her mind was muddling.

29

So, ask her.

I can't ask her.

Why not? The voices in her head argued back and forth. She'd dreamed about being married to Lucas and woke more sure than ever that they would not be suited. She was not attracted to him, let alone in love with him. The kind of love she felt was more gratitude and friendship. Not the romantic kind at all.

But perhaps you are worrying unnecessarily. He's not said a word to you. At least not made a proposal.

Be that as it may, the thought of that kind of conversation made her hurt. No one liked having a dream crushed. Her father never got to fulfill his dream, and now that she was here, her living it was iffy. *If*, that big word. She needed to take care of her sort-of family, and she'd counted on the shooting match to help them make it through the winter. And possibly participating in others, if she could figure out a way.

These early morning stewing sessions were getting old and getting her nowhere.

All she had to do was get back on her feet and start using that arm—the arm that right now was still securely wrapped to her chest. Wiggling her fingers no longer sent screaming pain up her arm, but it still hurt.

All. Another big three-letter word. Mavis had said to pray about the housing situation. If God had sent the fire or simply let the incident happen, how could she trust Him to take care of this part? Was it His fault she had a shot-up arm? No. That was the fault of those three men out on a spree. But if God was indeed all powerful, as both Mavis and her mother always said, He could have kept that from happening.

That was the clincher. He could have, but He didn't.

But it could have been a lot worse. True. So was that thanks to God and His provision or . . . ?

Or what?

"Cassie, are you ready for breakfast?"

"As soon as I've, uh, been up. Perhaps I can manage myself, but I'd feel better if you were here to keep me from falling."

"I'll be right in."

Cassie moved her feet to the edge of the bed and levered herself to a sitting position with her good arm. She was moving better, so the weakness seemed to be fading. She inched forward to let her feet over the edge and finally to sit with her feet on the floor. She looked up when the door opened and Mavis entered the room.

"You look a lot better today. Better color. Rosier."

"I feel better. We'll see how long that lasts." With Mavis standing in front of her, Cassie tried to stand, and then reached for a hand. "Just to balance." She made it, standing on her own. She heaved out a breath and nodded. Together they accomplished what was needed, and she sat back down on the bed.

"How about hot water to wash your hands and face?"

"Please." She was glad she couldn't see in a mirror. Her braid looked ratty enough on her chest. And clapping her hat on her head was not appropriate, not that she had it there. Like all her other things, the hat was still up in the cabin.

"I'll brush and braid your hair after your bath. Helping you sit in that tub is going to be a challenge. Maybe we should wait another day?"

"Whatever you think best. How come I feel so much stronger until I try to do something?"

Mavis smiled at her. "That will go away too. It is hard to take it easy when you start to feel lots better."

"Better and lots don't fit well together yet. Is Gretchen already gone to school? I thought I heard her moving around."

"Yes, and the boys are getting the hog-butchering supplies together for tomorrow. I'll bring my coffee in here, and we can talk while you eat your breakfast. Then I'm sure you'll be ready for a nap again. After that we could do the bath, if you feel up to it."

By dinnertime, they'd accomplished the bath and let Cassie sleep again, and Mavis had fried pieces of bread dough to go with the elk roast she'd put in the oven earlier. She brought some in to Cassie as part of her meal.

Cassie held up a piece of golden fried what?

Mavis smiled. "We dip it in the gravy or honey or syrup, depending on the time of day. It can be dessert too. I used to have that for the boys as a treat when they came home from school."

Cassie dipped it in the gravy, took a bite, and dipped it again. "This is really good."

"It's amazing the things you can do with bread dough. I've heard that some Indian tribes call it fry bread when patted out like a pancake and fried on each side. The bread will be out of the oven in a while, the regular loaves."

"Someday I will learn how to make bread." *Someday.*

The next day she joined the family at the table for dinner, with Mavis walking beside her. They'd started the butchering right after first light and had four hogs scalded, scraped, and hanging in the barn. Sheaves of fat lay in the sink, and one of the hog heads was already simmering on the stove for headcheese. The allspice, cloves, and other spices simmering with it filled the kitchen with appetizing smells.

"As soon as I grind some of that lard, I'll get it into the oven to render. I have a crock down in the cellar just waiting for it."

Cassie listened to the discussion as if looking into a pictograph of another life. Obviously butchering hogs was different from butchering elk. She had so much to learn, and they all took it for granted as part of their lives. She'd heard the saying "Living off the land." To Runs Like a Deer it meant finding wild things to eat. The Engstroms did that too, but not wild things; here they raised much of it. To eat and to sell or trade.

Between mouthfuls, Lucas said, "I'll take one of the hogs to the Hill City Hotel tomorrow, so I hope it's plenty cold. I know Chamberlain is going to want some smoked too. Perhaps he can find someone there to do that. Anyway, I'll tell him we can bring some more in when it's smoked."

"Is the elk done smoking?" Cassie asked, thinking of the last butchering day.

Mavis nodded. "Pretty much. We have the last batch in now. You could take some of the smoked elk to him. I'll take some in to the Brandenburgs and some to Molly Beckwith. Did anyone ask JD if he wants some for the store?"

"Nope. I thought you did." Lucas smiled at Cassie. He had a nice smile. But no sparks. He explained, "Some we sell, some we give away, and some we keep. That's the way of life here."

"Don't other people go hunting too or raise animals?"

"Oh yes. Most everyone does." Lucas waved a hand. "Every spring, Cal Haggard over in the next valley raises a flock of chickens. We have laying hens and butcher out the cocks when they reach fryer size. Or we swap, say, a side of bacon for chickens. When Mor has too many eggs, she takes them in to JD, and he applies the trade to our account there. When we have cows that are milking, she turns the extra cream into butter that can go to the store too."

Cassie listened carefully. Thoughts were coming to her. "So no one has to have real money that way."

"Right."

"But what about those who have nothing to trade?"

"We try to help them out. So do other folks. The churches help. We all do what we can."

Cassie thought to her life in the show. She'd never needed any cash because all her needs were taken care of. Was it like that for the cast and crew, the ones who were not related to the owner? And if so . . . Her mind refused to fit around the idea. Maybe Talbot hadn't lit out with hidden money. Maybe there really wasn't any to take care of all those people anymore. What had her father done to make it work? Now all his records were burned in the fire. There was no place she could go to ask questions. Other than to Jason Talbot. And she had no idea how to contact him.

But really what difference did it make? That life was over and done with. She glanced up to see Lucas watching her, his eyes gentle along with the smile he gave her. She tried to smile back, but her mouth didn't want to. *Don't encourage him*. Now, where did that come from?

After Lucas and Ransom went back outside, Mavis helped her back to bed. Somewhere during the time she was sitting in the chair, her knees had gone weak on her. "Have you seen Micah or Chief today?" she asked.

"Yes, they were helping with the butchering and were going to cut more firewood this afternoon. That's why they didn't stay for dinner."

"Oh."

Each day she grew stronger, and several days later Dr. Barnett showed up. Mavis brought him into Cassie's room, where she'd just woken up from another nap. At least this was the first one of the day.

"Hello, young lady. I thought I'd better check on that arm. I see you're in a regular sling now, not strapped down so tight."

"She was threatening to rip it off if she couldn't move it some."

Dr. Barnett smiled at Cassie. "Good for you for toughing it out. I hear that every day you are stronger. That you did not get an infection is the best news of all. Let's unwrap it and see how it looks."

Cassie gritted her teeth at the pain when he moved her arm, even though he was very careful and gentle.

"How is it compared to earlier?"

"It hurts, but there's no comparison."

"Good." With all the bandages off, he studied the stitches and the wounds they'd sealed. "Looks very good." He turned to Mavis. "You could take the stitches out the day after tomorrow, I think. Then leave off the sling at night. And begin using that arm. It will be weak, so be patient with it. Those muscles in there were really ripped up. Flexing your fingers and making a fist will help the strengthening progress. But if you do too much, you could strain it and have to slow down again."

"When will I be able to hold a rifle?"

"Hold it or shoot it?"

"I'm to be in a shooting match December fifth in Hill City."

"And this is November twentieth?" He shook his head. "You could maybe start holding the rifle by then. Were you planning to use your revolvers too?"

"And the shotgun."

His voice toughened. "Miss Lockwood, I hate to be the bearer of bad tidings, but you nearly got to chat with the angel of death. You lost a lot of blood, yes, but had the slug torn a major vessel, you would have bled to death. And it easily could have gone either way if infection set in."

"But all that didn't happen. And I need to be in that match."

"I can tell you are a strong young woman, but this time your body is not going to do what your mind tells it to do. Torn muscles take time to rebuild. Have you ever had a broken bone?"

She shook her head. "I've gotten plenty bruised a few times when I fell off my horse but I've never broke anything."

"Well, I'm just telling you what I know." He turned to Mavis. "It might bleed a little when you pull the stitches out. Wrap it up again if it does." He gathered up his things. "Just use some common sense, Miss Lockwood."

"Do you have time for a cup of coffee?" Mavis asked.

"I'd like to, but I need to get right back. We have a baby thinking on coming any time."

"How much do I owe you?" Cassie kept her voice controlled with effort. His news had hit like a mule kick.

"I'll send you a bill."

"All right." She watched him leave the room with Mavis and sank back down on the side of the bed. Tears welled and made her nose run. What was she going to do now? She had no money to pay a doctor bill, let alone buy supplies at the store. JD had said he'd like to sponsor her with ammunition, but she doubted that included supplies like food and kerosene.

She had to get ready for the shoot. She *had* to! That was the only way.

Two days later, after the others returned from church, Cassie winced when the stitches came out, but she could make a fist without too much pain. She had bent her arm now and again, drawing her hand to her shoulder. But not too often. No longer light-headed, she walked out to visit with Wind Dancer and George, taking them both carrots.

"Been awhile, hasn't it?" She stood between them as she had so often, rubbing their ears and noses. They each munched their carrot and nosed for more. "Sorry. The carrots are needed for food. When I plant a garden, I'll plant a long row just for the two of you. Or we might have to find something else you like. I'll ask if I can bring you some oats."

Buying a bag of oats, like a bag of beans, was beyond her means.

She brushed Wind Dancer with the brush held in her left hand. Two short swipes with her right were all she could manage. When she finished, they followed her back up to the fence by the barn. Lucas was there; he'd been watching. He took the brush.

"It's hard to believe that big old buffalo stood there with you like that. But I saw it happen, so I have to believe it."

"I bottle-fed him and raised him. I wouldn't expect him to treat anyone else that way. He's used to Micah and Chief too, but they don't handle him."

When Lucas took a step closer, George snorted and raised his head. "I hear you, big boy." He chuckled, stepped back, and shook his head. "I wouldn't trust him within a twenty-foot pole."

"You are smart. George has chased more than one person out of his corral." She patted both her friends and waved them off to the pasture.

"How's the arm?"

"Better." *But not better enough. Why couldn't my left arm be the one that was shot?*

That night she sat with Mavis by the fireplace. "I really need to get back to the cabin with the others."

"I hate to see you go. Have you talked with the others yet? About using the bunkhouse?"

"No. And maybe they have other ideas. I'm thinking to ride up there tomorrow."

"On Wind Dancer or by wagon?"

"Wind Dancer. I know I can't saddle him yet, but I've ridden bareback for years with him. I used to ride him without a saddle or bridle. It surprised a lot of folks to see us walking outside the corrals, but those in the show took it as part of life there."

"What if I invited them all down here for supper tomorrow night? We could talk then."

"Thanks, but I think they'll talk with me better alone." As if they ever talked a lot. But if they never talked with outsiders, who would know or care about them sharing the cabin? It wasn't like they had neighbors next door.

But she remembered how gossip spread through the show crowd. A town like Argus might be just like that, even though they did not live in town. When she brought that up with Mavis, she only said, "Think on those three men who saw the wagon burn. Rumors have started with far less."

Would those ignorant haters and liars never quit deviling them?

The next day Cassie climbed up on the rails of the corral and mounted Wind Dancer. She had put a bridle on him just to be careful, and she was wearing her britches again so she could ride easily. It felt like forever since she'd wrapped her legs around warm horseflesh and felt his muscles moving beneath her. With the sun on her face and the wind in her hair, she loped across the valley. Micah saw her coming and came down to open the gate, smiling up at her.

"Good."

"It sure is good. Is Chief up at the cabin?"

"Yes."

"Do you want a ride up?"

"No, I'll walk."

When they crested the rise to the level stretch where the cabin stood, she saw what had been the pile of split wood stacked all along the north wall. Posts had been set for a new wall that would be a lean-to, once for the wagon but now for the wood and a shelter for a couple of horses. "You've been working hard," she said to Micah, coming up beside her.

"Lucas and Ransom helped. Tomorrow we plan to add the roof poles. If the weather holds, we can get the roof on. The slabs cut from the pine trees will finish the sides."

The wagon wheels leaned against the cabin walls. All that was left of the fancy wagon, the one she'd lived in with her father and mother, the one that had carried them to the valley. She swallowed hard. The wagon was not worth crying about, and crying would not bring back any of the things in it. She sniffed and blinked and slid off her horse. At least she still had her memories, and now they were more important to her than ever. Was that why God gave them memories, as both a comfort and a challenge? She leaned against Wind Dancer, letting his warmth and the rich horse fragrance bring back all kinds of memories, a kaleidoscope of wealth.

Finally, feeling immensely comforted, she stepped back. "You go try out your almost stall," she said to him as she slipped off his bridle. "There's plenty to graze on here, so don't go away."

Pushing open the cabin door, she stepped inside. "Hey, I'm back, for a while at least."

Chief and Runs Like a Deer both smiled and nodded. Chief held up his coffee cup in question.

"No, I don't think so. You've sure gotten a lot done around here." She turned when Micah came in the door. "Mavis says for you to come down and get some of the pork. I could have carried some up, but she has other things for you too."

"I'll go down tomorrow."

"Any word from the sheriff?" Chief asked.

Cassie shook her head, flexing and stretching her fingers, a habit she'd grown into. Might as well get it over with. "Thanks to those worthless pieces of humanity, Mavis is concerned about the four of us living up here in the cabin, that rumors will fly and our lives will be harassed. So we need to talk about what to do. The Engstroms have offered either the men or the women the bunkhouse."

Micah shook his head. "You two cannot stay up here by yourselves. Look how those three got through."

"But that was a deliberate thing by cruel men. Why would we think that would happen again?"

"Better safe than sorry." Micah seemed to have taken on the job of spokesman.

"Runs Like a Deer, what do you say?"

"White people have different rules than Indians."

"Especially white women," Chief added.

"You mean me?"

"No, fancy white women."

For some strange reason, his comment made her feel a tiny bit better. She knew what he meant and she was grateful not to be included in the "fancy white women" category.

"We have talked about this." Micah pulled out a bench at the table, another new thing in the cabin. "I will marry Runs Like a Deer." He smiled at the woman setting the coffee cup in front of him. When she laid her hand on his shoulder in passing, Cassie felt the smile welling up from someplace deep within. Such good news to counterbalance the sad that tried so hard to take over.

"And I will return to the reservation." Chief never looked at her. "We need to finish the lean-to first. You stay at the ranch house for now. Or the bunkhouse."

But—"she stared from Runs Like a Deer to Micah—"but that is wonderful news. I hoped this could happen when I saw you together." She turned to Chief, the other side of this news that flipped and spun like the aspen leaves when they left the tree. "But I thought you didn't want to go back."

"This is best."

She struggled to keep from crying yet again. "You know you will always have a home here, if you want to come back." Another part of her life ripped away. Comforted one minute and bleeding the next.

"I know."

"But you won't leave without telling me."

He nodded.

"Then I guess I will get some of my things. When will you get married and how?"

"We'll ask Pastor Brandenburg. Or you could."

A short time later Cassie and her bag of clothing, along with her mother's Bible, rode back down the hill. What another strange turn her life had taken. *But much as I love these people, I don't want to stay at the ranch house. I want my cabin back.*

30

When would the pain go away?

"Cassie, dear, please don't overdo. You'll keep it from healing if you're not careful."

"But I have to be ready for the match." *That's all there is to it. It's my chance to earn some money.* Even if Chief left, she still hoped he'd change his mind. There were three of them with the same needs she thought of so often. So far the weather had stayed cold, but the snow was holding off, allowing them to get more done in preparation for the winter.

She'd ridden back up the hill again yesterday, needing to ride, to see her friends, both two-footed and four.

Othello had been in his element, running beside her, then leaping on the horse's rump so he could snuggle his nose under her armpit. George had galloped along with her and Wind Dancer for a short distance, making her dream of a Wild West show act again. The big bull could scare the strongest man, but here he was running with her and Wind Dancer just like they'd been doing for years. Three friends, three close friends.

The men had brought down the remainder of the hardwood trees felled higher on the hill, ready for them to start up the sawmill again. The supports for the roof of the lean-to addition to the cabin were in place, and Runs Like a Deer was using a froe to split cedar butts into shakes for the roof. With her weakened arm, Cassie couldn't even offer to help. How disgusting.

"You want coffee?" Runs Like a Deer asked.

"No thanks. Where are the men?"

"Micah is bringing down another dead tree to cut for firewood. Chief is hunting."

Cassie looked at the cabin wall where Chief had nailed the rabbit hides that Runs Like a Deer was turning into warm clothes for them all. An elk hide took up a large chunk of the wall, a deer hide another.

They seemed to be doing fine without her. "Well, I better get back. Lucas set up some targets for me." While she'd been working on strengthening her arm, earlier she had lifted her rifle with her right hand for the first time. That's when Mavis reminded her to be easy on the arm.

"Do you need anything?"

Runs Like a Deer slammed the froe into the cedar stump, and another shake fell to the ground. "No, we are good."

"See you tomorrow," Cassie said. "Oh, I nearly forgot. We are invited to Thanksgiving dinner. And yes, you all have to come. This is special."

Leaving those instructions, she rode back down the hill. But her shooting practice proved short. After three shots, her arm had refused to hold the gun up long enough for her to pull the trigger.

Cassie woke on Thanksgiving morning when the house was still. With no idea of the time, she threw her covers back and, stepping into slippers, crept out to the kitchen. The stove was still emitting some warmth, so perhaps she'd not been asleep as long as she thought. Should she start the stove and begin breakfast? The clock in the big room bonged, and she counted four strokes. Four o'clock—too soon to make noise to wake up the others. She crept back to her room and into bed.

After flipping from side to side and flopping on her back again, she fumbled for the matches and lit her lamp. The light sparkled on the frosted window, letting her know the room was so cold that the frost had painted patterns on the inside too. Snuggling down further under the quilts, she opened the Bible that used to be her mother's and turned to the Psalms. Mavis said she always found comfort and wisdom in the Psalms.

Over and over she read, *Praise the Lord. Praise His holy name.* Not always in those exact words but meaning the same. That's what this day was all about. She thought of picking up pencil and paper to make a list of the things she was grateful for but stayed in her warm cocoon instead and kept on reading.

Sometime later she realized she'd been hearing morning noises in the kitchen, so she got up, belted her warm robe, and with slippers on her feet again, walked into the kitchen to find Mavis starting the stove.

"Happy Thanksgiving," she said with a wide smile.

Cassie caught back a yawn. "Yes, happy Thanksgiving. What would you like me to do first?"

"You start the oatmeal, and I'll slice the ham. Ransom brought one in from the smokehouse last night. I think we'll scramble the eggs. Once the oatmeal is going, please go down to the cellar and bring up some of that raspberry syrup and a couple jars of string beans. I need to get the geese into the oven by about eight if we plan dinner for noon. After I slice the ham, I'll get to the stuffing and you finish up the breakfast. We'll let Gretchen sleep in for a little while yet."

The morning flew by as the house grew rich with delicious smells emanating from the oven and the pots cooking on the stove, all overlaid with a coffee aroma. The men finished the outside chores and gathered in the big room, where the women joined them for a while, taking turns jumping up to go baste the geese.

Runs Like a Deer, Micah, and Chief joined them a few minutes before they put the dinner on the table. When they all were seated, Dan Arnett spoke up. "We had a tradition at our house that the youngest and the oldest would each say grace." He smiled at Gretchen. "That okay?"

"Sure, and here we always go around the table and say something we are thankful for. But that lets the food get cold, so now we do that at the end of dinner."

"I'll go first, then." Arnett bowed his head and waited for quiet to fall on the gathering. "Lord God, today I'm so full of gratitude I don't think I even have room for this wonderful dinner. So thank you for the food and this family who have taken me in and made me part of them. Thank you for the hands that prepared this all. Amen."

Gretchen cleared her throat. "Thank you, God, for all of us and our home and my family. And that there is no school today and tomorrow. In Jesus' name, amen."

Lucas leaned over and tugged on her braid. "That was a good prayer. And you didn't even have to milk this morning."

Cassie swallowed a lump in her throat. Her mother used to love Thanksgiving and made sure everyone in the show received something special. This was her first holiday away from the show and the folks she knew and loved. How were they all doing today? Did any of them miss her? She looked down to keep the others from seeing her wipe away a tear.

Ransom picked up the big knife at his place and sliced into the crisply browned skin of the stuffed goose on the platter before him. As the plates were passed to him, he laid slices of meat on them, digging out the stuffing at the same time.

The others passed the bowls and platters around, and for a bit the only noises were the ring of silverware on the plates and the appreciative murmurs of the eaters.

When they all had eaten their fill and Mavis quit asking if anyone wanted more, Ransom pushed his chair back. "Let's go around the table now, so everyone can say their piece."

After they each had spoken, Ransom nodded. "It has been a good year. You are right, Gretchen. Now, I think we should wait awhile longer for dessert. But coffee in the big room, Mor?"

"Yes. You men go on, and once we put things away, we'll bring it in."

"Good. I was hoping you'd say that."

"Chief, I have a favor to ask," Lucas said when they were all gathered in the big room.

Chief nodded.

"Would you please tell us more about the night Mr. Lockwood won half the Wild West Show? I mean, like what happened after that?"

Chief narrowed his eyes, as if looking back in time. "Lockwood tried to tell Talbot that he didn't want half of the show. He had all he could do with the work he already had."

Ransom got up and tossed another log on the fire. "So what happened then?"

"Talbot got real insistent. Said he had been looking for a partner, and this looked good to him.

"Then Lockwood said, 'But I don't know anything about running a Wild West show.'

"Talbot wasn't giving up. He said, 'I hear you're a pretty good shot. What if you were to make up a shooting demonstration? You ever thought of trick riding? You get good enough and you could be the star of the show.' Talbot leaned closer to Lockwood. 'Just think, we could take our show all over the United States, maybe even to Europe.'

"Talbot looked over at me. I was standing against the wall, waiting to see how this was going to end. Pointing at me, he said, 'Maybe we could even hire some of *his* people. You have no idea how the folks back east get all excited about seeing Indians riding around and whooping it up.'

"Lockwood asked, 'How many people in your show now?'

"'We're pretty small,' Talbot said. 'Thirty people or so. Got a couple of buffalo, some longhorn cattle. A real fancy wagon, like the Gypsies have, and a fine team to pull it.'

"Lockwood asked if he had a tent.

"Talbot explained that they did the show out in the open, but they had a cook tent and smaller tents for the members to stay in. He said it looks like an army encampment when they're all set up. He told Lockwood he could give it a try, and if he didn't like it at the end of a year or two, maybe Talbot could buy him out, and he could come back here. He said, 'You would have made some money to buy stock and things for your ranch.'"

"Ivar Engstrom had been quiet so far, but finally he spoke up. 'You're not really going to do such a harebrained thing, are you, Adam?' He leaned forward and grabbed Adam's arm. 'Just let Talbot have it. We got plenty to do here.'

"I could see Adam was considering it 'cause he said to Ivar, 'But think, if I could get money to buy that herd we talked about and to build a barn and—'

"Ivar cut him off. 'We'll get those things without you going off like this. Just take a bit longer is all.'

"Then Lockwood leaned back in his chair and said, 'We can't work the mine, so there's no money there.'

"At that Ivar pushed his chair back and stood. I could tell he was some riled. But three days later we climbed on that train with ten Indians from the reservation, and we joined up with Talbot's show in Pierre."

"And that was it?" Lucas looked at his mother. "You knew them all. Right?"

Mavis nodded. "We'd been friends for a year or so. Ivar didn't talk about it for months because he said it made him so angry. He holed up at the ranch, and I didn't see him for several weeks. Then he came to town and asked me to marry him. After some thinking about it, I said yes."

Cassie sat back in her chair, trying to put it all together. She stared down at her mother's opal ring that she had found in the wagon early on the trip south. "But I thought . . ." She paused and sat still for a long moment. "My father loved the Wild West Show, and the years that he was running it, Talbot did the front work and my father worked on new acts, not only for his and my mother's, but those for other members of the cast too. But he dreamed and talked about this ranch, that someday . . ." She lifted her head. "Someday never came for him."

"On that note, I think it is time for pumpkin pie. I'll whip the cream." Mavis stood. "Lucas, you come get the coffeepot and make sure all the cups are full."

Cassie followed her out.

"You know one thing that would have made today absolutely perfect?" Mavis stopped with a faraway look on her face.

"What?"

"If Jesse could have been here. Maybe he'll make it for Christmas. He said he would try. Three years since he's been home." She shook her head, as if the memory were too heavy. "That's too long."

Cassie wished she could do something besides just nod. She'd heard the letters read to the family. Gretchen missed her brother too. Perhaps Ransom and Lucas did, but they never mentioned it. She didn't have a response for Mavis, so she simply said, "I'll cut the pie."

"Today I will shoot again." That became her vow for each day.

Every night she rubbed some salve that Mavis gave her into the weakened arm, and every morning, she exercised the pain-free arm. Pain free until she forced herself to add more shots.

"You are doing really good," Lucas told her the seventh day.

"Thank you, but . . ." Cassie laid her rifle down and picked up the shotgun. It was a good thing she had learned to shoot ambidextrously, thanks to her father, who had insisted she do so, especially for a portion of her trick riding and shooting act with the Wild West Show.

But shooting in an act like that and shooting in a match were two different things.

"Okay, throw," she instructed Lucas and blasted some more chips of wood, the one thing they had plenty of. Every miss made her more determined to keep going.

"Cassie," Mavis called from the back porch. "Time to stop again."

Lucas grinned at her. "See, you have to obey the boss lady." He took her guns and laid them in the leather satchel. "Do you want me to clean these?"

"No, I'll do that. Thanks for your help." She knew that his assisting her like this was causing more problems between the two brothers, especially since today Mr. Arnett had come to help them with the sawmill. They'd heard the whine of wood succumbing to the spinning blade until the men came down for dinner, ate, and returned to the mill. All except for Lucas, who stayed to help her.

He carried her satchel into the house and set it by the fireplace, where Cassie cleaned her gear every night. Then he took the basket of rolls and cookies Mavis had prepared for the men and went out the door whistling a tune.

"I'm ready for a sit-down. What about you?" Mavis nodded to the kitchen table.

"I guess." The fragrance of fresh-baked rolls had made her stomach growl in spite of the hearty dinner they'd eaten two hours earlier. "I feel so guilty that Lucas spends his time helping me rather than getting the work done."

"If he didn't want to do this, he wouldn't. He . . . we all want this shoot to go well for you. And before you remind me that you need the money, let me remind you that we are now your family and families take care of each other." She held up a hand at Cassie's almost reply. "Don't even bring that up."

Cassie swallowed her *but* and just nodded. Right now her arm hurt, though it wasn't screaming in pain, and sitting here in this warm kitchen with a woman who had become more like a mother than a friend seemed like a glimpse of heaven.

The barking of both dogs announced a visitor.

Mavis shrugged and went to the front door. "Why, Dr. Barnett, come on in and get warmed up. Coffee is hot." Her call made Cassie get up and fetch another coffee cup and plate from the cupboard. She dished up one of the rolls and poured the cup of coffee to set them both at the table. Western hospitality was another one of those things she was learning from Mavis.

"Hello, young lady." He set his hat on the table and stood for a moment, basking in the heat from the stove, before taking the chair at the table. "I think I followed the fragrance of fresh-baked rolls clear from town."

"I don't bake them every day, you know." Mavis sat back down. "So how are things in town?"

"Well, if by *things* you are referring to the three sitting in jail cells, the judge won't be here until next week."

"I'm sure their wives are pining for them."

"Not that I've noticed. My wife met with the women the other day to try to discern what they need. They all seemed in real good spirits." He and Mavis exchanged a look that made Cassie smile inside.

"What do you think will happen to them?" Cassie asked.

"Do you mean the men or the families?" Dr. Barnett nodded his appreciation when Mavis set another roll before him.

"The men." *I hope they rot in jail.* Cassie knew about

forgiveness, but every time she thought of that night, pure fury took over. Every time her arm gave out on her, she felt the anger rouse in her middle. Banking it was an act of will. She knew that anger wouldn't help her shooting any.

"Well, the circuit judge will convene court, and the sheriff will haul them over to stand before the judge, and the judge will decide whether this is cause for a trial by jury, and he will sentence them."

"So the shooting match will be before the court convenes?" Cassie asked.

"Yep. By the way, did you know there are flyers around about the match? And if they are in Argus, they must be in Rapid City too, and probably the other small towns around. Porter is determined to build up the appeal for guests to come to Hill City and all of our area."

"He, well, he and we are planning a Wild West show for next summer. All thanks to Cassie coming to town." Mavis smiled.

"Really?" He turned to Cassie. "So how is the arm doing?"

"It would probably be better if she were not shooting every day."

Cassie glared at Mavis. What a tattletale.

"Will you let me look at it?"

Cassie recognized an order when she heard one. She heaved a sigh and unbuttoned her sweater, rolling up the full sleeve of the shirt she wore under it.

Dr. Barnett settled his glasses more firmly on his nose and took her hand, raising her arm. She tried not to flinch when he got it nearly as high as her shoulder, but the man didn't miss anything.

"Squeeze my hand."

She did.

"Hold it. Squeeze hard."

But she couldn't hold it long enough.

"Good." He raised it again, then bent her elbow and moved the lower arm back and forth. "You have good motion. I have a feeling I don't need to tell you to keep raising it higher."

Mavis snorted.

He palpated her underarm, albeit very gently, but still she flinched. And gritted her teeth. "So you've been doing lots of shooting?"

She nodded. "I have to."

"No, you don't *have to*. But I don't figure telling you not to participate is worth my breath," the doctor said.

She shrugged.

"I figure your arm is going to tell you enough. And when you get home again after the shooting match, plan on the fact that you will have taken several steps backwards and the arm will need rest and gentle"—he looked at her over his glasses—"and I mean *gentle* exercises. No shooting again until you can feel it is back to where you are now."

His voice compelled her to look at him.

"Do you understand?"

Cassie nodded.

"That's one of the good things about the body God gives us. It tells us what it needs, sometimes rather forcefully." He laid her arm back on the table and patted her shoulder. "You are in the right place at the right time. God is like that with His children."

Cassie thought again on his words not only that night but every time her arm no longer screamed at her but yelped. Sometimes she even caught herself thanking God for her progress. Sometimes.

31

Cassie could hear her father's voice as if he were standing right off her right shoulder.

"*Ignore all that is going on around you. Think shooting. See yourself hitting the clay pigeons. Take a deep breath and let it all out. Good. Now take another. Good, and a third. You will do well, Cassie. You are a top marksman. You will do well.*"

She took another deep breath. *I've done this before. I can do it again.*

"Are you ready, Miss Lockwood?" Josiah Porter asked.

"I am."

"Good, then I will call the match." He raised his voice. "Ladies and gentlemen, we are ready to begin. We will shoot by turns, beginning with Miss Cassie Lockwood, formerly of the internationally known Lockwood and Talbot Wild West Show. She is followed by . . ." He continued with the introduction of the four other contestants.

Cassie gave a slight nod, and at the drop of his hand, the clay discs catapulted into the air. She raised her shotgun, shattered the first two, and handed her gun to Micah to reload. Her arm was getting its odd vibrating feeling too soon. In practice, that hadn't happened until near the end. She shot clean until the last round, when she missed one.

"First place of this round goes to Ty Fuller, second to Cassie Lockwood, and third to our own George Sands. Let's give them a round of applause for a match well shot." At the end of the applause, he nodded and smiled. "Our second event will be held over by the shed. This time they will be shooting live birds that we imported from Texas, since most of our birds had the wisdom to go south." He led the way with the contestants, the spectators following dutifully.

Cassie thought only of the shoot. With Micah walking beside her, she ignored the tiredness already making itself known in her right arm. Tired she could ignore. She was thankful for no pain. This time she would have to shoot even more quickly. Perhaps her having shot quail and partridge in the wild would be an assist here.

At the end of this event, she dropped to third, but with the first two contenders in a tie, she was only off by one bird. But that was one bird too many.

The one with the lowest score would win the day.

"We will have an intermission while we finish setting up for the revolver events. There is hot coffee and doughnuts available at the table behind us. Please help yourselves."

"Can I get you some, Cassie?" Mavis asked.

"Please, with cream and sugar." Cassie smiled her appreciation. Micah finished wrapping her shotgun and put it back in the case, removing the wooden box with her matching revolvers nestled in soft bags in the cotton nest. At least she could shoot this round left-handed. She was grateful now that she'd learned to do so. Often she'd outshot with her left. Today had to be a repeat of those performances.

She accepted the mug of coffee and wrapped both hands around it. She needed it as much for warmth on the outside as on the inside. Sipping, she smiled at Lucas, who'd been the runner. "Thank you."

"Can I get you anything else?"

"Other than a chair in front of the blazing fireplace, I can't think of a thing."

"At least the sun is out and the wind has died down. For a December day, this is positively balmy." Mavis glanced at Cassie's right arm and raised her eyebrows.

"I'm doing all right," Cassie assured her. "Tiring and a little tingly, but holding up." While Cassie appreciated her concern, all she really wanted was her father beside her, giving suggestions but at the same time making little jabs at the other contestants so that she laughed. *"Keep it lighthearted,"* he always told her. *"If you're having a good time, you will shoot far more accurately."* He also bet money on her. The knowledge of his betting always made her tighten up, just a little. Something she'd never told him, but he must have sensed it, because after a time, he'd never mentioned it again.

Cassie took first place with revolvers, bringing on a burst of applause.

"But you're right-handed." Mavis stared at her, her eyes wide. "That was amazing shooting."

"I trained myself for the Wild West Show. My father said being ambidextrous was a helpful skill, and today I proved him right."

By the time they'd completed the revolver rounds, Josiah announced there would be a break for the noon meal. "We'll offer a full dinner tonight at my hotel, but the staff has set up a table with sandwiches, hot soup, and various other delicious items. Please help yourselves. There are plenty of tables and chairs inside the building here." He led the way and from the doorway instructed, "Please allow our contestants and their associates to go first."

Gretchen sat next to Cassie with her mother on the other side. "You were so good out there."

"Thank you." Cassie rubbed her sore arm. It wasn't quite as bad as she had feared it would be, but the hardest event was yet to come.

"Excuse me. Could I speak with you, Miss Lockwood?"

Cassie looked up to see the man currently in first place smiling at her. "Of course."

"I'm sure you do not recognize me, but I met you and your father some years ago at another shoot." He squinted his eyes to remember better. "Maybe seven years ago?"

'I'm sorry, but you are right. I don't remember you, but I'm glad you came for our shoot here. Where are you from?"

"Now I live in Kansas City. I used to live near Oklahoma City. I always wondered what happened to you when news filtered out that the Wild West Show had disbanded. Pardon me for being nosy, but is there a reason you have not kept in contact with any of the other shooters? Or the matches that are held?"

She shook her head slightly. "The plain and simple fact is that I never had a list with names or addresses. For years my father took care of all that, and after he died, Jason Talbot did. I was trying to put a list together, but a few weeks ago our wagon with all the papers burned, and I had no idea where to turn. When Mr. Porter saw me give a shooting demonstration, he came up with this idea. We hope to make this and possibly a small Wild West show yearly events."

"That is surely good news. Is the rumor true? That you've been shot in the arm?"

"Yes. Embarrassingly so."

"And you are still shooting this well today. That is amazing." He held out his hand with a paper in it. "Here is my address, and now that I have yours, I will send a list of upcoming shoots to you. Perhaps you will decide to participate."

Cassie blinked at him. Was this man for real? "How kind of you." She took the card and put it in her pocket for now. "I'll look forward to hearing from you."

"You are interested then?"

"I am. Absolutely."

"Good. We always need younger shooters coming into the meets, especially a woman like you. I remember your father with esteem. He was a fine gentleman and an exciting challenge when shooting."

Cassie hoped her smile stayed in place. "Thank you. It is good to know he is missed."

"I need to get ready. Good luck."

"Yes, I wish the same to you."

"Cassie, that is so exciting." Gretchen stared from Cassie to the figure walking away.

"It is." She nodded. "It is beyond amazing."

"You need to eat some more." Ever the mother, Mavis smiled as she said it.

Cassie took a bite of a delicious sandwich and chewed thoughtfully. She'd never expected anything like this to happen. While the man didn't mention it, she wondered if she had outshot him. She won most of the matches she'd entered, both with her father and then when Jason went with her. Interesting that she'd never seen any of the money she won. But things would be different now. She rubbed her arm and continued chewing, ordering her mind to concentrate on the upcoming events.

Everyone cleared their things away and headed back to the event area, where more targets were set up. The hillside they'd been shooting into would be peppered with lead.

Mr. Porter called for the first event, indicating that Cassie should continue to be the first to shoot. Micah picked up her gun cases and walked alongside her to the shooting line. She smiled up at him. "Thank you, Micah. You make this feel some like it used to be."

"You are welcome, Cassie. As your father always said, 'Keep your eyes on the target and forget the world.'"

"You know, it was really a treat to meet someone who remembered him."

"I'm sure there are many that do. He was one of the stars."

"I want to do him proud." She rolled her shoulders, and the injured muscle complained. "Let's go." She took the rifle he held out to her and stepped to the line. She nailed the first three targets and stepped back for the next contestant.

"That's great shooting." Lucas stood beside Micah, who took her gun from her and began reloading.

Cassie rubbed her arm gently.

"Would you like me to do that for you?"

She glanced up at Lucas to see laughter dancing in his eyes.

"Thank you, no." But he made her smile.

"Good. You need to relax and enjoy yourself."

"It's hard to enjoy yourself when your arm wants to give up."

"I'm sure that is true, but you are holding up well," Mavis said when she'd strolled over to stand beside her. She laid her wool shawl around Cassie's shoulder. "Some heat might help. I think it's getting colder."

When Cassie's turn came again, she took her rifle in her left hand and walked to the line. Mr. Porter explained the routine so that all could hear. Clay pigeons would be fired nearly overhead.

"Any questions?" he asked her.

"No, thanks." This wasn't new, but like some others, she hadn't thought about it. Overhead shooting required different muscles and a quicker eye. By the third pull on the trigger her upper arm was yelping—at least that's what it felt like—even though she was shooting left-handed. She finished the round and lowered the gun. Tracking the clay birds overhead like that and shooting so high took all the willpower she had. Still, she missed one.

On the next round, she missed two out of five. In the final round, the simple act of lifting the gun made her groan. Pain streaked up and down her whole arm whether she was shooting right-handed or left. She missed the last three.

I let them all down. She watched the others shoot and knew she had fallen way down in the line. If her mental point count was anywhere near accurate, she was next to last. One other contestant did worse than she did. Only by keeping her eyes straight forward and on the other shooters could she keep the tears from running. They were paying prize money only to the first through third placements. Was there any chance she might have come in number three? Her one chance to earn some cash to help them through the winter. Micah needed a warm coat; he'd not lived through a winter like this before. And all of his and Chief's clothes, their show apparel and equipment were taken by the fire. And now she'd have no way to help them. Nor would she be able to repay Mr. and Mrs. McKittrick for their investment in shells for her guns.

Her worry must have leaked out onto her face, for Mavis leaned close and whispered in her ear. "Cassie, don't worry about those things. God will provide. You have all of us to help you."

Cassie reached for her hand and clenched it tight.

"How bad is it?"

"Bad." The arm throbbed like it had in the early days after the shooting. The pain of it ran over and around her head and down to her fingertips. *Home, I want to go home.*

She applauded with the others when Mr. Porter announced the winners and handed out the prize money. He thanked everyone for coming and reminded them about the dance scheduled for after dinner. "Remember, you will see more entertainment like this at the Hill City Wild West Show this summer over the Fourth of July weekend. We look forward to seeing you all then. And please, pass the news to all those you know! There will be rodeo events too; the whole program is still being worked on. Miss Cassie Lockwood will be both riding and shooting this summer, just as she used to do in other shows. Come and have a good time."

More applause followed his announcements, and the crowd began to disperse. He joined the group around Cassie.

"I'm sorry you didn't win, but for someone with a wound like yours so recent, I'd say you did amazingly well. You can be proud of yourself."

"Thank you. I wish it had been different. I have a favor to ask. Do you mind if I—we—do not attend the festivities tonight? I really need to go back to the ranch."

"I understand. I will come calling sometime soon, and we'll set up meetings to prepare for this summer. South Dakota winters are a good time to think up exciting things for summer." He bid them all farewell, talked with Lucas a couple of minutes, and then waved good-bye when Micah arrived with the wagon.

Lucas helped Cassie and his mother into the bed of the wagon and made sure Cassie was well wrapped in a quilt and his mother was comfortable. "I'm thinking you might have done better staying at the hotel. The weather isn't looking too good right now."

Dark gray clouds had been moving in, and now the sun was disappearing into them.

With a wave Lucas headed back to the hotel. Did he ever let a dinner or dance go by?

Ransom drove, and Micah took the seat beside him. They left the streets of Hill City behind at a trot, and in spite of the jolting ride, Ransom kept them to the pace.

Maybe they should have stayed in Hill City, Cassie thought, as the wheels ate up the miles. Darkness crept in and the wind tugged at the quilts, making them shiver. With their backs propped against the wagon wall behind the seat, Mavis put an arm around Cassie and wrapped them closer. Gretchen snuggled in too, so the heat made them all drowsy.

"I'm sorry I asked to go back to the ranch. All I could think was I needed to be home."

"That's all right. If Micah and Ransom felt it was impossible, they would have said so. We'll be fine."

"I wish Chief and Runs Like a Deer had come along." Cassie winced when they hit a bump. "Oh."

"Bad?"

"Yes."

But the worst part is that I let you all down.

32

I failed.

I failed!

The words tromped through her mind first thing in the morning and the last thing at night. They beat her over the head every time they caught her during the daytime. When she laid down to rest because she was too tired to keep moving, they echoed again. She'd counted on the money from the match to help get them through the winter, and now they had nothing

If her people didn't get warm clothes for the winter, they might freeze when and if the blizzards came. She had no idea what Chief needed, but according to him, he was going back to the reservation, and she had nothing to send with him.

Runs Like a Deer had come to them with the clothes on her back and that was it. She needed warm clothes too. At least the two dogs were getting along all right, and they had a cabin to live in, but with the wagon gone . . . The load grew heavier.

And then there was the dream thing. Sometimes she couldn't figure out what were dreams and what had really happened. After the night of the attack, had Lucas said what she thought he'd said, or had he not?

She sat in Mavis's kitchen three days after the shooting match, paring apples, lost in all these dark and clutching thoughts.

"Mavis? I have a question to ask that's really been bothering me." Asking it took every bit of courage she could muster. Cassie wanted to look Mavis in the face, and she could, for Mavis sat near her paring apples as well, preparing pies for Sunday dinner. But instead, she stared at her own hands because that was all her eyes would do.

"Just get it off your chest. It's much easier that way." Mavis started quartering, coring, and slicing the peeled apples into a big bowl of water while Cassie kept on peeling.

Cassie had learned that you keep peeled apples in water to save them from turning brown. So many things to learn. "You know that I'm not clear at times between dreams and the reality of that night."

"Understandably so."

"Well, it seems I remember when we were at the doctor's that Lucas made a reference to after we were married. Is that true?"

Mavis hemmed and hawed, took in a deep breath, and finally answered, "Yes, that was not a dream. He said it."

"Have I said or done something to make him think I want to marry him?"

"No." She chuckled. "He decided that the first time he saw

you, before he even met you. You see, Cassie, he falls in love two or three times a year, on the average. That's just Lucas. It passes. I figured this time it would pass too, but so far it has not. He's still smitten." She picked up another apple. "But he should be having this discussion with you, not me."

"Well, I can't ask him. That wouldn't be proper."

"True."

"Besides, I'm not in love with him, and he hasn't known me long enough to know that he is."

"Well, I can't answer to the first part, but I've heard of love at first sight, and it can last."

Water splashed from the bowl when Cassie dropped in another apple. "Everything feels like a mess. And there doesn't seem to be anything I can do to fix it. When you go to church on Sunday, will you ask Reverend Brandenburg if he will come out here to do a wedding ceremony for Micah and Runs Like a Deer? They don't dare go to town right now."

"So they're getting married? I was beginning to wonder if something was brewing between them. I've seen how Micah cares for her. But why don't you ask Reverend Brandenburg?"

"Because I don't want to be the cause of any more commotion. Let's let this all die down first, and then we'll see."

"But I thought you enjoyed going to church."

"I do, but I don't like feeling that someone wants to stab me in the back."

"Becky's sister?"

"Yes. Ever since I came, there has been nothing but commotion."

"I'm sorry you feel that way. I don't. I love having you here. We all do."

Cassie shook her head but didn't answer. She knew one,

several, who didn't. Glancing out the window, she saw white flakes floating down. Snow. Her last memories of snow, when they were snowed in for three days, were not good. She used to think it was beautiful; now she knew the dangers of it.

"Will Lucas stay in Hill City if it's snowing?" He had shot an elk yesterday, and today he was taking it in to the Hill City Hotel.

"Depends on how hard it's coming down. He'll be careful. Like all of us, he has a healthy respect for winter weather. But it can snow like this for hours and not really stick. We'll see."

They worked in silence for a few moments, Cassie's thoughts darting around. "I feel guilty, taking Gretchen's bed."

"I haven't heard any complaints from her. She and I have had some good talks on our way to sleep. Cassie, please, you have to quit worrying about all these things. Worrying and feeling so guilty. God will take care of you all. He promised, and He never goes back on His promises."

I wish I could believe that. After all that has happened, the shooting and the wagon burning, if that was an example of God's protection . . . She heard boots stomping on the back porch, and Ransom stepped inside.

"The temperature is dropping. I hope Lucas is paying attention." He hung his sheepskin coat, muffler, and hat on the pegs on the wall by the door. "I just added more wood in the smokehouse. Sure smells good in there." He laid a string of sausages in the sink. "Thought these would taste good for supper tonight. I sent some home with Micah too." He realized what they were doing. "Apple pie?"

"Thought we better use up the ones with spots so they don't rot the whole barrel. I knew Lucas would be happy."

"He's not the only one who likes your apple pie, you know. Gretchen better get a move on. It's getting dark fast."

Just then they heard the welcoming bark from the front porch. "Good. She's here."

"Could it be Lucas?" Cassie found herself worrying again. She dropped the last pared apple into the water.

"Not likely yet, but soon. Snow like this brings the dark on quicker."

The dog announced Lucas's arrival about the time they finished supper. Ransom hurried out to put the team away so that his brother could come in and get warmed up. Lucas stomped the snow off his boots on the porch, came in and shed his coat, and then stood close to the kitchen stove, warming his backside.

Mavis handed him a cup of hot coffee. "I'll dish you up a plate."

"Thanks, Mor. It's starting to come down harder now. I made it just in time. Good thing those horses know the way home." He cupped both hands around the mug and smiled at Cassie. "Mr. Porter said to tell you he's heard nothing but raves about the shooting match. It got more of the townsfolk fired up for the show, rodeo, whatever we want to call it this summer. He thinks this will help put Hill City on the map for easterners to come visit."

"Good." Cassie realized she was clenching and releasing her fingers. Now it didn't make her arm hurt, not much anyway. For the first two days after the shoot it had been really painful. Just today it had begun to let up, so she was hoping to go out and practice shooting tomorrow. And ride Wind Dancer up to the cabin to see the others. The doctor and his predictions had been right.

"I almost forgot. Porter sent you a letter. I guess he's in contact with someone else who is setting up a shooting match, much larger than this one was." Lucas dug in his pocket and pulled out an envelope. After handing it to her, he plopped down in his chair as his mother set a plate of food before him. "He wondered how your arm was doing. He said he sure admired you for shooting as well as you did."

Mavis poured coffee all around, filling Gretchen's half full. "That's all, Gretchen. Fill it with milk or cream."

"But then it will be cold."

"So set your cup on the reservoir to warm up."

Gretchen rolled her eyes but did as she was told. "I should just pour it in a pan and heat it."

"You could do that if you want." Mavis set the coffeepot back on the stove. "Do you have any homework?" When Gretchen nodded, her mother added, "You better get going on it then. The odds of no school tomorrow are pretty slim, if that was what you were banking on."

Gretchen poured the contents of her coffee mug into a small pan and set it on the stove. "If the snow is too deep, we'll need the runners put on the wagon."

Ransom sniffed. "Thanks for your advice. We never would have thought of that. Has Jenna's brother said anything about picking you up yet?"

"Nope," Gretchen threw over her shoulder as she went down the hall to get her books.

"Runners?" Cassie asked.

Ransom explained. "Sleigh runners replace the wagon wheels, but they don't work real well until the snow is deeper and the ground is frozen. We usually just pay into the wanigan."

"The wanigan?"

"Every year Jenna's father, one of our neighbors, hauls out an enclosed box that he fits on his sledge tracks. He uses it to haul all the ranch kids into town for school. The box has a small stove and window and door, more like a small room. You can see that we and the other ranchers appreciate it. So we all pay what we can so that the driver gets a bit for the extra work. I was one of the first to ride in it, before he installed the stove. In the dead of winter it was mighty welcome, even without the stove."

"I see." This was all new to Cassie, these winter routines. She thought she knew about severe winter, but the more she heard about it, the worse it got. No wonder everyone had woodpiles all over the place.

"If the snow is too deep for the cattle to graze, we'll start hauling hay out to the fields too. It's all part of winter life in South Dakota." Lucas grinned at her. "I brought a newspaper from Hill City too. There's a big article on the match. Josiah was really pleased with the coverage. I guess the newspaper in Rapid City ran an article too. We'll have to see if JD has a copy of that."

Cassie read the article. She was listed as a contender, and the writer mentioned that she'd been shot in the arm in a freak accident. Freak accident? She supposed that was one way to describe it. She zeroed in on the list of prize money paid. If only she could have held up for just a few more rounds.

When she read Mr. Porter's letter, she caught her breath. Here was the name and address for her to contact if she was interested in taking part in the match Josiah had mentioned. But it was down in Omaha, Nebraska. How would she have the money to get there? She folded the paper and put it back in the envelope. The match wasn't until spring. She looked up to find Lucas smiling at her. One more thing to deal with. She'd write a letter to be mailed the next time someone went to town. Omaha. It might as well be in Chicago or New York or Atlanta.

In the morning the snow was only three inches deep, so Gretchen rode off into a sparkling white world. Cassie stood looking out the window as the sun turned the world to brilliant, eye-watering glitter. She'd seen pictures of snow-laden trees and land, but this was more like the morning after the blizzard. She'd been too concerned about their journey being stopped then, but right now she could marvel.

"You should see the horses," Ransom said when he came in from checking on the stock. "They're running around and rolling in the snow like kids let out of school. George and the other buffalo are out there throwing up snow so they can reach the grass, giving the cattle a lesson in winter living."

"I saw them do that on the road down here. The snow disappeared so fast, though, that they didn't have to do it much."

"This might too, but we're nowhere near up to freezing yet. It's down in the twenties. Oh, did you know that the buffalo are all wearing a mantle of white? Their coat is so dense the snow doesn't melt on it. I remember reading that somewhere. Now I saw it with my own eyes."

"Really?" If that had happened before, the snow didn't last long enough to make her aware of it, not that she'd been out with the livestock like the men had.

That night she was adding wood to the fireplace when Lucas wandered into the room. He came to stand beside her. "Feels good, doesn't it?"

"I like keeping the fire going. I never used to think of watching a fire burning in a fireplace as being peaceful, but it makes me feel that way." She sat down on the stone hearth at the end away from the hottest part.

"Cassie, we need to talk."

She looked up at him. He pulled a chair around and sat down so their knees were nearly touching.

"I thought I could wait awhile, but . . . yes, I did mention 'after we are married.' You weren't dreaming it. But it is a dream of mine."

Her face felt almost as hot as her backside. "Your mother told you." On one hand she'd wanted Mavis to talk to him, but on the other she wanted to jump up and go hide in her bedroom. What could she say? Mavis—could she call her Mor like the others did?—was right, though. It was best to get this out in the open.

Lucas took one of her hands in his. "Cassie, I care for you deeply. You are my dream come to life."

"You feel sorry for me is all." She wanted to take her hand back but sat still instead.

"No. I want to marry you. I've wanted to marry you since the first time I saw you." He cleared his throat. "That is—will you marry me?"

"Lucas, you might think you love me, but you don't know me." *And besides, you've not even said you love me, not that it would make a whole lot of difference.*

"Ah, but I would love getting to know you better."

"But you see, I think of you as a brother or good friend. I

don't love you." There, she'd said it. Hard words but so true. While his hand was warm, she didn't feel any different. Where were the tingly feelings she'd read about, the attraction that her mother said she'd had for Adam the first time she saw him ride into the ring on that stunning white horse of his? Cassie stared at her hand, shaking her head.

"Cassie, let me make you love me. Give me—us—time. What can it hurt?"

This was so confusing! How could he make her love him? Was it possible? Could she come to love him? Or was love not such an important part of marriage? Did it happen sometimes later on?

Or does he just want clear title to the ranch? That thought sneaked in like a snake in the woodpile. She sighed. What choices did she have? Other than to go back to the cabin as soon as she could work it out, where was she going?

"I don't think this will work, but—I'm not saying yes—but we shall see. Just don't get your hopes up." Well, that was certainly a definite way to handle this. *I have a lot of thinking to do. And praying, as Mavis would say, most likely will say.*

She stared at the handsome young man in front of her. Why couldn't he just love Betsy, as they all thought he did? She rose and he did too. But he was standing right in her way. She looked up at him, realizing he wanted to kiss her. Instead, she stuck out her hand and shook his. "Thank you. I think." And sidestepping him, she headed to the kitchen and the safety of the others. One more thing to worry about. *What does God have to say about this,* she wondered.

That night, looking out on the moonlit snow, she took Mavis's advice. *God, I give up. This is all too much. If you have a plan for my life, a way for me to take care of my people,*

I need to know that for sure. And marriage to Lucas? That would solve a lot of problems, but I'm so afraid it would create more. I just don't know what to do. I guess I would like some sign that you are indeed listening. Trust doesn't come easy for me anymore.

She sighed and crawled into bed. If Lucas could make her love him, that would solve a lot. But right now she needed winter clothes for Micah and Runs Like a Deer. Probably not rainbow-colored coats like the one Joseph's father gave him, but something plenty warm.

Nagging thoughts stole sleep from her. *I let them all down. Can someone make someone else love him?*

"Cassie, what's troubling you?" Mavis asked the next afternoon when the men were all up at the sawmill. The sun was shining like it wanted to make up for the snowfall that was fast leaving the ground bare again.

"Lucas asked me to marry him. I know that shouldn't be troubling to a woman, but . . ." She paused, trying to think of a pleasant way to frame her concerns. Mavis picked up her mending basket. The warmth of the fireplace felt good, since outside it was still colder than chilly.

"Take your time. No hurry."

"Thanks. I guess that's one of the things bothering me. Is Lucas always in such a hurry?"

Mavis smiled around the yarn she was threading through the darning needle with the large eye. "When he knows what he wants, he goes after it."

Cassie took the iron poker and stirred the fireplace, then added another chunk of wood. As the sparks flew up the chimney, she exhaled. "I told him I don't love him. Shouldn't there be some kind of spark? Did you feel something special for the man you loved?"

"Oh, did I ever." Mavis's face took on a dreamy quality. "I thought he was the most handsome man I had ever known, and sparks seemed to jump in the air when we got close to each other."

"How long was it before you married him?"

"I didn't marry him. I married his best friend. For you see, I needed a home, a place to put down roots, and Adam Lockwood had the itch for adventure like you wouldn't believe."

Cassie stared at her friend. "Adam Lockwood? My father?"

"Yes. He asked me to go with him, but I couldn't do that. I just couldn't. Did Ivar know how I felt?" She stared into her mending basket, or perhaps it was into the past. "We never discussed it. We married, and since we were already very good friends, love came. He loved me, and I don't know when, but one day I realized how much I loved him."

"Did he make you love him?"

"I don't think so. I kept praying and I believe God opened my eyes to His plan for me. This land, this ranch, my three fine sons and daughter. A man as steadfast as those rocks at the end of the valley. Once he gave up the drinking, he was everything God wanted him to be. When he died, the light went out around here for a while, but then God reminded me that He would be my husband and the father for my children, three of whom who were already men. I have found that God always lives up to His word. Men leave and make mistakes and love and die, but God never changes. He said, 'I love you,' and He meant every word."

"Trust isn't easy."

"No, it never is, but my land, it is worth it."

"But where was God when those men attacked the cabin and destroyed my wagon?"

"He was right there. Someday when you look back, you will see that He worked good out of that evil, just like He promises. That could have been so much worse. I shudder to even think about it—bullets flying up there, your wagon burning." She heaved a deep sigh. "Cassie, I am so thankful He brought you here, into my life."

Cassie stared into the fire. A fire burned up her wagon, but this fire was heating the house and keeping her warm. Two sides of the same thing. God was using one for good, while the other had happened by evil.

Trust. Could she trust Him? What if something bad happened again?

She thought to some verses she'd read that morning. Jesus had promised that He was going away to get a home ready for His disciples, His friends, people in the world. Like her. She had a heavenly home to look forward to. And she had an earthly home now too. That cabin up the hill was her home, this ranch, this place. Hadn't He given her this, the dream she'd asked for—a home? A real home with sturdy walls, a fireplace, wood for the winter, friends to grow with. Staring into the glorious red and gold and yellow of the flames, she could almost hear a voice. *I brought you into a new land, to a home I prepared for you. Can you—will you—trust me for the rest?*

Cassie leaned over and took the mending basket from Mavis's lap. "I can't cook and do all the things you do, though I'm learning. But I can sew and mend. And I will choose to trust Him as you did. But one thing I ask."

"What is that?"

"Will you remind me sometimes?"

"Oh, never fear, God will remind you, and He will give you the peace that passes all understanding. Ah, Cassie, let Him lead, even though sometimes His answers come like whispers in the wind."

Lauraine Snelling is an award-winning author of over 60 books for adults and young adults. Her books have sold over 2 million copies. Besides writing books and articles, she teaches at writers' conferences across the country. She and her husband make their home in Tehachapi, California.

More Heartwarming Historical Fiction from Lauraine Snelling

To learn more about Lauraine and her books, visit laurainesnelling.com.

Leaving behind her father's Wild West Show—and a bundle of heartache—trick rider Cassie Lockwood sets out with two unlikely companions on a wild and daring new adventure: searching for her father's hidden Valley of Dreams.

Valley of Dreams
WILD WEST WIND #1

BETHANYHOUSE

Stay up-to-date on your favorite books and authors with our *free* e-newsletters. Sign up today at bethanyhouse.com.

Find us on Facebook.

Free, exclusive resources for your book group! bethanyhouse.com/AnOpenBook

More Heartwarming Historical Fiction from Lauraine Snelling

To learn more about Lauraine and her books, visit laurainesnelling.com.

Facing the untamed but beautiful Red River Valley, the Bjorklund family must rely on their strength and faith to build a homestead. Through the challenges of this difficult land, the Bjorklunds suffer tragedy and loss, but also joy, hope, and a love that continues strong.

Red River of the North
An Untamed Land, A New Day Rising, A Land to Call Home, The Reaper's Song, Tender Mercies, Blessing in Disguise

Astrid Bjorklund loves Blessing, the prairie town settled by her family. Yet if she pursues her passion for medicine, will she have to leave her beloved town—and chance for love—behind?

Home to Blessing
A Measure of Mercy, No Distance Too Far, A Heart for Home